'So you advise me to take a wife?'

'Yes, my lord, I do.'

'Then, ma'am, will you do me the honour of accepting my name and whatever fortune may come my way?'

To her utter amazement Miss Julienne-Eve Lawrence hears herself saying, 'Yes, my lord, I will.'

The new Lord Rotherham desperately needs to produce an heir to gain his rightful inheritance, for his grandfather has left his fortune to whichever of his grandsons first has a son.

The prospect of the dim-witted Sir Trevor, Rotherham's cousin, inheriting all is too appalling to consider, so this is one race Julienne-Eve is determined to help her new husband to win!

GW00701574

Bridal Path
Patricia Ormsby

MILLS & BOON LIMITED
London · Sydney · Toronto

First published in Great Britain 1982
by Mills & Boon Limited, 15 – 16 Brook's Mews,
London W1A 1DR

© Patricia Ormsby 1982
Australian copyright 1982
Philippine copyright 1982

ISBN 0 263 73876 0

04/0682/

Set in 10 on 10 pt Linotron Times

Photoset by Rowland Phototypesetting Ltd
Bury St Edmunds, Suffolk
Made and printed in Great Britain by
Cox & Wyman Ltd, Reading

Belatedly for Josephine,
with my thanks for her
unfailing interest.

CHAPTER
ONE

DESPITE spirited efforts by the compilers of local guide-books to enlarge upon its attractions, Leyswood Towers could not be described as other than a Gloomy Pile. To its owner, looking out from his business-room window across his wide acres, it represented nothing so much as an albatross hung about his neck.

'It's an infamous will, Ainsley, and you know it!' he ground out from between clenched teeth. 'My grandfather must have been far gone in senility to have entertained such a notion. My cousin Trevor is as near a simpleton as makes no matter, but his mama will see to it that he discharges his duty.'

The plump rosy little man, seated behind the big desk, bore all the appearance of an eager robin. 'Indeed, my lord, I have no doubt of it,' he replied in his precise lawyer's voice.

'You've told her, then?'

'I called at Hever Court this morning.'

Captain Lord Rotherham swung round on his heel and began to pace the room. ''Fore God, she could marry him off to her kitchenmaid! It's not likely that any lady of sense or breeding would wed such a sapskull, even for a fortune.'

'Which is why I urged your immediate return, my lord.' The little man placed the tips of his fingers together and studied them dispassionately before continuing. 'His late lordship, your grandfather, was by no means senile but, with the dual encroachments of age and failing health, even so independent a spirit might be forgiven a slight—softening towards those of his family who—er, cared to approach him.'

'Which I did not! Are you saying that my Aunt Elspeth did?'

'From what your housekeeper tells me, my lord, it would

appear that Lady Heathcott visited here on at least two occasions during the last weeks of your grandfather's life and may well have caught a hint of what was in his lordship's mind. I am of the opinion that she was not vastly surprised at what I had to tell her this morning.'

Rotherham laughed shortly. 'So she has had time to lay her plans, is that what you would say?'

'The thought had occurred to me, my lord.'

Rotherham stood, hands plunged deep in pockets, eyes drawn once more to the colourful September landscape.

'Maybe I do my dear aunt an injustice,' he said dryly, a humourless twist to his lips. 'She has, I am persuaded, too great a sense of family pride to permit ignoble blood to flow in her grandson's veins. A female of genteel birth would answer, I fancy, one with no influential connections and small hope of worldly advancement.'

'There are many such, my lord, who would count it no sacrifice to provide Sir Trevor with a son in exchange for a life of comfort,' pronounced Mr Ainsley.

His lordship's stormy dark eyes flashed scorn and the lawyer was instantly put in mind of his client's grandfather. Old Lord Rotherham had been just such a figure of a man in his youth, tall above the average with deep-chested shoulders and well-turned legs that had no need of parchment calves to improve their shape. His grandson had the same proud carriage of head and assurance of manner nor, Mr Ainsley noted gratefully, did he show sign of the indecision and dilatoriness that had so marred his father's character and put the old lord out of all patience with him.

'I haven't enquired after your lady mother, my lord. Did you find her in good health?'

'Well up to snuff, I thank you. She has even offered to give up her establishment in Bath and come to look after this mausoleum for me—a mighty heroic gesture since she loathes every stone of it.'

Mr Ainsley was momentarily lost in legal conjecture. 'Though your father never held the title, having predeceased your grandfather by many years, Mrs Saville will, doubtless, be granted the courtesy title of Lady Rotherham.'

'She'd not wish for it,' said her son quickly. 'The name has ill associations for her.'

Mr Ainsley cleared his throat gently. 'But she'd not repine if there was a Lady Rotherham?' he suggested.

'Are you trying to talk me into wedlock?' wondered his lordship with deceptive sweetness of tone.

'If the name is to be carried on, my lord, it is an eventuality that must be considered.'

'I'll not be bribed into it! When—*if* I marry, it will be to a lady of my own choice in my own time!' Rotherham smiled suddenly, an impish grin that transformed his rather austere countenance and made him look immeasurably younger than his twenty-seven years. 'And I know just what you would like to say—that, without a fortune, my choice could be damnably limited!'

'Thirty thousand pounds a year, my lord, is a great deal to whistle down the wind!' said Mr Ainsley severely.

'I'll leave you to practise whistling!' retorted his lordship with callous indifference. 'I'm for a gallop before dark. Challis will see to your comfort.'

With that he was gone, and his lawyer settled to contemplation of his immediate task. It was one in which he could take little pleasure for, in his opinion, the late Lord Rotherham had unjustly penalised his heir for the supposed faults of his parents. Small wonder the young man was incensed when he learned that, only by marrying and producing a son in advance of his cousin, Sir Trevor Heathcott, could he gain control of the bulk of the Saville fortune. Yet he should have no difficulty in finding a bride, the true difficulty lay in the urgency of the affair. His lordship would not be easy to please and there was the future to be thought on—no point in shackling him to some vapourish female who would bore him in a week. And, of course, there was Lady Heathcott. Mr Ainsley chewed his thumb and considered her ladyship. As forceful as her brother had been ineffective, she would waste little time in procuring a wife for her son. Crack-brained fribble he might be, yet there was no saying but that marriage to a sensible young woman might not be the making of him.

Mr Ainsley sighed and, drawing a chair to the fire, gave himself up to enjoyment of the excellent port which Challis, Rotherham's elderly butler, set at his elbow, while the object of his concern, astride a magnificent black stallion, eased the irritation of his nerves in urging the beast at full stretch across the fields.

The sky was heavy and the air cooling with the threat of rain as Rotherham reined in his horse and dropped down a steep bank to the road to head for home. Then it was that sounds of a lively altercation came to his ears and he perceived a cabriolet, tilted at an alarming angle, standing by the roadside. The driver of the vehicle was endeavouring to soothe his agitated steed and fend off a furious verbal attack being directed upon him by a young woman who stood, hands upon hips, upbraiding him.

'Now we *are* in the basket!' she declared. 'You have quite lost your direction and it is getting dark!' The culprit was understood to protest in his own defence that they could not be above five miles out of the way, and how was he to know that the axle would choose that very moment to break? But the lady was not to be pacified. 'We had as well be fifty miles as five off our course,' she pointed out, 'nor, I'll be bound, would the axle have broken had the wheel not run dry! If you had given it sufficient oil—oh!'

Hearing the sound of hooves behind her, she swung round to confront the rider.

'Servant, ma'am.' Rotherham pulled off his hat and made her a slight bow. 'Can I be of service?'

'Indeed, I pray that you may, sir,' she replied candidly. 'For this foolish fellow appears to be quite incapable of dealing with the situation and has no notion of which way to turn.'

'Whither were you bound, ma'am?' enquired his lordship with reluctant civility. To be obliged to play the rôle of Good Samaritan to a distressed damsel was not at all to his taste at that moment, there being a sufficiency of trouble on his shoulders already.

'I am on my way to Hever Court, sir,' she replied in a manner to match his own. 'To Lady Heathcott's residence. You are, perhaps, acquainted with her?'

That caught his interest and he eyed her with rising curiosity; a slight figure in a sensible wool travelling cloak and a deep-brimmed bonnet that effectively obscured what little he could see of her face in the gathering dusk.

'I have that pleasure, ma'am.' He swung down easily from his saddle. 'You are paying her ladyship a visit?'

'No, sir.' Her voice, he had to allow, was remarkably clear and pleasing. 'My visit is not a social one. I am to be employed as her ladyship's companion.'

'What, in heaven's name, is a child like you going for companion to my—to Lady Heathcott?' Rotherham was startled into exclaiming.

She stiffened and her chin came up in so defiant a manner as to bring a twinkle of amusement to his eyes.

'Some of us, sir,' she informed him in condemnatory tones, 'have to earn a living and I, being what you would doubtless describe as an indigent female, am one of those unfortunates.'

He looked down upon her upturned face which, even in the indifferent light that prevailed, gave promise of being uncommonly well-favoured.

'Indigent if you say so, ma'am, but surely so fair a lady could never be termed unfortunate?' His cool appraisal of her as he stood, hat in hand, the breeze gently ruffling his dark locks, plainly was not to her liking and, smiling a little, he turned his attention to the damaged cabriolet. 'Hmm. I'd best send my fellows to move it off the road, for we'll not get a wheelwright to attend to it before morning. Devil take it, here comes the rain! You'd best accompany me back to my house, ma'am, and I will have you conveyed to Hever Court in one of my own carriages. I am Rotherham, by the way.'

'And I am Miss Lawrence, Miss Julienne-Eve Lawrence,' said she with a dignity that sat quaintly upon her slim shoulders.

'Julienne-Eve? That smacks of French blood,' he commented, but wasted no more time in idle speculation as heavy drops of rain were beginning to fall. Mounting his horse again, he held out a hand to her. 'You'd best come up before me.'

'Wot about my money?' expostulated the driver for whom events were moving altogether too fast. 'Don't you let her tip me the double, sir!'

'If that means what I think it does, I have no intention of tipping you anything!' Miss Lawrence informed him. 'Here is your fare and be grateful that I am making no deduction for an uncompleted journey.' Grandly, she bestowed the money upon him and turned to the amused Rotherham. 'My valises—' she began tentatively.

'Will be brought to the house. Come, ma'am, it grows damper by the moment.'

In a twinkling Miss Lawrence found herself firmly, if a shade uncomfortably, established in front of his lordship, held close in the crook of his arm. Never before having been in such intimate proximity to a gentleman—and, while vaguely resentful of his autocratic manner, she was obliged to allow that he was a very personable gentleman— she was, not unnaturally, stricken dumb. To her relief, once they had left the road and passed between a pair of impressive entrance gates standing open and untended, the journey was a brief one. Through the semi-dusk and now searing rain, she got the impression of a well-ordered estate, pleasantly diversified by gentle eminences and fine trees. Then all her attention was captured by the great house, dominating the entire landscape like some primeval monster. As they came to a stand before it, the front door opened to loose a thin stream of light upon them and a footman came running to assist her.

'Bid Mrs Challis see to the lady's comfort. I'll join you as soon as I may, ma'am.'

Then he was gone and Miss Lawrence, feeling oddly forlorn, was ushered into the hall where a spare, elderly woman came to fuss over her, exclaiming aloud at sight of her sodden condition.

'You're like to catch your death of cold, miss! Thomas, take the lady's cloak to the kitchen to be dried and send Lucy with hot water and towels. If you will accompany me upstairs, miss, we'll have you comfortable in no time.'

Feeling that the last statement could well be over-optimistic, Miss Lawrence meekly followed this personage,

who announced herself to be Lord Rotherham's housekeeper, to a bedchamber on the first floor. Glancing about
her, she could not help but observe that her surroundings,
while sombrely impressive, yet bore all the appearance of
disuse. Only one of the fine cut-lustre chandeliers in the
pillared hall was lit, and no fire burned in the handsome
neo-classical Italian chimneypiece. The bedchamber was
equally cheerless, being swathed in Holland covers, and the
housekeeper apologised anxiously for its appearance.

'His lordship—I mean the late Lord Rotherham—lived
solitary here for many years, and bade us close up all rooms
not in use.'

'It seems a very large house,' ventured Miss Lawrence,
shivering slightly and wishing she had thought to snatch a
shawl from a valise before being carried off.

'Twenty-two bedrooms, miss,' said Mrs Challis proudly,
sweeping the cover off a dressing-table and setting down
her branch of candles. 'And only Challis and I and Thomas,
with a couple of chits of maids, to look after it. I'm sure I
don't know how we shall go on if Master Nathan—I mean
his lordship, intends to open it up again. Which, stands to
reason, he well may, being young and newly home from the
wars.'

'He has been in the Peninsula?'

'Yes, indeed, these four years, with His Grace of Wellington.' It was plain that Mrs Challis, as befitted a loyal
servant, considered that His Grace was the one deserving
of congratulation in this arrangement. 'Not that he would
have lived here while his grandfather was alive, for they
were ever at outs—but that is nothing to the point. Did you
have a mishap on the road, miss?'

Miss Lawrence then related the sad tale of the broken
axle, and accepted Mrs Challis's commiserations on the
general inability of the lower classes to make provision for
such contingencies while she refreshed herself with the
welcome hot water and dragged a comb through her gleaming brown locks.

'There's only the one good fire and that's in the business
room, miss. I make no doubt Mr Ainsley's still sitting over
it. That's his lordship's lawyer who has been shut up talking

with him since coming from Lady Heathcott this afternoon.'

'Lady Heathcott?' echoed Miss Lawrence in surprise.

'Yes, his lordship's aunt, over at Hever Court. Now, if
you'll come with me, miss.'

Before the young lady had time to comment upon this
circumstance, Mrs Challis was leading her downstairs and
across the hall into a well-lit room with heavy drapes closed
against the evening air. In a chair drawn up to the fire dozed
a rotund gentleman, his feet propped up on a stool and a
glass of port on a table at his elbow.

He sat up at once, blinking owlishly at the unexpected
intrusion but, when Mrs Challis had explained the matter to
him, he was most assiduous in seeing to the visitor's comfort, drawing up another chair for her and insisting that she
partook of some wine.

'Port rarely being to a lady's taste, no doubt you would
prefer Madeira? His lordship declares this to be a very
tolerable one,' said he, busying himself with the decanters
on a side-table, while his alert gaze approved the lady's
appearance. 'You have travelled far today, ma'am?'

'From the London side of Sevenoaks only,' replied Miss
Lawrence, stretching out her toes to the blaze and revelling
in its warmth. 'From my late employer's residence.'

'Indeed?' Mr Ainsley's eyebrows all but disappeared into
his hairline. 'Your—late employer?'

As he seemed expectant of further confidences, Miss
Lawrence kindly enlightened him. 'Yes, my dear Mrs
Crawford, to whom I was companion, passed away very
suddenly and I was forced to seek another post without
delay. By a happy chance Mr Baynton, her legal advisor,
also deals with Lady Heathcott's affairs and recommended
me to her.'

Mr Ainsley was all attention. 'I—ah, I am slightly acquainted with Mr Baynton.'

'Since I have no one of my own to advise me, I was most
grateful for his help,' stated Miss Lawrence firmly, trying to
shut from her mind the memory of her last encounter with
that smooth-spoken gentleman, when he had explained
delicately that Mrs Crawford had, despite his warnings,

lived far beyond her income for many years.

'I am well aware, my dear Miss Lawrence, that she wished to make provision for your future—indeed, this charitable intention was a constant theme of conversation with her, but when her affairs are settled up I fear there will be little, if anything, left over for you.' He then, with all the air of a gracious benefactor, had presented her with fifty pounds. 'Should there be more to come, I shall know where to find you.'

From his discouraging manner Miss Lawrence got the distinct impression that there would be nothing more to come, but she pocketted her pride and the fifty pounds, thanked him for his good offices and left him in order to make immediate preparation for her journey. Despite his civility towards her, she found she could not like Mr Baynton, and gloomily supposed it to be some basic flaw in her own character that precluded her from feeling the gratitude she ought for one who had befriended her.

Mr Ainsley, closely observing her as she sat, lost in these unhappy recollections, experienced a sudden apprehension. To his knowledge Lady Heathcott, for whom he occasionally acted in the Saville connection, had never before employed a companion, and for her to engage so youthful and taking a young lady in this capacity was beyond anything strange.

'You—ah, you are quite alone in the world, ma'am? No parents or other family?'

She shook her head rather dolefully. 'My father was a naval officer. He lost his life at the Battle of the Nile.'

'And your mother?'

'Was the daughter of a French émigré,' she replied, wondering that she should not resent his interest, but rather liking the friendly little man. 'My father's family cast him off when he married her. I have no knowledge of them.'

'And this Mrs Crawford—how did you come to be in her employ?'

She hesitated, sensing that something other than mere curiosity lay behind this courteous inquisition. 'She was godmother to my father,' she said at last, 'and could not approve of the way in which my mother and I had been treated. She invited my mother to join her establishment as a—a sort of housekeeper and companion. Then, after my mother failed to return from France, I took over her duties.'

'Your mother went to France?'

'Yes, above three years ago, to seek out any that might have survived of her father's family.'

'To attempt such a thing at a time when this country was at war with France!' Mr Ainsley shook his head in astounded disbelief. 'Does Mr Baynton know of all this?'

'Well, yes, I suppose he does.' Miss Lawrence looked her surprise at the lawyer's obvious agitation but, before she could discover the reason for his concern, Lord Rotherham entered the room.

'I must inform you, ma'am, that it is blowing up for a storm. I do not advise your continuing your journey tonight and have instructed Mrs Challis to prepare a bedchamber for you.' He stopped short as she set down her glass and turned to face him. The wine and the warmth had combined to bring a soft flush to her cheeks, while melting blue-grey eyes and a delicately retroussé nose lent an air of distinction to a countenance that was further enhanced by an exquisite complexion and a mouth that, for all its sweetness, showed firm above a rounded chin. Rotherham, seeing her clearly for the first time, experienced a rare surge of admiration but, unwilling to parade his feelings, continued speaking with cool unconcern. 'We keep country hours here and dine at six. I will ring for Mrs Challis to take you to your room.'

'Th-thank you, my lord, but I fear I am putting you to a vast amount of trouble,' stammered Miss Lawrence, also experiencing a slight shock at sight of him. He had changed from buckskins and riding-coat into pantaloons and a long-tailed coat that looked to be moulded to his person. His neckcloth, as near to perfection as was possible, was fashioned in a *Trône d'amour*, his striped toilinette waistcoat showed never a wrinkle, while the dancing firelight was reflected back off gleaming Hessians and a single jewelled cravat pin, nestling amid snowy muslin. It was, she knew, only fashionable morning dress, but it made her miserably conscious of her plain stuff round dress and

sensible low-heeled shoes, and she fancied she read cond-
emnation of her appearance in his brusque dismissal of her.

'It is not of the least consequence, ma'am,' he returned
indifferently. 'Does Lady Heathcott expect you tonight?'

'No, for I had the intention of availing myself of the
coach service to Tunbridge Wells to-morrow, from whence
she kindly offered to fetch me, but when I set about
arranging with a driver to take me into Sevenoaks to pick
up the stage, he said he was making the journey on his own
account to the Wells today and would carry me on to my
destination for a small sum. That being yesterday,' she
added, 'I have had no opportunity of acquainting Lady
Heathcott with my change of plan.'

'So she will not look for you before tomorrow?' interposed Mr Ainsley thoughtfully.

Rotherham shrugged as if the matter was one of small
significance and, to Miss Lawrence's relief, Mrs Challis
then appeared in response to his summons and bore her off.

Returned once more to the bedchamber to which she had
first been conducted, she found the covers removed and the
bed made up, while one maid applied a bellows to a
smouldering fire and another slid a warming pan between
the sheets. Perceiving that her valises stood open upon the
floor and that most of her small wardrobe had already been
unpacked and put away, Miss Lawrence declared that she
was well able to look after herself and beyond doubt Mrs
Challis had a better use to put her girls to—which fact the
housekeeper did not dispute but hustled them off with
almost unseemly haste.

Left alone, Miss Lawrence sat ·down to consider her
situation. She was not at all sure that she ought to be
accepting Lord Rotherham's hospitality though, to be sure,
the noise of the wind and the rain beating against the
windows convinced her that she had no choice but to
remain under his roof. Well, if she was forced to be his
guest she must put herself out to be agreeable and give him
no cause to look at her in that odiously condescending way
that had so provoked her. He might be a nobleman of the
first stare but she, Julienne-Eve Lawrence, was not quite
nobody and so she would show him! Then she recollected

that she *was* nobody, a paid companion, and most unlikely ever again to be treated like a daughter as had been her good fortune when in Mrs Crawford's employ. She mused over what Mr Baynton had told her of that lady's sadly depleted income and wondered anew at it, for she had always believed Mrs Crawford to have been fully awake upon every suit, nor could she begin to understand how a woman of such admirable commonsense had allowed herself to become so behindhand with the world.

A glance at the hurrying clock informed her that, if she was to make a timely appearance at the dinner-table, she had best bestir herself and, going to the closet, she was about to pick out a sober gown of dark green tabbinet when her attention was caught by the silken sheen of a cream figured florentine. Wistfully she stroked its soft folds, her thoughts dwelling on that happy day the previous June, her twenty-first birthday, when Mrs Crawford had made her a gift of the frock, together with an exquisite shawl of the finest cobweb wool, interwoven with gold thread, which set if off to perfection. Then her eyes lit up with a gleam of the purest mischief. Why not put his top-lofty lordship to the blush by appearing at his table in full evening rig? The next moment she was standing in her petticoats, her sensible shoes kicked off, searching feverishly for slippers and mittens, and praying that Rotherham would not put down her determination to outface him as mere ignorance on her part of the suitability of such a get-out for so informal an occasion.

'He may disapprove of me—he shan't ignore me!' she muttered fiercely as she tied up the knots of gold ribbon with which the dress was adorned and debated whether or not to wear the rose-cut pink garnet pendant of French design that was the only piece of jewellery she had ever had from her mother—and that, most likely, because in her hasty departure Mrs Lawrence had quite forgot it.

Belowstairs Mr Ainsley was endeavouring to engage his lordship's attention on the subject of their unexpected guest.

'I tell you to your face, my lord, I don't like it. Here is a young lady of undoubted breeding and no fortune—just the very one for Lady Heathcott's purpose.'

Rotherham looked faintly sceptical and helped himself to Madeira. 'I do not suppose there is anything we can do to alter the outcome,' he said mildly. 'Or had you in mind to kidnap Miss Lawrence and keep her here by force?'

Mr Ainsley drew a deep breath, indicative of extreme exasperation. 'My lord,' he got out at last, 'I beg of you to consider your situation. Without money you cannot hope to maintain this house or your position.'

Rotherham watched him over the rim of his glass, dark eyes alight with perverse amusement. 'Oh, I shall come about, never fear,' he murmured.

'And you cannot sell the place without the consent of your heir, it being entailed,' continued Mr Ainsley in the same reproving vein.

'And my heir is cousin Trevor who'll not wish to forego the consequence that being the owner of Leyswood Towers would confer upon him—nor, depend upon it, will his mother.'

'Lady Heathcott dotes upon the place,' agreed Mr Ainsley.

'Then she is heartily welcome to it! I can always go a-soldiering again.'

'But the war is over, my lord! Bonaparte is confined to his island—'

'Aye, like a tiger in a cage. One false move on the part of his gaolers and the trap will be sprung!'

'What? You cannot believe that—that Monster will be loosed upon us again?' gasped Mr Ainsley, shocked out of his habitual composure.

His noble client's views on the likelihood of the ex-Emperor providing further employment for the armies of the allied sovereigns were not destined to be revealed, for Challis presented himself at that moment to announce that dinner awaited their convenience.

Miss Lawrence, who had also been advised of this welcome event, was descending the stairs just as the gentlemen stepped into the hall. Despite the inadequate lighting, nothing could have been more effective than the picture she presented, one hand holding up her skirts sufficiently to afford a glimpse of gold-sandalled feet and neatly-turned ankles, the other making play with an elegant ivory *brisé* fan. Challis, who had seen nothing like it in that house for more years than he cared to remember, stared in open-mouthed fascination. Mr Ainsley, though scarce less be-wattled, yet retained sufficient wit to observe the effect of this apparition upon Lord Rotherham.

That gentleman stood as if rooted to the ground before saying with a decidedly steely edge to his voice: 'How delightfully you look, ma'am!' and, moving forward, offered the lady his arm.

Mr Ainsley, following behind them into the dining-room, could not withhold a secret smile of satisfaction, and dared to hope that the girl's quite remarkable looks might prove more persuasive in influencing his lordship's opinion than would any arguments he might venture to put forward.

CHAPTER
TWO

DINNER—though, in Miss Lawrence's opinion, such an appellation did more than justice to the simple repast set before them—proved an unexpectedly animated meal. Mr Ainsley exerted himself to be agreeable and, though Rotherham spoke little, she was nonetheless aware of his eyes constantly upon her while he lounged back in his chair, his long fingers playing with the stem of his wine-glass.

For her part she did her best to follow Mr Ainsley's lead, and was rewarded by a chuckle from his lordship when she recounted how Mrs Crawford, having been assured by a friend that a *trou-madame* table was just the thing for a lady in her circumstances, had ordered one of these indispensable pieces of furniture from Mr Gillow.

'A most handsome affair it was,' conceded Miss Lawrence, 'covered with superfine billiard cloth and complete with balls and pins, for only a little more than nine pounds, which gave us many a happy evening's entertainment, but not precisely what Mrs Crawford had in mind, having envisaged something more in the nature of a folding bagatelle board.'

'Why, then, you won't take it amiss, ma'am, if Mr Ainsley and I repair to the billiard-room for a time after dinner?' Rotherham spoke pleasantly enough.

'Indeed, my lord, if you should not dislike it too much, it would give me pleasure to accompany you.'

It was mortally cold in the billiard-room, but Mr Ainsley had had the forethought to produce his fur-lined travelling rug and, enveloped in its folds, Miss Lawrence presently found her eyelids drooping and an overwhelming desire for sleep come over her. After a time her silence was so marked that the gentlemen came to look at her.

'Safe in the arms of Morpheus,' pronounced Mr Ainsley. 'A beautiful innocent, do you not agree, my lord?'

'Beautiful? Yes, unquestionably.' Rotherham spoke with slow deliberation as he studied his next move upon the table. 'Innocent? Of that I am not so sure.'

'What do you mean, my lord?'

'If your suspicions are correct she could well have been directed here, either to spy out the land or to foster alarm and prompt me to do something ill-advised.'

'Like rushing into a hasty marriage against your better judgment?' enquired Mr Ainsley, gently sarcastic, though much relieved that his lordship had perceived the dangers attendant upon Miss Lawrence's advent.

Rotherham grinned. '*Touché*,' he admitted. 'But then my aunt knows little of me, she and my mama having taken each other in strong aversion from the very first.'

Mr Ainsley, carefully setting down his cue and drawing away from the sleeping Miss Lawrence, spoke quietly.

'Baynton, the lawyer who advised her—you'd not know of the fellow, my lord, but I do—is no better than a Captain Sharp, and is as close as inkle-weavers with Lady Heathcott. I have a new clerk in my office,' he added slowly, 'one who, in spite of his excellent testimonials, I hesitated to engage because he had once been in Baynton's employ. But time and the devil drive so I hired him. In the light of hindsight, maybe I was at fault. If her ladyship suspected his lordship's intentions then Baynton would be the very one to help her.'

'The clerk could have read my grandfather's will?'

Mr Ainsley nodded rueful assent. 'Which was to be kept close until you were returned to this country and the contents divulged to you and Sir Trevor on the same day.'

'Why did you leave me until the last, I wonder?' The apparent irrelevance of the question did not disconcert the little man in the least.

'Because here I could be sure of a comfortable bed, a good glass of port and a game of billiards,' he explained blithely. 'At Hever Court I would have had to listen by the hour to that coxcomb—your pardon, my lord!—your cousin discoursing upon the latest whim of fashion or some gastronomical delight that his chef had concocted to titillate his appetite.'

'Who said physicians should be good cooks?' Rotherham straightened up to observe the effects of his carefully placed ball. 'Now, see what you can do with that, my friend.'

'Mandeville, I believe.' Mr Ainsley surveyed the table from every angle before bringing off a stroke of consummate delicacy. 'But to plain facts, my lord. Do we warn this young lady of the danger she may invite in joining the household at Hever Court?'

'Danger? You don't think my aunt would force her to the altar at pistol point?'

'There are more subtle methods of persuasion.'

Rotherham looked from the sleeping girl to his grave-faced lawyer. 'You infer that it could be made impossible for her to refuse to marry my cousin?'

'Yes,' said Mr Ainsley baldly and left it at that.

Miss Lawrence stirred and sighed, and a curl dropped from its confining ribbon to rest upon one cheek. Rotherham's hard eyes betrayed a momentary flicker of something like pity.

'She is very young,' he allowed.

'Could you truly wish her wedded to your cousin?' persisted Mr Ainsley.

'God, no! But for all we can tell she may readily accept what is offered her—may have done so already.'

'I believe her to be free of any blame in the matter.' Mr Ainsley spoke with confidence. 'Have you a trustworthy connection in that house?'

Rotherham thought for a moment. 'Yes, Adam, my aunt's groom. He was in my grandfather's employ until the old man, in one of his rages, flung a carriage lamp at him and near killed him. He taught me to ride and my father and aunt also. I fancy he only stays with her out of devotion to the family. I spoke to him the other day. He'd most likely be happier here if I'm to remain. Now I come to think on't, Mrs Challis said something about taking on one of his granddaughters here—the girl, Lucy, I think.'

'Providing that circumstance is not known to Lady Heathcott, as of now the girl Lucy is appointed Miss Lawrence's maid,' decreed Mr Ainsley.

Rotherham raised a derisive eyebrow. 'Do companions have maids?' he asked.

'Not in the general way, but we can make up a story that

will fit the case. Lucy can convey a message to her grandfather and enlist his aid. If we are mistaken in our premoni-
tions then no harm is done. If not—'

'Yes, what do you propose to do—if not?' enquired his
lordship curiously.

'I don't know,' confessed Mr Ainsley. 'But, to be on the
safe side of chance, let us take the worst possible view of the
case. It is best that Lady Heathcott should not know of Miss
Lawrence's lodging here tonight. I will deliver her and Lucy
to Tunbridge Wells tomorrow and deposit them at the
Royal Sussex Hotel as if they had come off the London
coach. There they will be collected and brought to Hever
Court as previously arranged.'

'And how do you propose to explain all this to the young
lady?' Rotherham plainly was still unconvinced, either of
Miss Lawrence's innocence or of the need for such subterfuge.

'I shall tell her as much as I think fit,' returned the little
man calmly.

He was spared further explanation by reason of Miss
Lawrence opening her eyes and murmuring: 'Oh, dear, I
have been asleep! How very ill-bred of me—I do beg your
pardon.'

'It has been a long day for you, ma'am, and a very trying
one.' His lordship was all affability as he handed her out of
her chair and rescued the rug which had fallen to the floor.
'You'd better have this with you,' he added wryly. 'This
house is as cold as charity. Come, Ainsley, let us light the
lady to her bedchamber.'

Seeing Miss Lawrence to be a shade bewildered, as well
she might, by this apparent *volte-face* on Rotherham's part,
Mr Ainsley gallantly offered her his arm and, with her host
bearing the candles, they proceeded in dignified procession
upstairs. Then, his lordship having satisfied himself that
everything possible had been done for her comfort, they
bid her a respectful goodnight and withdrew.

Julienne-Ève, quite overcome by fatigue, was struggling
with the fastenings of her gown when a timid knock on the
door announced the arrival of a breathless Lucy.

'M'lord says I'm to lady's maid you, miss,' she gasped,

'and sleep on the truckle-bed here in your room.'

'Goodness me, whatever for?' wondered Miss Lawrence sleepily.

'Well, I expect he has his reasons, miss,' said Lucy who, though younger than her new mistress, was a deal wiser in the ways of the world. 'Now, if you'll turn your back, I'll have you out of that gown in no time.'

Miss Lawrence, her hair brushed and a warming-pan put once more between the sheets, was asleep before she knew herself to be in bed, nor did she wake when Lucy left the room to return some time later, looking thoughtful, to settle down upon the truckle-bed.

The morning was a raw and gusty one, with sharp spatters of rain punctuating brief bursts of sunshine. For a blissful moment Julienne-Eve lay, idly stretching, eyes still closed, savouring the anticipation of a new day. Then Lucy's voice, bidding her good-morning, brought her to full awareness and she sat up quickly.

'Mr Ainsley begs the privilege of a word with you, miss, as soon as you have broken your fast.'

'Why, whatever is the time?'

'Close on nine o'clock, miss, and he is wishful to be on his way. Would coffee and rolls and honey be all right, miss?'

'Yes, yes, anything.' Miss Lawrence, perceiving that a state of some urgency obtained, scrambled nimbly out of the big four-poster bed and into her clothes.

Little more than half-an-hour had passed before, leaving Lucy to pack up her possessions, she presented herself in the business room where Mr Ainsley awaited her.

'I trust you slept well, my dear young lady? His lordship sends his apologies but the gale has wrought damage in some far part of the estate and he has been out since daybreak.' Julienne-Eve experienced a distinct sense of disappointment which, she was quick to remind herself, was perfectly absurd, for how should his lordship be expected to wait upon a mere servant of his aunt's whom he had been obliged to shelter for one night? This last circumstance formed the basis of Mr Ainsley's next remark. 'I beg you will acquit me of impertinence, ma'am,' he said, 'but does anyone—apart from those in this house, of course—know of your being here last night?'

'How should anyone know of it, sir?' she asked, frankly
puzzled. 'Since I could not foretell it myself! Oh, there is
my driver, to be sure.'

Mr Ainsley waved that individual away with an impatient
gesture of the hand. 'His vehicle is being repaired now and,
I am given to understand, he should be gone within the
hour. I myself propose to carry you to the Wells so that you
and Lucy may be taken up by Lady Heathcott's carriage.'
He checked her as she was about to speak. 'Hear me out, if
you please. We have decided, Lord Rotherham and I, that
it would be best if her ladyship did not know of your being
here. I grant you all has been conducted with the utmost
propriety, but the presence of an unmarried and—if you
will allow me—most taking young lady in a bachelor establishment could give rise to—er, adverse comment.'

Miss Lawrence thought this over and decided there was
much in what he said. 'But why is Lucy to come with me,'
she required to know. 'Will not Lady Heathcott think it a
presumption on my part?'

Mr Ainsley took some little time to phrase a careful
reply. 'I am sure we can contrive a good story between us to
account for Lucy,' he said. 'An employee of your Mrs
Crawford's, devoted to you, resolved to see you safely to
your destination—something of that sort? Incidentally, her
grandfather is employed at Hever Court. If her ladyship is
prepared to take her on, so much the better.'

'Mr Ainsley,' said Miss Lawrence rather unsteadily, 'why
do you feel it necessary to provide me with a—a body-
guard?'

He smiled. 'I am happy not to have been mistaken in my
reading of your character, ma'am. I am of the opinion that
nothing less than the truth will satisfy you, though his
lordship is not in agreement with me on this. So I will effect
a compromise and give you the bones of the business
without all the reasons.'

She sat silent while he recounted to her with commendable clarity as much of the story as he thought fit to disclose.

'It is essential for Lady Heathcott's purpose that her son
should marry and produce an heir without loss of time. A

great amount of money is involved. Should Sir Trevor not fulfil this requirement before—before too long, then he stands to lose this fortune. You, being without family or expectations, are the ideal subject for the unenviable position of his wife.'

Miss Lawrence, her head in a spin, began to wonder if Mr Ainsley, whom she had taken to be a very sensible sort of man, might not, after all, be a candidate for Bedlam.

'Surely—some lady of his acquaintance—' she began.

'You have not met Sir Trevor,' he cut in brusquely. 'An unfortunate accident while an infant—he was thrown out of a carriage on to his head—has retarded his mental processes. He is like an overgrown child—a capricious child, I may add. What little wit he has is directed solely towards the adornment of his person and the demands of his stomach. Physically, he appears perfectly normal and, as is often the way in such cases, enjoys excellent health. But for a young lady like yourself to be obliged to endure a lifetime of subjection to such a man is beyond all reason.'

She turned so pale that, for a moment, he feared he had said too much and that too hastily. 'But if he should pay his addresses to me,' she said in a voice little above a whisper. 'I cannot be forced to accept his offer?'

Mr Ainsley regarded her with all the pity of his greater experience. 'There are ways, my dear, of overcoming even the strongest resolution, and alone in that house you would be helpless. Hence my intention to provide you with some assistance in the shape of Lucy and Adam.'

'Did Lady Heathcott know I had spent last night under this roof would she still be disposed to consider me as a future daughter-in-law?' enquired Miss Lawrence hopefully.

He darted her a sharp glance. 'From what I know of the lady, ma'am, she would most like lay stress on your tarnished reputation, and point out that your only hope of re-establishing it would be to marry Sir Trevor before—'

'Before what?' she asked, mystified by his sudden silence.

'Before Lord Rotherham conceives it to be his duty to do so,' he said reluctantly.

'Lord Rotherham? But why—he—is this some sort of jest, sir?'

'Far from it, ma'am, but I cannot say more.' Mr Ainsley, knowing himself to be on very thin ice, beat a hasty retreat. Miss Lawrence, however, was not minded to give up so easily.

'In what way is Lord Rotherham concerned in all this, if you please?' she demanded to be told.

Mr Ainsley drew a deep breath and decided that only frankness would answer. 'He stands in the same position as does Sir Trevor. Whichever one of them marries first and begets a son wins the fortune. Should neither produce a male child or, indeed, any child at all after a set period of years, then the money is dispersed in a more general way throughout the family. Nonetheless, I can assure you, ma'am, you need have no fear of his lordship forcing his attentions upon you.'

Strangely, this assurance did not afford the lady any consolation, and she was only half-attending to her mentor's advice on how she should conduct herself at Hever Court when they were joined by Rotherham in mud-splashed riding boots and coat, the raindrops glistening on his dark hair.

'Well,' he rapped out, looking keenly from one to the other. 'Have you told her? Yes, I can see you have. Which is it to be, ma'am? If you do not care for the prospect that lies ahead of you I will engage to convey you wherever you wish to go.'

'But I have nowhere to go,' said Miss Lawrence dolefully.

'You have no friends who could be of assistance?'

She thought over her meagre stock of acquaintance and shook her head. His lordship looked thoroughly exasperated then his expression changed to one of watchful scepticism.

Mr Ainsley quickly intervened. 'We could be mistaken, of course, in our reading of the matter,' he offered.

'If you have any doubts, ma'am, Adam'll take a message and I'll have you out of there in no time,' drawled Rotherham.

She began to thank him, but Mr Ainsley cut her short by consulting his watch and declaring they must be away if she was to give the appearance of having stepped off the London coach. Then she was being handed up into the waiting chaise; Lucy, round-eyed with excitement, was seated opposite her, while the gentlemen exchanged a few last-moment confidences. The steps were put up, the door shut, and they were away at a lively pace down the drive, the curve of which presently hid the sight of the great house and of its master, standing before it, from her view.

As Tunbridge Wells was not above seven miles distant and Mr Ainsley's cattle were a pair of fast goers, the journey was accomplished in a remarkably short time. Miss Lawrence was not unfamiliar with the town, having spent a month there on one occasion, lodging at the house of some old friends of Mrs Crawford's who, being in somewhat reduced circumstances, were obliged to take in lodgers to supplement their income. This information, for a reason she could not precisely define, she preferred to keep to herself. However genteel and amiable, the Misses Beresford could scarcely be expected to extend the same cordial reception to her in her present situation as when she had been Mrs Crawford's favoured companion. At every turn a reminder of her sadly changed way of life was being thrust upon her, and she was obliged to blink back the ready tears and make civil response to Mr Ainsley's cheerful discourse. That gentleman, having deposited them at the Royal Sussex Hotel, took himself off without delay, it being no part of his plan to be recognised by any of Lady Heathcott's staff, and again Miss Lawrence felt a lump rise in her throat as she watched the smart little chaise dash away.

She had small opportunity for repining, however, for Lucy, who had never before been to the Wells, was so loud in her admiration of everything she saw that there was nothing for it but to leave their baggage in the porter's charge and take a turn along the Parade. There they viewed the busy shops and marvelled at the press of people going to visit the chalybeate springs for, in the opinion of many astute judges, Tunbridge Wells had numerous advantages to offer the visitor which gave it a decided preference over all other watering-places, of which it was the most ancient in the kingdom, Bath only excepted.

They got back to the hotel in good time to witness the arrival of the stage-coach and watch its passengers alight. As they did not appear to be looked for yet, Miss Lawrence ordered coffee, and they were sitting, sipping it and observing their companions in the busy coffee-room, when Lucy suddenly stiffened and rose to her feet.

'It is—yes, 'tis granddad!' she exclaimed, staring over Miss Lawrence's head out of the window at a carriage that had drawn up outside. 'I'll go fetch him, miss!'

'Be careful, Lucy! You know what Mr Ainsley said—' began Julienne-Eve, but found herself talking to thin air.

Lucy returned a few moments later with a tall, grey-haired man, dressed in groom's livery, whom she proudly presented to her mistress. Adam, who appeared to be a man of few words, knuckled his forehead and made a leg.

'You'll be the young leddy, then, come from Lunnon?'

'From Sevenoaks, to be exact.' Miss Lawrence, wondering who he supposed she might be if not Lady Heathcott's new companion, experienced a decided lowering of the spirits at sight of her new ally.

'He bain't such a buzzy old fool as he looks!' Lucy assured her in a piercing whisper once they were settled in their seats. 'He don't talk the dog's head off, but he's peart enough.'

Miss Lawrence was quite prepared to accept this limited encomium until she could judge of the matter for herself. For the moment, her attention was held by the handsome barouche drawn by a pair of sleek dapple-greys, its panels picked out in pale blue to match the silk lining and cushions, and its shining silver-plated ornamental work. If this was the style in which Lady Heathcott proposed to support her companion, then that young lady had no fault to find with it. Nonetheless, as she sank back thankfully into the deep cushions and Lucy placed a rug over her knees, she could not quite put from her mind the memory of another mode of travel which she had experienced the previous day, held close by a gentleman's strong arm—less comfortable, perhaps, but somehow more reassuring.

CHAPTER
THREE

EVEN to Miss Lawrence's untutored eye, Hever Court was a gentleman's residence of outstanding elegance, its perfect proportions proclaiming the hand of Mr Holland as surely as did the flowing symmetry of its landscaped gardens that of his father-in-law, Mr 'Capability' Brown.

Within the house, the same sense of affluent good taste prevailed. A bracket-faced female in rustling bombazine led the travellers upstairs to a bedchamber which, to Julienne-Eve's way of thinking, was more suited to a lady of fashion than to a humble companion; the furnishings, from the draped tent-bed to the boat-shaped couch with crocodile feet, being in the very first style. Once again, she could not help but compare her circumstances with those of the previous evening, but she was allowed little time for reflection for the woman, whom she discovered to be Lady Heathcott's dresser, informed her that she would return in half-an-hour to escort her to her ladyship.

'An' you'd best be ready and up to the rig,' advised Lucy sapiently. 'That one's as sharp as she can stare and she'll soon know I'm no lady's maid! Out of those clothes, if you please, miss, and let me put you to rights.'

Prompt to the minute, Miss Lawrence, discreetly dressed in a simple cambric gown with a Paisley shawl folded about her shoulders, was conducted to Lady Heathcott's drawing-room where her ladyship received her, reclining upon a chaise-longue.

Her air of fragility accorded well with the muted hues of the satin drapes, the delicate shading of the silk-lined walls, and the Savonnerie carpet, all of which combined to form a picture worthy of the brush of Watteau, the subdued tones lending a pleasing touch of melancholy to the scene. A superbly carved harp, with painted sound-board, occupied one corner of the room; beside it was placed a gilt chair and foot-stool, as if awaiting the musician whose fingers would bring the instrument to life.

Observing the young woman's wide-eyed interest, Lady Heathcott smiled faintly and waved her to be seated. As Julienne-Eve moved to a nearby sofa there was an upheaval among the cushions and a large marmalade cat revealed itself, who glared at the newcomer out of malevolent green eyes and, tail twitching, sprang to the floor and stalked across to its mistress to establish itself upon her lap.

'So you are Julienne-Eve Lawrence?'

'Yes, ma'am—my lady.'

'Ma'am will do, or Lady Heathcott.' The light clear voice was as impersonal as water dripping from a stone. 'I had not thought you to be so young.'

Miss Lawrence felt she might well say the same of her employer. 'I am in my twenty-second year, ma'am.'

'Quite an age, to be sure.' Her ladyship sounded amused. 'Now tell me all about yourself. Mr Baynton gave me only the scantiest details and, man-like, left out what was of first importance.' She listened without interruption to Miss Lawrence's account of her existence from an early age, her pale eyes fixed unwaveringly upon the girl's face. 'I see,' she said, when the recital was complete. 'No family and no—attachments of any sort?'

'No, ma'am,' said Julienne-Eve, then added quickly to account for the inexplicable colour that had flooded her cheeks, 'I have an apology and a request to make to you, ma'am. Lucy, the girl who accompanied me—'.

'Ah, yes, Lucy,' murmured Lady Heathcott, her slender beringed fingers digging deep into the cat's thick fur to which it responded with loud purrings. 'Tell me about Lucy.'

It was clear that word of Lucy's presence had already reached the drawing-room, and Miss Lawrence told her—or, rather Mr Ainsley's—story in what she hoped was a convincing manner, ending up with a plea that, if a place could be found for her, the girl might be kept on at Hever Court.

'Adam's granddaughter, is she? Well, I shall see what can be arranged but, for the moment, keep her for your own convenience. And now,' Lady Heathcott went on, raising a hand to the bell-pull and cutting across Miss Lawrence's expressions of gratitude, 'you must be sharp-set after your journey. I will arrange for a nuncheon to be sent to your room. Do you ride, by the way? You do? Capital! Adam will be delighted to have someone exercise his horses. Send Lucy to inform him whenever you wish for it.'

Miss Lawrence, knowing herself to be dismissed, yet had to ask a further question. 'But—my duties, ma'am?'

Again she was subjected to that unblinking scrutiny. Even the cat had turned its head to look at her, and she could not help but observe how like to the animal's eyes were her ladyship's and was put uncomfortably in mind of a witch's familiar.

'They need not concern you to-day, I believe. Spend the afternoon in settling in and getting to learn your way about. We will meet again at dinner.'

All perfectly agreeable, Julienne-Eve had to admit as she made her way back to her room, yet there lingered a persistent suspicion at the back of her mind that she was being assessed in terms of usefulness to her ladyship's designs and for no other purpose. In just such a way had her mother been used to—of course! That accounted for the odd sense of recognition she had experienced when speaking to Lady Heathcott! They were two of a kind, maman and her ladyship, cool, poised, and sparing of affection. To children and animals, perhaps, some warmth might be shown since they offered no threat of rivalry, but towards a daughter growing into womanhood or, maybe, a companion with looks above what was ordinary, no generosity could be expected.

The unfortunate fact of that country being at war with England had not deterred her mother from getting to France. With superb aplomb, she had connived at the escape of a French prisoner-of-war and, in recompense for her assistance, he had offered to marry her and take her with him. Having been in Mrs Crawford's household for two years apparently supplied a good and sufficient reason, in Mrs Lawrence's eyes, for leaving her daughter in that lady's care. There had been one brief message from her announcing her safe arrival in France but, after that, nothing. Despite her natural anxiety, Julienne-Eve had to confess that things were infinitely more agreeable that way. The strong bond of affection between her daughter and Mrs Crawford had been a constant source of affront to Mrs Lawrence, who was a lady capable of imagining a slight or insult if a sufficient one was not offered. No doubt her equivocal position and lack of fortune did much to nurture this unhappy trait, or so her daughter charitably supposed.

A tap upon the door interrupted these unprofitable musings, and Lucy entered, bearing a tray piled high with food. Both young women promptly set to, with good appetite, to sample the cold meats, cheese and fruit set out for their approval.

'One thing, miss,' said Lucy when the first pangs had been assuaged. 'I can't sleep here with you. Her ladyship won't have it, says the women servants must sleep in the West wing and the men here in the main building, else they'll be gettin' up to larks.' As the girl seemed to find her ladyship's precaution perfectly reasonable, Miss Lawrence said nothing, but she was the more surprised when Lucy, having finished her meal, removed the key from the lock and laid it on the dressing-table. 'Granddad said to keep it by you, miss. The wind's in the west to-night and blows through these windows fierce enough to rattle your door. Best lock it than stay wakeful.' Miss Lawrence, unimpressed by the excuse—for how should Adam be supposed to know how the wind might affect her bedroom door?—thanked her and put the key away in a drawer, but the incident caused her to speculate on just how much Mr Ainsley had told Lucy of his fears for her mistress's safety. 'Granddad did say that if you cared for a ride, he'd saddle up a mount for you whenever you wished,' added Lucy, heaping the empty dishes together. 'I can tell him when I take these back to the kitchen.'

So that instruction had reached the stables already! 'For today I think a walk around the gardens will suffice,' said Miss Lawrence firmly, 'and then, with your aid, we will go through my wardrobe.'

'Aye, you'll need all your gowns here, miss,' Lucy warned her darkly as she edged her way out of the room with the tray. 'Full rig for dinner every evening, I'm told.'

Miss Lawrence was to discover that Lucy's informant had not been at fault when she presented herself that evening in the small ante-room which gave on to the dining-room. Here she found Lady Heathcott and her son awaiting her. Having pictured Sir Trevor to be something of a zany and quite ineligible in every way, she was much taken aback to find him to be the epitome of a man of fashion. From his pomaded hair to his satin knee-breeches and striped silk stockings he was a delight to behold, for Nature had blessed him with an excellent figure which displayed to advantage the sartorial triumphs of his tailor.

He greeted the newcomer to his household with a lack of interest that bordered on the discourteous, scarcely raising his heavy-lidded eyes from contemplation of his gold-mounted shell snuffbox which appeared to afford him much gratification.

'Servant, Miss—er—'

'Miss Lawrence, Trevor,' supplied her ladyship.

'Oh, yes, Miss Lawrence.' The indolent drawl was almost an insult in itself and he capped it by turning to consult the Viennese black-and-gold mantel clock behind him. 'Three minutes past the hour. Late, wouldn't you say?'

The indignant Julienne-Eve was about to speak up in her own defence when Lady Heathcott interposed smoothly.

'Miss Lawrence has but arrived today. It is not at all an easy thing, let me tell you, my dear Trevor, to be obliged to make one's first appearance at a strange table and look as charmingly as she does.'

Far from being set down by this reproof, Sir Trevor merely grunted and offered his arm to his mother to lead her into the dining-room. The mortified Miss Lawrence was about to follow when Lady Heathcott, her good humour quite dissipated, reprimanded him once more.

'I am out of all patience with you, Trevor! You have two arms, have you not?'

'What? Oh, yes, of course.'

Reluctantly accepting his other arm, Julienne-Eve pri-

vately marvelled that Lady Heathcott should be so busy in
her defence but, as the meal progressed, she began to
understand that her ladyship used her son as she would any
peevish spoiled child. He was like a beautifully-dressed
puppet that danced to her touch on the strings, nor did he
appear to have an opinion in his head that was not placed
there by her.

During the excellent meal of fried river trout with shrimp
forcemeat, supported by a saddle of mutton with its attendant vegetables and sauces, and an assortment of jellies,
creams and cheeses, Lady Heathcott kept up a light, unforced conversation, to which Miss Lawrence responded as
best she could. Sir Trevor spoke only when spoken to and
sometimes not then, his whole attention seemingly concen-
trated on his food of which he consumed a vast amount, the
unobtrusive butler being swift to anticipate his every wish
and keep his plate and glass filled to capacity.

Fascinated by the spectacle, Miss Lawrence was startled
back to awareness by her ladyship enquiring if she was at all
acquainted with the town of Tunbridge Wells and its en-
virons.

'I visited there on one occasion with my late employer,'
she replied, deciding that a half-truth would meet the case.
'But I cannot pretend to any great knowledge of the place.'

'It has, of course, fallen greatly out of favour since the
Regent brought Brighton into fashion but, for myself, I
prefer it.' Sir Trevor, his mouth full of succulent meat, was
understood to mutter that Brighton was all the crack. 'Not,
of course,' continued his mother, disregarding this conversational gem, 'that we are without entertainment here, did
we choose to avail ourselves of it, for there are many houses
of distinction in the neighbourhood. The nearest is that of
Lord Rotherham, but five or six miles away. He is my
brother's son,' she added, 'and now, since his grandfather's
death, the head of the family.'

'Rotherham? Ain't seen him in an age,' pronounced Sir
Trevor, moved to something like animation. 'Good sort of
fellow, Rotherham.'

'Well, there could be two sides to that opinion.' Lady
Heathcott's icy tone left at least one of her listeners in no

doubt as to which side she favoured. 'It is to be hoped that his years in the army will have rendered him a little more—amenable.'

She turned to address a request to her butler and Miss Lawrence glanced towards Sir Trevor, hoping that he might have something more to add about his cousin. To her alarm, she found him to be staring at her fixedly, his eyes no longer blankly disinterested but filled with a sort of lustful eagerness that threatened to strip the very clothes from her person. Instinctively, she put a hand to her bosom as if to protect herself from this visual assault, but his interest in her seemed to have passed and he was once more absorbed in the delights of the table.

Pleading fatigue, she retired to her room soon after tea had been dispensed. A footman lighted her upstairs and saw to the replenishing of her fire. She asked him where Lucy was and received a very odd look in reply.

'None o' the girls sleeps in the main house, miss,' she was informed.

'Oh, of course,' she agreed, feeling suddenly grateful for the key lying secure in her dressing-table drawer. 'Thank you, that will be all. Goodnight.'

He looked as if he was about to say more, but changed his mind and left her. At once she ran to her dressing-table to get the key. Surely she had put it in the top right-hand drawer? But it was not there and, though she turned everything out upon the floor, nor was it in any of the other drawers.

Sternly repressing the urge to indulge in a fit of strong hysterics, Miss Lawrence sat down to consider her situation in a rational manner. Who should have removed the key save one who wished to enter her room at will, or permit another to do so? The thought of who that other might be sent a cold chill down her spine, and she looked round the big, well-lit bedchamber in a sort of wonderment as if incapable of believing her own fears. Then, from somewhere below, came the sound of the deep, throbbing notes of a harp.

Drawing back a curtain, she perceived light streaming from the room beneath on to a terrace and realised that her

bedchamber was situated directly above Lady Heathcott's
drawing-room.

'All the more reason for not spending a night in this
room!' she muttered as the music rose to a crescendo, and
going to her door, peered out into the passage. Most of the
candles in the wall-sconces had been extinguished, but there
was sufficient light for her to discern another door across
the way from hers. Cautiously she tried the door-knob and
sighed in relief when it yielded to reveal another bedchamber, bright with moonlight, and containing only a few
necessary pieces of furniture. The whole bore a neglected
air and smelled slightly musty.

'There are worse things than the smell of must!' she
informed herself severely, ascertaining that there was not
only a key on the inside of the door but also a bolt. It was
the work of moments only to collect blankets and pillows
from her own bed and substitute a warm robe-de-chambre
for her thin gown. All the while the music from below
swelled and ebbed, sometimes in a light, tripping melody,
at others as mournful as a dirge. Miss Lawrence, though
grateful for anything that might cover the sound of her own
movements, vowed that never again would she listen to the
notes of a harp with an easy mind. Then, extinguishing all
the candles, she stole across the passage to her refuge.
After a slight struggle, she managed to open the window a
few inches and the brisk cold wind explored every corner of
the room.

'Depend upon it, it is better to freeze than suffocate!' she
sighed, dwelling with longing upon the memory of the good
fire she had left behind her. Having secured the door, she
wrapped herself up closely in the blankets and, despite her
agitation of spirit, shortly fell asleep and knew no more
until she awoke the following morning at her accustomed
early hour.

The wind had risen to a gale during the night and,
shivering, she hastened to close the window. There
appeared to be no sound of movement in the house and she
resolved to get back to her own room before the staff
should commence their daily duties. The first thing she saw,
on looking out into the passage, was that the door to her

own bedchamber stood wide open. Presuming that Lucy or some other servant was already astir, she hurried across, only to stop and stare in utter stupefaction at the scene of disorder before her. Chairs were overturned, the remaining covers had been ripped from the bed, and her few toilet possessions set out upon the dressing-table had been swept to the floor in a confusion of broken glass and china. It was as if a wanton child had stormed about the room, destroying everything in his path. A wanton child! She recalled Mr Ainsley's description of Sir Trevor and, again, experienced a chill of apprehension.

'Try for a little sense,' she urged herself. 'There was a storm last night—an open window—?' But a glance confirmed that the windows were firmly shut and, coming to a swift decision, she returned to her refuge and removed every trace of her overnight tenancy.

She had almost completed the task of putting her room to rights and was on her knees, trying to collect together the débris from the dressing-table, when Lucy's voice sounded outside, asking if she might enter.

'Goodmorning—Lord have pity on us, miss! Whatever's happened?'

'It would seem I did not pay sufficient heed to your grandfather's warning about the wind last night,' explained Miss Lawrence ruefully, sitting back on her heels, 'but unwisely left a window open—with what result you can perceive.'

Quite why she did not wish to tell Lucy the truth she could not be perfectly sure. It was not that she did not trust the girl, but until some explanation of the occurrence was forthcoming she felt the least said the better.

'Don't be troubling yourself with that, miss. I'll fetch a broom and scoop when I come to do your fire. Do you wish for chocolate or tea, miss?'

Miss Lawrence declared for chocolate and drank it gratefully, huddled up in her cold bed and nibbling a Naples biscuit, while Lucy swept up and laid the fire.

'Oh, by-the-by, did you happen to remove the key from my drawer yesterday evening while I was at dinner?' she enquired artlessly.

'Me? 'deed, no, miss! D'you mean you didn't lock your door last night?'

'I couldn't very well without a key, could I?'

'But you put it—' Lucy went to the dressing-table and opened the top drawer. 'Here!' And she held up the key for Miss Lawrence's startled inspection.

'How—how very stupid of me!' she managed to get out. 'How could I have missed it?'

'Lying under a scarf, it was,' nodded the maid. 'Best keep it with you to-day. I'm to take you to her ladyship at nine o'clock so I'll be back again about five minutes to the hour. I've sponged and pressed your riding habit and it will be all ready for you when you want it.'

The interview with Lady Heathcott proved unexpectedly brief. She protested that, never having had a companion before, no doubt Miss Lawrence knew more of her duties than did she. Her present housekeeper was a stupid woman and loath to suggest anything that might involve her in more work than she quite liked, perhaps Miss Lawrence would take over the arrangement of the dinner menus? Then there were the flowers to be seen to—the head gardener would cut her what blooms she required from the greenhouses.

'I am never in plump currant in the morning,' her ladyship confessed, lying back against a mound of lacy pillows, her bed strewn with magazines and papers, and a suspicious bulge under the coverlet hinting at the presence of her cat. 'Find what you can to do and then have Adam escort you for a ride.' Julienne-Eve, reflecting that every-one seemed bent on getting her on the back of a horse, was about to go in search of the housekeeper when her ladyship spoke again. 'And how did you sleep last night?'

'Very well, I thank you, ma'am.'

'But not, I understand, in your own bed?'

Miss Lawrence braced herself. She had not been going to raise that issue but since someone, probably her dresser, had told Lady Heathcott, she had her answer ready.

'No, ma'am. I know it to be out of all reason foolish, but I am not at ease alone in a strange room unless the door be locked, and I had mislaid the key.'

'And have you found it now?'

'Yes, thank you, ma'am.'

Her ladyship nodded as if the conversation held no further interest for her and turned her attention back to *The Lady's Magazine*, leaving her companion with nothing to do but retire, closing the door quietly behind her.

She found the housekeeper to be a timid, rather than a stupid woman, who clearly was in dread of her mistress's disapproval. 'Living under the cat's tongue, that's what it is,' she animadverted bitterly. 'You'll find out, miss! Sweet as sugar-pie one moment and rakin' you down the next! And as for that dresser of hers, Miss Marchant, stick a knife in you she would, if it took her fancy! And there's nothing goes on in this house that she don't know about!'

While privately agreeing with this masterly summing-up of character, Miss Lawrence was careful to murmur something non-committal and suggest they had a word with the chef, who turned out to be a cadaverous Italian, with the eyes of a soulful spaniel but a strictly gentleman-like appreciation of a pretty young lady.

After that invigorating encounter, she dealt with the head-gardener, to such effect that his admiring underling had to assist her carry back her burden of blossom in a wheelbarrow. Once the flowers had been arranged to her satisfaction, she then felt at liberty to indulge in her own pursuits and, calling for Lucy, hurried to change into her riding-habit.

The sedate bay mare Adam produced for her approval brought a hastily suppressed smile to her lips, but she jogged off demurely enough until they were well away from the house.

'May I allow her to show her paces now?' she enquired with gentle malice.

'She hasn't many,' admitted Adam, respectfully eyeing the lady's straight back and admirable seat. 'But, then, I wasn't to know, was I, miss?'

'Well, now you do know, don't you?' retorted Miss Lawrence, urging her sluggish steed into as near a gallop as was to be hoped for.

His next remark revealed that Adam knew about things

other than horses. 'What took place last night, miss? Lucy told me you'd mislaid the key to your room.' The expression on her face prompted him to add: 'That lass is awake upon every suit, she knew sommat was amiss.'

Miss Lawrence decided that Lucy's grandpapa was no nodcock either, and told him of the condition in which she had found her bedchamber that morning.

'Thank God you wasn't in it,' he said when she had finished. 'But—'tis strange, that. He—well, he—' He stopped, plainly embarrassed at what he was about to say.

'You mean Sir Trevor, don't you?'

'Yes, miss. You'll have seen for yourself that he's a thought astray in the head, poor lad, but there's no vice in him, that I'll swear. In any case, he's shut up at night in the East wing with Stapleton, his valet. 'T ain't possible he could've found your key.'

Julienne-Eve was tempted to enquire why, if Sir Trevor was so harmless, was he confined at night, but the groom's words had touched a chord of memory and, in her mind's eye, she saw Lucy producing the key from a drawer as a magician would a rabbit from a hat. She glanced at Adam, but he was staring ahead of him, his face set in an uncommonly forbidding way. 'Awake upon every suit' he had said of his granddaughter. More so than her mistress, it would appear! But why should Lucy do such a thing? To frighten the lady away? And who would profit by her departure? Not Lady Heathcott if she was bent on having her as bride for her son. Lost in her thoughts, she scarce uttered a word for the remainder of their ride.

At the end of it, as Adam assisted her down from her patient steed, he said gruffly: 'I'll have a prime 'un for you tomorrow, miss.'

Tomorrow, mused Miss Lawrence, making her way back to the house. Who knows what might not have happened before tomorrow?

CHAPTER
FOUR

CONTRARY to Miss Lawrence's apprehensions, nothing very much happened, although dinner that evening was marred by a peevish outburst from Sir Trevor, deploring the dressing of one of his favourite dishes, and a thundering scold was delivered to be passed on to the kitchen.

Lady Heathcott, ignoring her son's complaints in a way which suggested she was all too used to them, remarked that she found her glove drawer to be sadly depleted and, if her companion would be so obliging, several new pairs could be purchased in Tunbridge Wells on the following day.

Miss Lawrence undertook the commission with delight and, with Adam handling the reins, was away from Hever Court before ten o'clock. It was a bright, clear morning, giving promise of a rare Autumn day; she was in the highest of spirits and much inclined to set down her previous doubts and fears as the products of a disordered imagination. In her striped sarcenet gown with a green velvet spencer to match the ribbons trimming her excessively becoming chip straw bonnet, she looked as fresh as the morning itself and, if much of this ensemble had been fashioned by her own skilful fingers, that in no way detracted from its elegance. Indeed, in the opinion of many gentlemen of taste and discernment taking their daily stroll along the Parade the sun, shining with impartiality upon all, yet chose no worthier object on which to lavish its radiance than Miss Lawrence.

Oblivious to the interest she had aroused in these male bosoms Julienne-Eve, having purchased her ladyship's gloves, allowed her attention to be captured by a striking display in a nearby mercer's window. Once inside the shop, the materials spread out for her inspection were so many and varied that she found herself wholly at a loss in making her choice. Arguably, the acquisition of fifty pounds justified some slight extravagance, but she was all too aware that, once her small capital had gone, there might be no more to take its place. With this constraint in mind, she was hesitating between the relative merits of a delicate leylock jaconet on the one hand and a fine heavenly blue poplin on the other when a soft hesitant voice spoke almost in her ear.

'Surely I cannot be mistaken? It must be—it *is* Miss Lawrence!'

The speaker was an elderly gentlewoman, dressed with neat propriety, who stood, hands clasped in a supplicating manner, regarding Julienne-Eve out of large mild blue eyes.

'Miss Beresford! Oh, what joy to see you! How are you, and how is Miss Anne?'

'Alas!' The blue eyes clouded with ready tears. 'My poor sister is laid upon her bed and is not like to leave it for many a day.'

'But how is this? What—'

'She would not be denied the apples from the topmost branch of the tree, the ladder slipped and she broke a leg,' explained Miss Beresford sadly. 'I am sure I don't know how I shall go on for, as you know, she did everything that was practical in the house. Despite the summer season being over, we have every room taken until the end of the year and after.' Miss Lawrence came to a swift decision in favour of the leylock jaconet and, while the assistant was parcelling it up, gave Miss Beresford her own news, which occasioned further tears in memory of Mrs Crawford. 'But how fortunate for you to have obtained a post in such an establishment as Hever Court! Lady Heathcott is of the very first consequence though, of course, Sir Trevor—' She disposed of Sir Trevor with a deprecating gesture and Julienne-Eve, her purchase completed, took her by the arm and led her outside.

'Miss Beresford, can we be private somewhere for a few moments? I would dearly like your advice upon a—a matter of importance.'

'Well, I must not linger. There is so much to be done with Anne indisposed,' fluttered the lady hesitantly. 'But I had intended to spend a few minutes in reflection in church.

There is rarely anyone there at this hour of day.'

'Then let us go thither.' Miss Lawrence took command of the situation and they hastened in the direction of the nearby Church of King Charles the Martyr.

They found the building to be quite deserted and established themselves in a discreet corner where they could talk quietly, unobserved. There Miss Lawrence explained, in the most moving way, that she could not be easy in her present employment and might well decide to relinquish it at no very distant date.

'I had thought of coming to you for a time as a guest,' she concluded tentatively. 'But, not to put too fine a point on it, I cannot afford to be without gainful occupation for very long at a stretch.'

Miss Beresford drew a deep breath. 'Miss Lawrence, I do believe you were *sent* in answer to my prayers! Would you—could you consider coming to live at Culver Lodge and assisting me while dear Anne is incapacitated?'

As this was precisely what Julienne-Eve had in mind, she lost no time in assuring Miss Beresford of her willingness to cooperate in such an undertaking.

'But how I am to extricate myself from Hever Court, I do not yet know,' she confessed, 'for there is nothing in her ladyship's conduct or treatment of me to justify my leaving her service.' She hesitated, then hurried on. 'I know I can trust to your discretion, ma'am?' Miss Beresford, all eager interest, gave the required assent. 'Then—I have been told that Lady Heathcott seeks a wife for her son—some question of a legacy lost should he not marry. To my mind, she is in no need of a companion, so what can be the true reason for my employment?'

'You mean—she would require you to marry Sir Trevor?' The clear eyes were wide with horror. 'Oh, no, Miss Lawrence! Not for any title or legacy!' A little surprised at hearing her own opinion so heartily endorsed, Julienne-Eve unfolded her plan in so far as she had thought it out, and the older lady nodded her approval. 'Rest assured I shall have a room made ready for you—not, I fear, as grand a one as you have been accustomed to, for the better bedchambers are all bespoke, but, depend upon it, it will be comfortable and you may come as soon as you conveniently can. I may inform Anne of your circumstances, may I not?'

'Of course but, if you please, no one else. You just chanced to meet me and I am looking for a post.'

Promising the utmost discretion, Miss Beresford hurried back to Culver Lodge, all aglow with her good fortune, while Miss Lawrence, equally relieved in her mind, rejoined Adam at the Royal Sussex.

Several times on the journey back was she tempted to confide in him, but the knowledge that his loyalties, if not with Lady Heathcott, must lie with Lord Rotherham, held her silent. How could she count on greater safety at Leyswood Towers than at Hever Court? Lord Rotherham, no less than his cousin, needed a bride and, while she believed Mr Ainsley to be speaking the truth when he declared his client would not force his attentions upon her, yet a fortune was a fortune and, by the look of things, his lordship stood in want of it.

For a moment she allowed herself to dwell wistfully upon the prospect of becoming Lady Rotherham, but commonsense quickly checked that line of thought. Once she had fulfilled her marital duty and an heir was assured, she had no doubt his lordship would go his way and leave her to her own devices. Dismissing all such notions as being quite unworthy of her consideration, she bent her mind to the problem of how to get herself to the Misses Beresford without anyone knowing of her intention. She was still wrestling with this apparently insoluble difficulty when they came to a halt with something of a flourish before Hever Court.

'Will two o'clock suit you for your ride, miss?' enquired Adam politely as he handed her down.

'Yes, so long as her ladyship does not require me.'

'Very good, miss. I promise to have something a bit livelier for you to-day.'

There was the nearest thing she had seen to a grin on Adam's face as he drove off, leaving her wondering just what sort of animal she was going to have to contend with that afternoon.

She at once discovered Icarus to be the most beautifully-mannered bit of blood she had ever had the good fortune to mount. A gleaming resty chestnut, never once did he allow her to feel that he was the master, but submitted gracefully to her lightest touch upon the reins.

'Oh, he is wonderful!' she cried out in sheer delight as she gave him his head, with Adam on his steady grey close behind her. 'To whom does he belong? Who rides him?'

'He mostly eats his head off, miss. I mount him when I can. The master bought him but—they don't deal very well together.'

Miss Lawrence could understand that, for how should so intelligent a creature readily submit to so doltish an authority? 'I am going to shake the fidgets out of him,' she called over her shoulder. As Icarus lengthened his stride the distance between him and the grey increased until she was flying down the greensward by the road that bounded the estate, with the groom left far behind.

It was then she felt the slightest movement of the saddle and immediately she checked her headlong course. Icarus responded obediently, dropping down to a canter when, without further warning, the girth parted and Julienne-Eve was precipitated to the ground, being given no time to do more than kick her foot free of the stirrup as she fell.

'Miss, miss, are you safe?' Adam, bending anxiously over her, looked to where Icarus had halted, the saddle trailing.

'The—the girth slipped, I think,' said Miss Lawrence, putting a hand to her spinning head and thanking her good fortune that she had landed on thick grass and not on the road.

'By the looks of it, the girth's broke, miss,' said Adam grimly. 'You just bide there while I fetch him back.'

Thrusting the grey's reins into her hand, he set off at a trot towards the troubled Icarus who, not being in the way of experiencing such untoward accidents was, nonetheless, behaving with the greatest good sense. Adam's perfunctory treatment of her brought a near-smile to Julienne-Eve's lips. His horse first, the rider a long way second, was the essence of a good groom, but the expression on his face when he returned, leading the chestnut, was not reassuring.

'Is it—oh!' Miss Lawrence, in attempting to rise, found she had not escaped entirely unscathed for her left ankle seemed disinclined to support her weight. Subsiding back upon the ground, she inspected it carefully. 'Nothing much,' she announced. 'A twist or slight sprain maybe. But we are a long way from home.'

'That girth has been cut through, miss.' Adam's voice was cold with shocked disapproval. 'To within an inch or two.'

'So that it would hold for a time?'

'Aye, 'til you were ridin' hard. Thank God, you reined him in, miss.'

'But how—who saddled him up?'

'I did, miss. And that girth was whole then, I'll swear.' He paused, reflecting. 'I gave him to the lad, Jem, to hold while I led out the grey and—yes, Lucy came by to have a word with me. Her ladyship required to know whether the barouche would be ready for her use this afternoon—some small repair was being done to the sway-bar.'

'So you went to look at the barouche, leaving Lucy to hold the grey?'

He stared at her stonily. 'What you're sayin', miss, is that either Lucy or Jem did it, for I left them together.'

Miss Lawrence was about to ask him what other alternative he had to offer when a loud hail attracted their attention, and they looked to see a gig, handled by Lord Rotherham, come bowling along the road.

'What's to do?' Then he saw the swinging saddle. 'Good God! A faulty girth?'

'Cut through, my lord.' Adam gave him details while Miss Lawrence rubbed her injured limb and wondered when anyone was going to show concern for her plight.

'You have taken no hurt, ma'am?' His enquiry, she was persuaded, was prompted, by the merest civility.

'Nothing to speak of, my lord, save for my ankle,' she replied as coolly as she dared, wishing with all her heart that it had been anyone other than Rotherham who had, once again, come to her rescue.

'Let us have that boot off—gently, so!' His long fingers lightly probed the injury while she watched his intent face.

At length he nodded as if satisfied. 'A sprain, nothing more, no bones broken. We had best make for Leyswood Towers where Mrs Challis can attend to you, it is only a mile or so distant. Adam, you can return to Hever Court with the horses and bring back a carriage for the lady.'

Miss Lawrence who, despite putting a brave face on it, was beginning to experience the after-effects of a severe fall, submitted meekly to being lifted into the gig while Adam, leading Icarus, set off back to Hever Court.

'It would seem,' said his lordship, deftly turning the little vehicle, 'that someone is ill-disposed towards you, ma'am.'

'That possibility had occurred to me also, my lord,' said she, struggling against an almost irresistible urge to burst into tears.

'I had a message from my mother this morning,' he went on, as easily as if he was tooling her around the Park at the fashionable hour and nothing untoward had happened. 'She informs me that she and a friend propose to join me at Leyswood Towers to-morrow for a time.' Miss Lawrence's head was beginning to ache rather badly so she did not give this intelligence the attention it deserved. He glanced at her sharply. 'What I am endeavouring to explain, ma'am, is that, once my mother is fairly installed, it will be perfectly proper for you to seek refuge under my roof, if such should be your need.'

Miss Lawrence stiffened. His mother, indeed! Did he really expect her to be taken in by such a Banbury tale?

'I cannot conceive of Lady Heathcott viewing my removal into your care with anything other than disapprobation,' she said primly.

'I allow it would be best if she did not know of your destination,' he agreed. 'For if she comes seeking you and meets up with my mama, I doubt that either of 'em will keep the line!'

She felt she ought to ask him what he meant by that remark, but a strange languor was stealing over her and, though she opened her lips, no sound other than a faint moan issued from them.

'Does your ankle hurt greatly?' he enquired. 'You are excessively fortunate, you know, to have fallen just where you did. Or, perhaps, very clever.'

The lady, who did not consider herself to be in the least fortunate, wished he would not speak in riddles and in just that cold, faintly sarcastic manner.

'It—it's not my hurt so much as someone wishing me harm,' she tried to explain. 'What have I done to deserve such Turkish treatment?'

'What answer would you wish me to give you, I wonder?' he mused, half to himself.

She was, by now, thoroughly bewildered. 'I—I do not understand you, my lord.'

'Then I will make myself perfectly plain, ma'am. I cannot conceive of any reason why anyone should wish to put a period to your existence—quite the contrary, in fact.'

She eyed him resentfully. 'Then whoever is so obliging as to make me the object of such attentions should be a deal more careful how they set about it!' she snapped. 'I could have broken my neck just now!'

'Yes, that was clumsy,' he agreed. 'Who d'you suppose did it?'

'According to Adam, it must have been either Lucy or the young undergroom, Jem. But for what reason?'

'To frighten you into leaving Hever Court?' he suggested.

'Who should want me away from Hever Court save only—' She stopped abruptly at realisation of what she had been about to say.

'Save only me? True enough, ma'am. And I did send Lucy with you, did I not? So here is your villain, all set up for you! And to complete the story, I am now abducting you and carrying you off to my lair!'

Regrettably, at this point Miss Lawrence lost her temper. 'It would not be to your liking if I married Sir Trevor, would it, my lord?' she flung at him.

He shrugged, as if finding the whole subject a dead bore. 'I am sure you have decided you had much better marry me.'

This pronouncement quite took her breath away but, while longing to box his ears, she rallied bravely.

'I have no desire to marry anyone,' she got out at last. 'I

had rather die a spinster than lend myself to such an alliance!'

'Then let me tell you, ma'am, your behaviour in general hardly bears out that statement!' said he harshly. 'First, you visit my house to see what I have to offer—oh, yes, a convenient little accident, was it not? Then you go on to visit my cousin, but clearly he is more than even you can stomach, so you devise a way to place yourself under my care once more—another contrived accident? What a gudgeon you must think me! That lawyer fellow, Baynton, put you up to it, didn't he? He, no doubt, to get his share of whatever price you demand for submitting to my embraces—or Trevor's! How high do you rate yourself, ma'am? Five thousand a year? I am not prepared to pay more.'

She gave a gasp and so far forgot herself as to hurl invective at him. 'You odious, arrogant beast!' she blazed, then, seeing his scornful smile, controlled herself with an effort. 'Be so kind as to stop this vehicle and allow me to alight.'

'What? Leave you by the roadside with a sprained ankle?' he mocked her. 'That's doing it rather too brown, ma'am.'

'I don't care!' she cried wildly. 'Why should you think this of me? Mr—Mr Ainsley believed my story.'

'Ainsley is a sentimental old fool where a pretty woman is concerned. And you are a damnably pretty woman, are you not, my dear? If you want to get away from Hever Court I said I would help you and that I'll do, word of a gentleman.'

'You are t-too kind, my lord,' she spluttered. 'But are you not setting yourself rather high?'

He raised his eyebrows at that. 'So the little cat has claws, has she? Beware lest I take you at your word and put you down in the middle of my park!' As he spoke, the gig was turning in at the gates of Leyswood Towers.

'Adam would pick me up again before too long!' she retorted defiantly.

'He wouldn't find you where I would deposit you,' his lordship informed her. 'But later—much later, you would be discovered or would drag yourself to the house where you would be obliged to stay, quite unchaperoned, for the night. But don't deceive yourself into thinking that your helpless state would appeal to my chivalry to the extent of inducing me to offer for you, Miss Lawrence! Nor, I fear, would my aunt regard you with any favour. The possibility of her son having to father my by-blow would stick even in her throat.'

Scalet-cheeked, her hand itching once more to hit him, Julienne-Eve realised that she was at a great disadvantage where insults were concerned and decided to alter her tactics. She leaned back comfortably in her seat and forced her lips to frame a smile.

'Now I call that pitching it a bit too strong, my lord,' she chided him. 'Removing from my grasp at one and the same time both a fortune and a title.'

'Depend upon it, ma'am, your only hope of achieving that ambition lies with my cousin,' he assured her. 'Not that I am unappreciative of your charms, but I am not so deep in the suds that I have to accept a cheating harpy such as you for wife.'

'I hope, my lord, that you may never have to accept worse,' she returned with a pathetic dignity that caused him to look at her in question. 'I can assure you that, even more than you, do I earnestly pray that our paths may never cross again.'

'Take the reins,' he said curtly as they drew up to the house. 'I will come round and lift you down.'

'Do not put yourself to that trouble, my lord.' If Miss Lawrence had been flushed before, she was now as white as the lace at her throat and, before the vehicle had quite come to a stand, she prepared to descend. Inevitably, her ankle gave way beneath her and, with a little cry of anguish, she fell to the ground.

The doors were opened and Thomas came running to her aid, but Rotherham was out of the gig and beside her before any other. Gathering her up in his arms, he snapped to the footman to look to the horse and strode into the house where a horrified Challis stood staring at this unprecedented arrival.

'Fetch your wife!' he was ordered and hastened to obey

while his master, commanding a wide-eyed maid to open the door of the saloon, entered there to deposit his semi-conscious burden upon a sofa. 'You foolish little ninny-hammer!' he scolded her. 'Why could you not have waited for me to assist you?'

'Because I—because I—' Words failed Miss Lawrence and, to her utter mortification, the long-stemmed tears would not be denied. An oddly helpless expression stole over his face as he knelt beside her.

'Don't cry,' he pleaded in a vastly softened tone. 'When I am out of temper, I say more than I mean.' She made no reply, merely closed her eyes while the tears still streamed down her cheeks. A certain bustle in the hall heralded the approach of Mrs Challis and he rose. 'I'll leave you now.'

She had a curious impression that something brushed her forehead, but when she opened her eyes he had turned away and was addressing the housekeeper.

CHAPTER
FIVE

Sɪʀ Peregrine Whittinghame settled his considerable bulk more comfortably into the corner of his well-sprung travelling chaise to the accompaniment of protesting creaks from his Cumberland corset, and eyed the lady sitting opposite him with some concern.

'D'you mean to tell me, Sybilla, that the boy don't expect us until to-morrow? Now, I call that behaving scaly! What if—well, he might have to make some—er, domestic arrangements before receiving us.'

'Nonsense!' said Mrs Saville with supreme confidence. 'He hasn't been at Leyswood Towers above a se'nnight. He'll not have had time to form any connections of *that* sort as yet.'

The large gentleman looked as if he was tempted to put her right on that point, but contented himself with saying: 'I shouldn't wonder at anything he might do after hearing the terms of that wretched will.'

'That's just it!' said Rotherham's mama, the tall ostrich plumes on her bonnet nodding emphatically. 'He must not do anything ill-advised—which, being Nathan, is more than likely, more particularly if he's in a rage.'

'Go off at half-cock, you mean, and marry the first wench that offers?' enquired Sir Peregrine. 'Thought he'd have more rumgumption than to do that. One thing I will answer for—he's going to ride mighty rusty when he hears what we have to tell him.'

'But he's not going to hear it, not yet at all events.'

Mrs Saville smiled sweetly upon her escort and smoothed her pale yellow kid gloves over her wrists. She was an uncommonly youthful-looking woman for her close-on-fifty years, with scarce a trace of grey in her abundant fair hair, a complexion that was the envy of many a lady twenty years her junior, and the brilliant dark eyes that also characterised her son. Her caped pelisse of sprigged taffeta, trimmed with Egyptian crape, worn over a poplin walking-dress, was in the first stare of fashion, even if it allowed no concessions to the rigours of travel. Sir Peregrine, while he could not fault her appearance was, however, less appreciative of it at that moment than was to be expected of a gentleman newly betrothed to the lady.

'You are not going to tell him?' he exclaimed. 'But why, my love?'

'Circumstances alter cases,' said she, leaning forward to pat his hand where it rested on one plump pantalooned knee. 'It must now be a prime object with me to secure a suitable match for Nathan before bringing our own felicitous arrangements to his notice.'

'He ain't going to like it,' predicted Rotherham's future step-papa gloomily. 'Never did care for me much, as I remember. Called me a fat fribble once.'

'Very discourteous of him, to be sure,' she soothed him, 'but when he marries and settles down at Leyswood Towers and we are at Bath, I daresay there will be no occasion for you to meet above once or twice a year. So, you see, it is of the first importance that I should arrange an alliance for him. That should not prove too difficult, for it is generally accepted that a single gentleman in possession of a fortune must be in want of a wife.'

'But he ain't in possession of a fortune, not yet anyway,' objected Sir Peregrine with the air of one who has produced an unanswerable argument.

'He will be.' Mrs Saville smiled upon him kindly. 'You don't imagine that I would permit my whey-faced sister-in-law and her goosecap of a son to chouse him out of that, do you?'

He shook his head doubtfully. 'Don't see what you can do if they win the Nursery Stakes. Not that I wish to throw any doubt upon Nathan's—er, performance,' he added hastily, seeing the militant gleam in his lady's eye, 'but it is a matter of who gets off to the best start. I mean it could well be a girl and no one to blame.'

'Miserable old squeeze-crab!' exploded the lady suddenly.

'I—I beg your pardon?' gasped the startled baronet.

'Oh, not you, Perry! I am referring to his late lordship of Rotherham. To so vent his spite upon my son is the outside of anything!'

'Just why did he hold you in such aversion?' tentatively enquired her betrothed.

'My father and he were at daggers-drawing for all of their lives, I do believe. I cannot be sure, but I am persuaded that the cause of it all was that they both loved the same lady and she chose my father. Rotherham, in a sort of defiance, then married some little nobody—oh, well-bred enough, he would make sure of that—who produced my husband and his sister and, having fulfilled her part in the tragedy—or comedy, whichever way you see it—she departed this life, doubtless thankfully.'

'But how did it come about that you married her son?'

'My own parents passed away when I was still a child. I was brought up by an aunt who knew nothing of any of this. Nor had Rotherham told his son, and when my poor Theodore informed him that he had offered for me he feared his lordship had taken leave of his senses so enraged. was he.'

'One might be forgiven for supposing that, as you were the daughter of the woman he loved—' began Sir Peregrine.

'To him, I was the daughter of the woman who had spurned him. There was little room for love in that cold heart.' Mrs Saville sighed. 'Sometimes I fear that Nathan resembles his grandfather too closely in that he distrusts any excess of sensibility or affection.'

'He's a cold-blooded young devil, if that's what you mean.'

'Not to those he really likes and esteems. When he takes a wife, I think it could well be for love.'

'Humph! Then you'll have to be pretty bobbish if you are to provide such a lady for him at the drop of a hat!' said Sir Peregrine with brutal frankness.

'Oh, that don't signify,' she returned airily. 'He need not stay married to this one if he don't care for it.'

Sir Peregrine bent a condemnatory glance upon his beloved. 'No, confound it, Sybilla, not at all the thing! The poor girl would—'

'The poor girl would be well repaid for her services.' Mrs Saville was in no two minds about that. 'Nor can I believe it would be so very disagreeable to be married to Nathan for a time.'

'Yes, well, you're the lad's mother so you're prejudiced in his favour—stands to reason you would be.' He sounded unconvinced but, fortunately, the lady was paying him scant attention.

'How like my obnoxious sister-in-law I must sound!' she chuckled. 'Depend upon it, she is laying her plans, just as I am mine, at this very moment!'

Had Mrs Saville the privilege of being present just then at Hever Court as Adam was recounting the afternoon's activities to Lady Heathcott, she would have been more than ever assured of the aptness of her prognostications.

'You say Rotherham has borne her off? She is even now at Leyswood Towers?'

'Yes, m'lady.' Adam was being at his most impassive. 'His lordship has required me to take a carriage over to convey miss back here.'

'Oh, he has, has he?' Lady Heathcott's eyes narrowed and her fingers tapped irritably on the arm of her chair. 'And so you shall, but I am coming with you! I would be failing in my manners did I not thank my nephew for his civil attentions to my companion. Just give me time to change my dress and we will take the barouche—it is repaired, is it not?'

'Yes, m'lady. I told Lucy this morning, seein' as how she said you'd be requiring it this afternoon.'

He was subjected once more to her cool, level stare. 'As it happens, I do require it, but who was so farseeing as to foretell that this morning?'

Adam mumbled something about having misunderstood Lucy and thankfully took himself off. Her ladyship, however, made no immediate move but sat where he had left her, her fingers still beating a gentle tattoo upon the chair-arm, her expression very thoughtful.

For his part, Adam was more angry than reflective as he went in search of his granddaughter. He found her at work in the laundry-room, singing away happily as if she had not a care in the world.

'A word with you, my girl,' he said, a jerk of the head drawing her out of the room and away from prying ears.

'Why, granddad, you're all on the fret! What's amiss?'

'Who put you up to cutting that girth?'

'What girth? What are you saying?'

'I'll have the truth from you by gate or by stile!' he growled. 'Miss's girth was cut through and nobbut you could ha' done it. An' what's more, there weren't no message from her ladyship about the barouche. 'Twere only a trick to get me away so as you could do your work!'

'There's no sort of use ringing a peal over me on that score!' she retorted. ''Twas her ladyship's dresser, that Miss Marchant, who hinted that I should find out about the barouche, and I know that one well enough to be sure that if I hadn't done it and her ladyship found the carriage not to be ready when she wanted it, I'd be the one to bear the blame. As for cut girths, no one put me up to anything and I don't know what you're talking about!'

Cheeks flushed, eyes sparkling with outraged innocence, she outfaced him so confidently that Adam experienced a qualm of doubt. Could Jem have been the guilty party? But that he could not believe for the lad knew well that the mere suspicion of his doing such a thing would earn him a thrashing and instant dismissal.

'Miss Marchant, eh?' he said slowly, as if turning over a new possibility in his mind.

'And she's one as has no love for Miss Lawrence,' Lucy further elaborated.

'Aye, to be sure,' he agreed. 'She wouldn't like another woman coming it over her in the house. But she wasn't anywhere near the stables.'

For the first time Lucy appeared to take in the full implications of her grandfather's disclosure. 'Miss Lawrence! Was she hurt?'

'Nothing to signify, a sprained ankle only. Lord Rotherham has her in his care.'

Lucy whistled soundlessly. 'Her ladyship won't care for that!'

'She don't. I'm to drive her over to fetch miss back.'

'And I'd best go prepare cold compresses and the like. Granddad, you'd be well advised to have the horses put to and not keep her ladyship waiting. I'll warrant she's up in the boughs enough already.'

Adam, feeling that he had been rolled up, horse, foot and guns, but unable to put his finger on just how it had been done, nodded his agreement and went away. It was as well for his peace of mind that he did not observe the self-satisfied smirk that flitted over his granddaughter's lively countenance as she watched his retreating back.

Meanwhile, at Leyswood Towers, all was in a state of confusion. No sooner had Mrs Challis made Miss Lawrence as comfortable as was possible than came the unexpected arrival of Mrs Saville and Sir Peregrine to add to her troubles.

'Thank the Lord all's ready for them,' she muttered to her harassed spouse as he hastened to fetch wine. 'And don't take that to the saloon! The young lady's not to be moved, his lordship says, until the carriage comes for her. The book-room's best, it's all clean and there's a good fire.'

To judge by the expression of disgust on Mrs Saville's face as she entered the book-room to be met by a cloud of smoke, the housekeeper's optimism was entirely unjustified.

'Faugh!' she exclaimed. 'What have you got here, Nathan? A rook's nest in the chimney?'

'More than likely.' He was struggling to open a reluctant window. 'Most of these rooms have lain idle for so long it is a wonder anything fulfils its proper function.'

'As I remember, this chimney always smoked,' said his mama with feeling. 'Cannot we remove to the saloon?'

'Not at the moment. A young lady is there, recovering from a slight accident.'

Mrs Saville blinked once or twice rapidly while Sir Peregrine darted her a glance of smug triumph.

'What young lady?' she asked in the most innocent way that did not deceive her son for one moment.

'Aunt Elspeth's companion,' he informed her blandly.

'Since when has Elspeth required the services of a companion?'

'Only a short time ago, I understand.'

Nothing was said while Mrs Saville gave this intelligence her full attention. Then, apparently quite oblivious to the smoke belching forth from the fireplace, she seated herself on the nearest chair, as if prepared to stay there all day if such proved necessary to get to the root of the matter.

'What is she like, this young lady? Is she pretty?'

'Very,' replied his lordship dispassionately. 'At least, that was Ainsley's considered opinion.'

'Mr Ainsley? What does he know of her?'

Rotherham was tempted to point out that the lawyer had also visited Hever Court, but the sure knowledge that his mother would have the whole truth out of Mrs Challis before the cat could lick its ear dissuaded him from such a course.

'She was forced to call here for assistance on her way to Hever Court a few days ago.'

'What? Another accident?'

'Yes,' said Rotherham, discouragingly curt.

'How unfortunate she appears to be,' commented his mother in the tone of one who reserves judgment, while Sir Peregrine helped himself very audibly to snuff. 'Is all being done for her comfort that should be?'

'Yes—that is, I have left it to Mrs Challis.'

'Then I'd best go to her. To be candid, Nathan, it sounds a very smoky tale to me.'

'Yes,' said his lordship again.

She nodded, as if satisfied. 'You think there's something out of true also?'

'I am of the opinion she was directed here by Baynton.'

Her lip curled. 'That man! He is Elspeth's creature, is he not?'

'Or his own. Ainsley suspects he had foreknowledge of grandfather's will.'

'I see.' Mrs Saville rose and stood, lost in thought for a moment. 'You had best leave this to me, Nathan.' So saying, she swept out of the room.

'As she says, leave it to her,' advised Sir Peregrine,

lowering his ample curves into a chair suited to receive them. 'Wonderful woman, your mother. She'll have the truth out of the chit in no time.'

Rotherham, venting his irritation upon the sulky fire, was not at all sure he wanted to hear the truth about Miss Lawrence. If she was innocent of any duplicity, as she protested, then an apology from him for his mistrust of her should suffice, and that would be the end of it. If she was guilty, then that also would be the end of it. He found this prospect not to be entirely to his liking and, once again, expressed his resentment by kicking at the smouldering logs.

'Not the best thing for your boots,' Sir Peregrine reminded him. 'Not for me to say, of course, but my man'd be in a rare taking if I did such a thing.' He stretched out a shapely leg and studied his glossy Hessians with justifiable pride. 'Swears he doesn't use champagne or any of that nonsense, but he used to be as thick as inkle-weavers with Brummell's valet and *he* used only the best vintage.'

The mention of champagne put Rotherham in mind of his duties as a host, and he at once thought to offer his guest some refreshment.

'Forgive me, but we are all at outs here, and your arriving a day early—why are you a day early, may I ask?'

'Your mother would have it that you were in need of guidance and, by Jupiter, it seems you are!'

Rotherham's face hardened and Sir Peregrine reminded himself that if he wished to turn his prospective son-in-law up sweet he would have to keep a rein on his tongue.

'I cannot conceive what has given my mother such a notion.'

'Well, that little pullet in the saloon—'

'She is not a little pullet!'

'No?' Sir Peregrine savoured the quality of the Madeira. 'A fine wine, my boy.'

'Yes, one of the few things for which I have to thank my grandfather.'

'If she's not a little pullet, then what is she?' For all his caution, Sir Peregrine's curiosity got the better of him.

'As I explained before, she is my aunt's companion and a

lady of breeding,' retorted Rotherham shortly, wondering why he felt obliged to uphold Miss Lawrence's character in any way.

'And pretty with it? Devil of a waste, ain't it?' sighed Sir Peregrine.

'Yes.' Rotherham spoke absent-mindedly, hardly realising what he said, and Sir Peregrine deftly turned the subject to horse-racing and if his lordship fancied anything for the Autumn meeting at Newmarket.

In the saloon Julienne-Eve lay, drowsy from the effects of a James's Powder, and very content to remain so until her aches subsided. A slight sound aroused her and she opened her eyes to behold a tall, elegantly-dressed lady standing by her couch, inspecting her in great detail. Feeling that something was required of her, she endeavoured to sit up, only to be pressed back upon her cushions while she struggled to reply to a string of smoothly-worded enquiries. It took her befuddled brain some little time to grasp that this solicitous lady was Lord Rotherham's mother—far longer, in fact, than it took Mrs Saville to get all the relevant facts appertaining to Miss Lawrence's presence at Leyswood Towers and draw her own conclusions.

'It's plain from what you say that Baynton and my sister-in-law intend that you shall marry Trevor, but why are you being subjected to this harassment?'

Miss Lawrence bit her lip. 'I thought at first—' she began.

'That it was Rotherham attempting to scare you off? No,' said his lordship's mama, 'not in his line, I assure you.'

'He—he condemned me from the very start!' complained Miss Lawrence, a break in her voice.

Mrs Saville sighed in sympathy. 'Was he very rude to you?' she asked.

'Atrociously! He said the most unforgivable things!' At thought of those things, Julienne-Eve blushed most becomingly, and the older lady regarded her with mounting interest.

'I wouldn't pay too much heed to what Rotherham says when he takes a pet,' she advised, then, seeing the glint of tears on the girl's lashes, 'use my handkerchief, my dear. He didn't offer for you, did he?'

Miss Lawrence choked into the handkerchief. 'Certainly not!' she gulped. 'He—he dislikes me amazingly!'

'He is personable, titled, and with the prospect of being excessively wealthy.' Mrs Saville enumerated her son's good points in an admirably detached spirit. 'You might do very much worse for yourself, you know.' Miss Lawrence drew a deep breath and reminded herself that here was another parent ambitious for her son's future, and she redoubled her resolve not to be used by either of them. Mrs Saville, watching her expressive countenance, guessed shrewdly at what the girl was thinking. 'Do you intend to return to Hever Court?'

'I suppose I must, for the time at least.'

'If you don't care to—why, there's nothing more simple than to plead indisposition and remain here.'

But Miss Lawrence was not to be persuaded into doing any such thing. Cajole he never so sweetly—and there seemed small likelihood of his doing that—she was not remaining under Rotherham's roof for one minute more than was necessary.

The ringing of the door-bell, followed by a considerable commotion in the hall, caused Mrs Saville to turn her head and listen acutely. The next moment the saloon door opened and Challis was ushering Lady Heathcott into the room.

'The young lady is resting here, m'lady. I beg pardon, ma'am, I did not know you were here!'

'It is of no consequence. Thank you, Challis, you may leave us,' said Mrs Saville, very much in the grand manner. 'I hope I see you well, Elspeth?'

Though taken aback at sight of her sister-in-law, Lady Heathcott replied with equal composure. 'I thank you, Sybilla, I am in as good health as can be expected. And you?'

Both ladies were conducting this opening skirmish with a light touch, gently flexing retaliatory muscles while testing the opponent's guard.

'I am happy to say I never felt better,' declared Mrs Saville. 'I wish the same could be said for this poor child.'

Her ladyship's attention being thus directed to the

shrinking Miss Lawrence, she at once began to question her.

'Whatever befell you? Adam spun me some tale of a severed saddle-girth and how you might have been killed.'

'Very true, ma'am. It would seem as if someone is bent on doing me a mischief.'

'But who? Who knows you in these parts?'

'My sentiments entirely, Elspeth.' Mrs Saville cut in smoothly. 'The child has had no one to stand for her—up to now, that is. But, since today, we are all her friends. If she should feel herself to be more at ease at Leyswood Towers, why she is very welcome to stay.'

Lady Heathcott's tongue flicked out, lizard-like, to moisten her lips. 'You forget she is in my employ, Sybilla,' she murmured.

'A most hazardous occupation from all I hear,' purred Mrs Saville, making play with her rings. 'She was directed to you on Mr Baynton's recommendation, I understand?'

The pale eyes gleamed momentarily. 'You are remarkably well-informed as to my affairs, Sybilla.'

'A sisterly interest, no more, I assure you,' protested Mrs Saville.

There was no saying how this exchange of barbed pleasantries might not have ended had not Rotherham entered the room at that moment.

'A pleasure, ma'am, none the less delightful because unexpected.' He bowed gracefully over his aunt's hand. Miss Lawrence thought he did it with considerable address.

'I have you to thank, I believe, Rotherham, for my companion's safe return.'

'Hardly that, ma'am,' he disclaimed. 'I but conveyed her here. Miss Lawrence has herself to thank for the conduct of her accident.'

Only one of his hearers fully understood his meaning and it served to confirm that young lady's resolve to be out of his lordship's house and beyond any need of his further assistance. This view clearly was also held by Lady Heathcott and, in no time at all, Miss Lawrence was being assisted to the waiting barouche and there disposed along the length of one seat, while her ladyship took her place opposite her.

Mrs Saville stood watching the handsome equipage pro-
ceed down the drive until, reminded by her son that the air
was growing chill, she went into the house to re-join Sir
Peregrine in the book-room. That gentleman, embarking
on his fourth glass of Madeira, was in a benevolent mood
and inclined to treat the whole episode with misplaced
humour.

'So her ladyship took the chit off, did she? Too bad,
m'boy!' said he, rolling an eye towards Rotherham whose
attention appeared to be centred upon the destruction of a
tassel depending from the cord of the window drapes.

'Yes, I am much inclined to agree with you there, Perry.'
Mrs Saville seated herself by the now brightly burning fire.
'Nathan, do stop playing with that thing and listen to me.
The girl has no malice in her that I could discover. Depend
upon it, she is being used, but Elspeth will play her cards
more carefully now that she knows I am cognisant of the
situation. Nonetheless, you must make haste.'

'Make haste to do what?' Her son was according her
scant attention.

'Offer for Miss Lawrence, of course. Then, when she has
accepted you, we can have her here.'

Rotherham's lips tightened. 'You are seeking an excuse
to remove her from my aunt's care?'

This way of putting the matter did not commend itself to
his mother. 'Don't be so absurd, Nathan!' she implored
him. 'I want you to marry her.'

'What? You must be all about in your head, mama!'

'She has, I am persuaded, a tendre for you, though she
may not yet be aware of it,' went on Mrs Saville, unmoved
by this aspersion cast upon her mental abilities. 'It surely is
not beyond your powers to ingratiate yourself with so
delightful a young lady?'

'I have no wish to marry her.'

'Then you are a fool, my son. She is an admirable choice
and one most unlikely to lower your consequence by
indiscreet connections. You, of course, providing you show
her a proper respect, need observe no such restriction.' She
waved away the protests that were trembling on his lips.
'Also, it seems that she is in some danger at Hever Court,

though from what source I am at a loss to discover. We must get her away from there before irreparable harm has been done.'

With something like a snort of derision, Rotherham strode from the room, closing the door very forcefully behind him.

Sir Peregrine looked doubtfully at his lady. 'Can't say he seems to care for the notion, m'dear,' he ventured.

Mrs Saville was not a whit put out by her son's abrupt departure. 'My dear Perry,' she said, as one explaining the complexities of the globe to a schoolroom infant, 'do you not recognise that his so-called distrust of her is his only defence?'

Sir Peregrine's understanding, never of the keenest, quite failed him. 'Defence against what?' he demanded to be told.

'Against falling in love with her, of course!' she responded gaily. 'Depend upon it, if I can contrive to get her into this house and he can be satisfied of her innocence in the business, then it will be all over for him.'

'You could be right,' he allowed. 'And there's much to be said for courting in your slippers, as the saying goes. But what of the girl?'

'She's half-way there already,' said Mrs Saville complacently. 'A sweet child, I do declare. It will give me great pleasure to take her in hand and instruct her in how she should go on as mistress of this—this museum piece!'

The object of her interest, having assured Lady Heathcott that her injury was of small account and she would be about and into everything in no time, was also giving her future some serious consideration, but her plans ran very contrary to those of Mrs Saville and hinged largely on how to remove herself into the Misses Beresfords' care without the knowledge of either of the noble households who had her welfare so much at heart.

CHAPTER
SIX

CULVER Lodge, the handsome mansion which had been purchased by the Misses Beresfords' parents in the later years of the previous century, was set in capacious and well laid-out grounds in that district of Tunbridge Wells known as Mount Ephraim. Some days after Miss Lawrence's unhappy accident, at an hour in the morning when few persons were yet abroad, one of Pickford's famous 'Flying Wagons' drew up before the impressive entrance gates to the house and that young lady was tenderly assisted to alight.

'Now, miss, don't you go for to lift them baggages. I'll carry 'em up to the door for you.'

'No, no,' she protested. 'I have taken you too far out of your way already, I must not detain you further.'

'Lor' bless you, miss, 'tain't nothin' to oblige a lady.' The big man shuffled from one foot to the other, rubbing at his flaxen forelock in an excess of embarrassment.

'Then get on wiv it, 'Arry,' advised his companion, leaning down the driving seat. 'Or 'twill be all dickey for us wiv Mr Mat.'

Quite unmoved by the threat of Retribution in the shape of the redoubtable Mr Mathew Pickford, Harry seized the two valises in his huge hands and stumped up the drive in the wake of the limping Miss Lawrence.

'There ye be, miss, all right an' tight—an' thank 'e, miss.'

'Thank *you*, indeed,' said Miss Lawrence with real gratitude, bestowing generous recompense upon him. She had no time to say more for a beaming Miss Beresford was greeting her cordially and drawing her into a cosy little room where breakfast was being set out by a trim maidservant.

Sighing her relief, Julienne-Eve subsided into a chair and accepted the cup of coffee poured for her by Miss Beresford who, when they were alone, leaned forward to hiss conspiratorially: 'How did you arrange it?'

'Quite simply, after all. I learned by chance that Pickford's were calling early this morning to collect some articles her ladyship was disposing of at the saleroom in Tunbridge Wells so, with the assistance of my maid, I persuaded them to take me and my possessions also.'

'Your maid?' queried Miss Beresford doubtfully.

'Yes, I fear I had to concoct a tale which, doubtless, has been made known to all the household by now. I allowed it to be understood that I was being deposited at the Royal Sussex where I would board the first coach that offered for London. I also left a letter for her ladyship—good manners required no less—begging her forgiveness for my precipitate departure and thanking her for her kindness.'

Miss Beresford expressed herself as being fully in agreement with these sentiments and, over a substantial breakfast of buttered eggs and crisply broiled bacon, the two ladies discussed in detail the requirements of the establishment and what should be Miss Lawrence's duties.

She soon discovered that several of those lodging at Culver Lodge were already known to her from her previous visits in Mrs Crawford's company and, so superior was their understanding of her character and behaviour, the fact of her being in a more humble position than formerly in no way affected their benevolent attitude towards her. Scarce a day passed without some pleasurable excursion or party to be enjoyed and, although her conscience prohibited her from accepting all such invitations, Miss Beresford insisted that she should take every advantage of the continuing benign weather.

The day unfailingly began with a stroll on the Parade to the music of the band, after which those who felt so disposed partook of the waters, while others occupied themselves in walking or reading, then all would reassemble in parties for breakfast later in the morning. The reminder of the day was spent in accordance with individual tastes; in viewing one of the many nearby places of interest; in riding; in visiting one's friends or resting, as inclination dictated. The evenings were amply filled by card assemblies or attending the theatre, at which there were performances on four nights in the week; balls, of which, in addition to the regular Thursday night occasions, there were those given by the Master of Ceremonies, and numerous private affairs held by people of fashion; concerts of an excellence to satisfy even the most demanding of critics, and countless other entertainments thought up by hostesses stimulated by the glorious weather and a keen spirit of competition.

Needless to say, Miss Lawrence did not avail herself of even a small part of these varied *divertissements*, chiefly because she felt it was not her place to do so, but also because she had a lively dread of meeting someone who might report her presence in the town to either Lady Heathcott or Lord Rotherham. October was well advanced when, on a morning that promised to turn into as brilliant a day as its predecessors, she set out, unattended save for Miss Beresford's brisk terrier, for her daily promenade.

The shop-keepers were taking down their shutters in the Parade and, despite the early hour, quite a number of persons were already about, tempted by the freshness of the air. Having changed her book at Mr Scragg's Library, Miss Lawrence continued on until the smell of roasting coffee drew her into Durrant's provision store at the corner of Pink Alley where, after some consultation with the proprietor, she laid out five shillings for a pound of the best sort. Sounds of violent canine altercation cut short the conversation and urged her out of the shop and down Pink Alley, where she discovered the terrier, who had slipped his leash, hurling abuse at a large hound of doubtful lineage and belligerent aspect.

'Oh, no! Nimble, come to me!' she implored, but it was too late, the terrier had launched himself into an attack upon his adversary, who was far superior to him in size and weight. 'Dear Heaven!' she moaned, visualising the prospect of having to carry home a battered and bleeding dog to Culver Lodge. 'Help, someone, please help!' She turned to go back towards the Parade in search of aid and all but ran headlong into a gentleman who came hastening round the bend of the alley. 'Oh, sir, if you would—your lordship!'

Rotherham took in the situation at a glance and, seizing the two closely interlocked combatants, one in either hand, he wrenched them apart. Then, speeding the departure of the stranger with his foot, he soundly cuffed Nimble before setting him down on his four paws.

'This is your dog, I presume, ma'am?' On receiving her affirmative nod, he continued: 'Where is his leash?'

'He—I—oh, dear! I left him tied to a post.'

The leash was retrieved and the outraged Nimble made secure, giving Miss Lawrence time to regain her composure and be thankful that the dog-fight had provided sufficient excuse for her high colour and general air of perturbation. Then she cried out again in dismay.

'My coffee!'

His lordship eyed the freshly-ground coffee, spreading freely over the alley from its burst package, and sniffed appreciatively.

'Good stuff, I'll be bound!'

'The best,' she sighed.

'Very proper, ma'am,' he said. 'Only the best would be acceptable in the circumstances.' Then, as if recalling the somewhat equivocal conditions that had prevailed at their last meeting, he went on in a more formal manner. 'I understood you to have left these parts for the greater attractions of the Metropolis, ma'am.'

'No,' she said in a small voice. 'Th-that was not strictly true.'

'So far from being true, I would suggest that it was an out-and-out rapper?'

She caught the quiver of amusement in his voice and took courage. 'I hope her ladyship—your aunt—was not too displeased with me.'

'She was as sick as a horse,' he informed her. 'Came rattling over to accuse my mother of having enticed you away. A memorable occasion, I assure you. Mama's fluency surprised even me.' He hesitated, then looked at her rather shamefacedly. 'I owe you an apology, I believe, ma'am. I should have listened to Ainsley.'

'It is of no consequence, my lord,' she said, her dignified pose quite spoiled by having to clutch at her bonnet which a mischievous breeze threatened to dislodge. 'How is dear Mr Ainsley?'

'I can answer that more precisely in a few moments since

I am meeting him from off the London mail, hence my being here at such an hour. One of his pair has gone dead lame which is the reason for his having to employ so plebeian a method of travel. But where are you lodged, ma'am? Not far from here, I'd judge.'

'I am at—' She bit back the too-ready words and looked engagingly confused.

'Quite right!' he approved. 'But, if it is of any comfort to you, you are no longer in danger of being importuned by either my cousin or myself. We learned t'other day that he got married a few weeks since.'

'Sir Trevor? To whom?'

'To Lucy, your one-time maid.'

'What?' Julienne-Eve felt as if the ground had been cut from under her feet. 'The deceitful cat! So it was she who tried to frighten me away so that she—oh!' Seething with indignation, she forced herself to listen to what he had to say.

'We had the whole story from Adam—poor fellow, he's taken it sadly to heart. Apparently, that first night you were at Leyswood Towers she overheard Ainsley and me discussing my grandfather's will and—other things, and decided to take a hand in the play.'

'Which included trying to put a period to my existence!'

'I'd say that was misjudged. I doubt she intended more than to frighten you. One good thing comes out of it, her ladyship may have gained a daughter-in-law but she has lost the services of her groom. Adam has come to me, having no wish to submit to his granddaughter queening it over him.'

'But how did she do it? Surely her ladyship could not care for so humble a connection?'

'I understand my aunt was presented with a *fait accompli*.' His tone was very dry. 'Lucy appears to be able to turn Trevor round her thumb.'

'That wouldn't be too difficult,' she agreed, 'when one recalls that he has been bullocked all his life by his mother.'

'No doubt it must be a refreshing change to have someone toad-eating him and deferring to his lightest wish. Yes, Spanish coin I know, but if it makes him happy, poor fellow, who should grudge it him?'

This amiable expression of opinion was so contrary to what she had expected of him that she blurted out: 'You, for one, I should suppose!'

He smiled and bent down to fondle the terrier's ears. 'Because he has lost me a fortune? What a mean-spirited fellow you must think me, Miss Lawrence.'

'The fortune is not yet lost, my lord,' she reminded him. 'If your cousin can marry, so can you.'

'By God, you're as bad as Ainsley! He tells me he has a lady in mind who should suit me! He might be speaking of a mare for his stallion to cover! I'll not do it.'

Miss Lawrence was so obsessed by consideration of Lucy's behaviour that she scarce noticed what he said.

'Of course you must marry, my lord,' she informed him severely. 'If only to give that chit a good set-down! You'll not let her rob you of your inheritance?'

He grimaced. 'She may have done so already. And how can I be sure—'

'You cannot, of course.' She marvelled at her own composure in discussing so intimate a matter. 'But neither can she be sure that her first-born will be a son.'

'So you advise me to take a wife?'

'Yes, my lord, I do.'

'Then, ma'am, will you do me the honour of accepting my name and whatever fortune may come my way?'

Though nothing about her had changed, the sun still shone and people still walked and talked a few yards away on the Parade, yet for Miss Lawrence the world had come to a stand. Then, to her utter amazement, she heard herself saying: 'Yes, my lord, I will.'

The ensuing silence was rent apart by the shrill note of a horn.

'Devil take it, it's the mail!' he rasped.

'And I must go else there'll be a search mounted for me.' Impulsively, seeing his worried frown, she laid a hand on his arm. 'Think nothing of it, my lord, you were only funning. Yes, yes, of course, that's it. You had no intention of making me a serious offer.'

He caught her hand in his. 'Oh, yes, I had, and you're not going to get out of it, my girl! I asked you to marry me and you accepted—there is our witness!' He nodded at Nimble who sat at their feet, ears cocked, observing them with a worldly-wise air.

'But—but I cannot! Not just yet. You see,' she hurried on, 'I have undertaken to assist some ladies who are in distress and I cannot relinquish my task for—well, I agreed to remain until Christmas.'

'Christmas? That's two months off and Trevor already married! Altogether too late, ma'am.'

Miss Lawrence devoutly wished that this very private conversation could be conducted in a rather less public place.

'Yes, I do see that,' she whispered.

He passed a hand over his brow as if collecting his thoughts. 'Let me have this perfectly clear,' he said slowly. 'I am offering for you in the hope of gaining back what I consider to be my rightful inheritance. You are marrying me—why, Miss Lawrence?'

'Because the very idea of Lucy enjoying what should be yours quite revolts me!' said she with devastating frankness.

'Well, I suppose rapacity and revenge are as good reasons for a marriage such as ours as any other.' He sounded uncertain, as if resentful of her sympathy, and what she had done to revive his resentment she could not imagine. She turned her head away and spoke hurriedly.

'If we are to go through with this, my lord, can it be kept secret for a time?'

He regarded her frowningly. 'It might be better so,' he allowed. 'The terms of my grandfather's will are now generally known and the betting-books are held ready, waiting for me to enter the race. You'd not care for that.' Miss Lawrence decided that she very definitely would not care for that, and said so. 'Then we cannot be wed here,' he went on, 'my name is too well-known. It will mean a special licence and London. Ainsley can see to that. Can you get away from your post for a few days?'

'I suppose so,' she said dubiously. 'But what excuse can I give for my absence?'

'I'll have Ainsley write you a letter, claiming to know of

something to your advantage which necessitates your waiting upon him in London. Let me see—if I turn round and send him back to-day, you could receive that letter at latest on Wednesday. Could you journey to town on Thursday to return, perhaps, on Saturday or Sunday?'

'Why not Friday?' she asked artlessly.

'Would you deny us so short a honeymoon, ma'am?' he quizzed her and was oddly touched to see the fiery colour stain her cheeks. 'Leave it to me to make the arrangements and when you receive Ainsley's letter, do your part.'

'Y-yes,' she faltered. 'I am sure you will know just what has to be done.'

He was tempted to inform her that he had not before arranged a wedding trip such as this was likely to be, but he contented himself with pressing her hand reassuringly. 'I must leave you now else Ainsley will be thinking I have forsaken him.'

'Good—goodbye, my lord.'

'Rather *au revoir*, my lady.'

With a little gasp, she snatched her hand from his grasp and fled, dragging the reluctant Nimble away from a promising rat-hole, down which he had been breathing in a manner calculated to keep its inhabitants cowering inside for the rest of the day.

Rotherham watched this hasty retreat, a half-smile softening the hard line of his mouth. The shock of seeing her so unexpectedly had provoked in him such a spasm of joy that his proposal had come almost unbidden to his lips and the very thought of losing her seemed quite insupportable. Why this should be so he could not be perfectly certain; doubtless the knowledge that he had cruelly misjudged her had so worked upon his sensibilities that he had felt obliged to make reparation. He wondered that he should be so strangely lighthearted, then slapped a hand to his thigh and exclaimed aloud: 'By Jupiter, I never took her direction!'

For a moment he stood irresolute, then entered the provision store and summoned the proprietor to look at the tragedy of Miss Lawrence's coffee.

'Oh, to be sure, 'tis the young lady that's helping out at

Culver Lodge. No, sir, I doubt Miss Beresford will pull caps with her on that score, so nice a lady as she is. You'd like another pound of the same sort sent to her? A pleasure, sir.' Laboriously he wrote down Miss Lawrence's name and address in full. 'I'll despatch it this minute, sir, so it'll be at Culver Lodge hard on the young lady's heels.'

Satisfied, Rotherham went to look for Mr Ainsley to find that worthy stamping about impatiently to ease his cramped legs.

'Thought you'd forgotten me, m'lord,' he grumbled. 'And we've none too much time.'

'No, that we haven't,' grinned Rotherham, taking the little man by the elbow and urging him into the Royal Sussex. 'So short of time are we that we are going to eat breakfast here while I tell you what I have in mind to do. Then you'll be off back to London by the next coach!'

The lawyer's voluble protests were muffled by the closing of the hotel doors behind the two gentlemen and, for the next few minutes thereafter, he spoke not at all as Rotherham disclosed his plans. When he had finished, Mr Ainsley sat back in his chair and regarded him with something like approval.

'I have thought all along, my lord, that she was the right one for you,' he pronounced.

'But it must be kept secret until—well, for as long as we may,' insisted Rotherham, and his companion observed with mildly malicious satisfaction that his lordship's colour was somewhat heightened. 'I'll not have my wife's condition made the subject of wagers by every rake and downie of the ton.'

'She'll go through with it?' Mr Ainsley's bright eyes were intent on his client's face.

'I believe so—she's as game as a pebble.'

Mr Ainsley put a hand over his mouth to conceal a smile and wondered just what had occurred so to change his lordship's opinion of Miss Lawrence.

Julienne-Eve, hastening up the hill to Mount Ephraim, was thinking along much the same lines. When her first fury at Lucy's duplicity had cooled, she began to doubt if she had not, indeed, taken leave of her senses. To accept

Rotherham's offer, tossed at her as carelessly as he would a penny to a crossing-sweeper, how could she have made such a cake of herself? Then she remembered that she had not told him where she lived. Oddly enough, instead of experiencing a powerful sense of relief at this providential reprieve, she found her heart to be descending to somewhere in the region of her trim half-boots.

'So that's the truth of it!' she accused herself aloud, heedless of the curious glances of passers-by. 'You have been in love with him from the very start and are only too glad to snatch at any opportunity to become his wife!' Then she reflected that he had fallen in very readily with her wish to keep their marriage secret. 'Well, what did you expect?' she muttered furiously. 'All he wants from you is a son as soon as Nature can provide, after which you will be pensioned off and—and forgotten!'

At this melancholy thought she felt the tears stinging behind her lids and relieved her feelings by tugging sharply at Nimble's leash, which so surprised that sagacious animal that he left off snarling insults at a supercilious poodle passing on the other side of the road and meekly followed the lady back to Culver Lodge.

Once there she had scarce time to put off her bonnet than the arrival of a pound of Durrant's best coffee put her to the necessity of explaining to a surprised Miss Beresford how she had come to leave it in the shop.

'It is only what any gentleman would do,' she told herself as she went about her household duties. 'Depend upon it, when he has had second thoughts, the only letter you will receive from him will be one asking to be released from our—our engagement.'

But when, on the following Wednesday morning, she took in the post and her trembling fingers unfolded the single sheet of writing-paper with Mr Ainsley's neat signature at its foot, her relief was so great that she had no need to feign astonishment at receiving such a summons. Miss Beresford was adamant that she should comply with the lawyer's request to present herself at his office without delay.

'Why, he even tells you what coach to take from here and

that you will be met by his clerk,' she pointed out, 'and apologises for not coming in person to discuss the matter, but owing to severe rheumatics—oh, most gentlemanly, I do declare! He mentions Mrs Crawford—can it be that you are to benefit from her estate? I must say it would be nothing out of the way if you did, for I know in what great affection she held you.'

'I had thought Mr Baynton dealt with all her affairs,' said Miss Lawrence with perfect truth. 'But perhaps I was mistaken. I see Mr Ainsley mentions having arranged a lodging for me in London for two nights. I cannot conceive why,' she added, lapsing once more into mendacity.

'These things take time, I am given to understand,' said Miss Beresford sagely. 'In any case, you are more than deserving of a little holiday, and I shall not expect you back a minute before you wish for it.'

So delighted was the good lady at thought of her young friend's expectations that it did not occur to her to wonder how Mr Ainsley could have obtained Miss Lawrence's direction, and Julienne-Eve's fertile imagination was not put to the necessity of inventing yet another rapper.

CHAPTER
SEVEN

THE journey to the Metropolis was in itself an adventure for one who had never before engaged on such an undertaking, and Julienne-Eve set out, much encouraged by the good wishes and advice of the household at Culver Lodge, all of whom were persuaded that she must be in expectation of a considerable fortune to account for so urgent a summons.

As hers was the last inside seat to be had, she was not surprised to discover the nine o'clock London-bound coach to be as full as it could hold, her slim person being firmly wedged between a large talkative lady on the one hand, and an even larger morose gentleman on the other. None of the other passengers had a great deal to say for themselves, so the large lady held forth without interruption until their destination was reached, her chief topic of conversation being herself and how excessively fortunate her husband was to have so admirable a spouse and her offspring so devoted a mother.

Miss Lawrence, whose good looks and solitary state had aroused this paragon's curiosity, was obliged to assure her that she was being taken care of from the moment she set foot in London and, on descending from the coach, looked about her in full expectation of seeing someone who would answer to the description of Mr Ainsley's clerk. Her travelling companion's mouth pursed into an 'O' of disapproval and her eyebrows rose to alarming heights when Rotherham's tall figure detached itself from the usual throng attendant upon the arrival of a stage-coach and came forward to claim the young lady. The sight of this elegant swell sufficed to discourage Miss Lawrence's new-found friend who went off, muttering under her breath certain observations which were not at all to her protégée's credit.

Beyond casting a whimsical glance in her direction, Rotherham paid her scant heed and, picking up Julienne-

Eve's small portmanteau, he led her to where his phaeton stood waiting.

'We will go at once to Ainsley's offices,' he said briefly. 'He wishes to speak to you concerning—but I must not steal his thunder.'

Miss Lawrence wondered what Mr Ainsley could have to say to her that was of pressing importance and, shivering a little, drew her cloak more closely about her.

'How very much colder it is here in London than at the Wells,' she commented politely. 'And how very civil of you to meet me, my lord.'

Rotherham, dropping a coin of sufficient magnitude into the grubby paw of the urchin holding his horses to cause that case-hardened scamp to blink in speechless astonishment, gave his attention to guiding his mettlesome pair through the crowded streets.

'If we are to exchange polite whiskers, ma'am,' he said, a shade impatiently, 'may I say how gratified I am to see you in such good looks?' He was tempted to add that he was gratified to see her at all, for the possibility that she might repent of her hasty decision had never been far from his mind despite his protest to Mr Ainsley to the contrary. 'Was your journey tolerably comfortable?'

'I doubt you would have enjoyed it, my lord,' she surprised him by retorting. 'But for me, who have never before experienced it, the delight of travelling to London far outweighed any discomfort.'

'You have never before been to London?' he asked incredulously. 'Why then it will be my pleasure to act as your guide and point out everything worthy of note. Here, as a prime example, is St Paul's Cathedral and, if you should care for it this afternoon, we may ascend to the dome and view the panorama of the city, lying spread beneath our feet.'

'Are—are we to be wed there, my lord?' she asked shyly.

He glanced at her and saw that, for all her pose of studied nonchalance, her mittened hands were clasped tightly in her lap and she was staring ahead of her in a fixed manner that seemed to take in little of her surroundings.

'No,' he replied gently. 'Ainsley has arranged for the

ceremony to take place at Bow Church. His offices are in Bread Street, only a step from there.'

She looked down then at her light travelling mantle, worn over a plain gingham gown. 'I had thought—my dress is hardly suitable for such an occasion,' she began, but he quickly intervened.

'I have presumed to purchase one or two articles of clothing which I hope will be to your liking, ma'am.'

'You have had clothes made for me?' she gasped, a little shocked. His teeth flashed in a sudden smile.

'I must confess I enjoyed doing it,' he admitted, 'and only pray I was not too far and wide in my judgment of—of your person.'

She sat, momentarily speechless. Never had she expected such consideration from his lordship but, of course, she reminded herself severely, he could not have his bride going about looking like a drab. Then he was handing her down from the phaeton before a tall, narrow house, and she climbed a steep flight of stairs to be greeted at the top by a beaming Mr Ainsley.

'I'll leave you to your discussion,' Rotherham called up to them from the foot of the stairs. 'We have close on an hour before we need be at the church so I'll go fetch a warm pelisse for you, ma'am.'

Without waiting for a reply, he was gone, leaving her to look in question at Mr Ainsley.

'Come, my dear Miss Lawrence,' said he, ushering her into a small, dark room that smelled of old books and older documents, and setting a chair for her by his over-crowded desk. 'I must tell you that my interest was greatly stirred by your story, and further titillated by my small acquaintance with Mr Baynton. I beg you will forgive me, but I took it upon myself to pay him a visit and represent myself as being your man of affairs.'

Miss Lawrence, who had never envisaged herself as being in need of anything so grand as a man of affairs, could find nothing better to say than: 'Indeed?'

'Indeed!' echoed the little man, shuffling through the mound of papers in front of him. 'I have here a copy of the late Mrs Crawford's will. Would you care to peruse it?'

Puzzled, but impressed by his portentous manner, she did as she was bid. After a few minutes she raised her head to look at him blankly. 'She—it says here that she left me forty thousand pounds!' she whispered.

'Invested in the five per cents,' confirmed Mr Ainsley. 'Which will give you a snug annual income, I am happy to inform you.'

'But Mr Baynton said that the money wasn't there, that Mrs Crawford had quite outrun the constable.'

'That,' said he carefully, 'was not strictly true. Certain it is that the poor lady made provision for a deal more money than she was possessed of at the time of her demise, but her house, furnishings and other assets were disposed of to advantage and you are the prime beneficiary of the will, to receive your bequest before any other. That is amply covered.'

Miss Lawrence laid the document down upon the desk and looked him straight in the eye. 'Mr Baynton, of course, did not know where I was to be found,' she said doubtfully.

Mr Ainsley spread out his hands in a gesture suggestive of his total inability to comprehend the deviousness of the human race. 'Nor, believe me, had he the least intention of looking for you, ma'am,' he sighed. 'He had every expectation that your marriage to Sir Trevor and—hopefully—the acquisition of a fortune, would so occupy your attention and satisfy your material needs that you would ask him no further questions.'

'In that he was perfectly right,' acknowledged Miss Lawrence. 'I quite believed him when he told me there was nothing more to be hoped for from Mrs Crawford's estate.'

'Why should you not? But I have had dealings with the gentleman before and am not generally thought of as being gullible. However, there is no case to be proven against him because, as you rightly say, he did not know where you were and could claim not to be able to assess the full value of the estate until the property was sold.' Mr Ainsley cleared his throat and appeared to be having some difficulty in choosing just the right words for his purpose. 'His lordship was insistent that you should be told of this without delay.'

Miss Lawrence pondered this statement. 'Why?' she asked, brow wrinkled in puzzlement.

'It could influence your decision to marry him. This bequest grants you an independence that you have not previously enjoyed.'

'But I am not marrying him for the sake of *my* independence, but to secure his!'

He beamed at her. 'Yes, my dear young lady, I was quite confident of that, but his lordship would have it that you must be given the opportunity to change your mind, if you so wished.'

Miss Lawrence experienced a moment of near panic. 'Does that mean he would like to change his?' she got out nervously.

'You must know that he does not,' Mr Ainsley assured her.

She reflected that she knew nothing of the sort and, observing her concern, Mr Ainsley summoned his clerk and sent him out for a pot of coffee. While awaiting its arrival, he discoursed upon the attractions of the Metropolis and how much he envied her, coming fresh to it, with everything a new delight.

'I have here a publication which, I venture to think, will please you, ma'am, and if you do not regard it as a presumption on my part, I would esteem it an honour if you would accept it as a small bride-gift. It is called *The Microcosm of London* and is published by Mr Rudolph Ackermann at his shop in the Strand. It depicts well-known London scenes—a hundred of them in all. Here,' he laid a hand on the open book, 'is the Guildhall, and here,' turning a page, 'the Royal Academy. In another picture we see Mr James Christie conducting a sale at his auction-room in Pall Mall, and this one portrays the Prince Regent himself, apparently escorting two military visitors around Carlton House.'

In no time Julienne-Eve was absorbed in the exquisite aquatints by Mr Pugin and Mr Rowlandson and, with a cup of coffee at her elbow, was seated, eagerly inspecting each while Mr Ainsley, well-pleased at his stratagem, watched her from behind his desk, when the door opened quietly to admit Rotherham.

For a moment he stood on the threshold, taking in the charming picture she presented, cheek resting on one hand, lips slightly parted in awed appreciation as she slowly turned the pages. Then his voice aroused her to awareness and she looked up with such an expression of ingenuous pleasure on her face that he experienced a stir of emotion that was something more than mere appreciation of her beauty.

'I have brought you your mantle, ma'am,' he said, and held it for her to slip into.

'Ooh!' she breathed, her hands reverently stroking the deep fur shoulder cape of the Russian pelisse. 'Is—is it for me?'

'For no one else,' he assured her gravely, buttoning her into it as if she was a small girl and standing back to view the result with narrowed eyes. 'Hmm. A shade loose, perhaps, but that is easily mended. These may not be so happy a choice.' From his pocket he produced an elegant pair of lavender kid gloves. 'You can carry 'em if they don't fit.'

'But they do!' she cried in triumph like a child as she drew them on. Again his heart ached strangely and, to conceal his feelings, he leaned forward to look at her book.

'What have you there? Oh, *The Microcosm*.'

'Yes, Mr Ainsley has made me a gift of it—is it not prodigious kind of him?'

'Not,' said his lordship with feeling, 'if he intends that I should escort you to more than half the places depicted therein in two days!'

Mr Ainsley cleared his throat and consulted his watch. 'If you are ready, ma'am, we should, I think, be on our way,' he suggested.

'I am quite ready, thank you,' she replied in a tolerably steady voice.

Frowning, Rotherham looked from her to the lawyer. The latter bowed his head affirmatively, then, collecting his hat and gloves from the top of a dusty cupboard and calling to his clerk that he should not be away above a couple of hours, he shepherded the lady and gentleman down the stairs ahead of him.

The ceremony in Bow Church was conducted as expeditiously as was possible by a parson who gave no appearance of taking the least interest in either of the parties he was required to link together in wedlock. Before Julienne-Eve quite realised it, the wedding band was on her finger, she was signing her new name 'Julienne-Eve Saville', and Mr Ainsley was bestowing a decorous kiss upon her cheek. Then they repaired to a nearby inn where, in a small upstairs parlour, an inviting cold repast was offered for their approval. But first Mr Ainsley insisted on toasting the newly-wed pair in champagne and smiled to see the bride's nose wrinkle a little in distaste as she sipped the wine.

'A toast to your good fortune also, my lady,' said Rotherham, raising his glass to her.

'Th-thank you,' she responded, 'and to yours, my lord.'

Belatedly realising how intimately this last lay in her power to bring about, in her confusion she hastily drained her glass and all but choked on the heady stuff. A moment later, she was conscious of a warm, pleasurable glow stealing over her, and found herself to be sustaining her share of the conversation with commendable aplomb. Nonetheless, she was grateful when Rotherham did not offer to refill her glass for, though it would have been an unforgivable breach of good manners to have said so, she had not greatly enjoyed her first taste of champagne and was very happy to follow it up with lemonade.

'I cannot answer for you, Ainsley, but I find myself uncommon sharp-set. Now, ma'am, how may I tempt you?'

Julienne-Eve, having had nothing pass her lips other than a cup of coffee since her very early breakfast, was more than ready to be tempted and made an excellent meal, only pausing when his lordship remarked that it was clear he would have to set back the hour arranged for their dinner at the Pulteney in order to give her appetite time to revive.

His lady gulped nervously. 'W-we are lodging at the Pulteney, my lord? Is it not very fashionable?'

'It is the best, I am given to understand,' said he, hesitating over the choice of anchovy toast or cheesecake to round off his meal. 'But if you prefer any other you have but to say.' Hastily, she disclaimed any such desire and he went on. 'Now, I believe Ainsley wishes to discuss a few legal complexities with you and then, if you still have a mind for it, there is St Paul's to be conquered.'

He was treating her with a sort of amused deference that seemed to hold her at arm's length, and for that she was grateful. In fact, she was left with very little time to indulge in misgivings for it was past six o'clock before she had had her fill of sightseeing and they arrived in Piccadilly outside the Pulteney which, to her unsophisticated eye, presented an appearance of awe-inspiring magnificence. She was further confounded when an impressive major-domo led them upstairs to a superb suite of rooms on the first floor, and she was informed that it was the very one occupied by the Grand Duchess Catherine of Oldenburg, sister to the Tsar of all the Russias, during the state visit of the Allied Sovereigns earlier in the year.

She was scarce able to take in the tasteful appointments of the saloon before a prim maid was bobbing to her and leading her into a bedchamber done out in the very first style, a fine four-poster holding pride of place, with ivory satin drapes depending from its tester.

'His lordship said as how your dresser had been taken ill sudden, m'lady, so I am to wait upon you, if you please.'

Julienne-Eve nodded dazed acquiescence and allowed herself to be disrobed. Rotherham had disappeared into his own bedchamber, which lay on the farther side of the saloon, but his absence, instead of affording her relief, aroused quite a contrary emotion. His conduct throughout the day had been unexceptionable and, insensibly, she had come to accept his presence at her side and felt absurdly bereft when it was removed. Discovering that the maid was addressing her, she forced herself to make coherent reply.

'What to wear tonight? Oh, the cream florentine, I should suppose.'

'Well, if you're set upon it, m'lady, but I would have thought this would be more suitable.'

She was laying out a confection of lace over figured satin, with full sleeves of diaphanous gauze and fastened down the front with pearl buttons; the whole in a love-in-the-mist blue that accorded perfectly with Julienne-Eve's widely incredulous eyes.

'But that isn't—I don't—oh!'

The sensation of living in a dream world that was as ephemeral as a bubble and as likely to evaporate at the touch of reality intensified as she submitted to being put into the gown, having her hair skilfully dressed with a tiny spray of artificial rosebuds placed among the dark curls, and a shimmering length of silver net draped about her shoulders. For an instant, as she stood before the cheval-glass, she fancied that a stranger looked back at her out of haunted eyes. This top-lofty lady of fashion, one white-gloved hand switching the train of her full skirts, the other resting by the deep-cut neckline of her gown, was not of her world, and she experienced a strong urge to tear off the beautiful dress, don her own clothes and take the first coach back to Tunbridge Wells.

'Quite charming. My felicitations, ma'am.'

Rotherham dismissed the maid with a gesture and came to lay two jewellers' cases on the dressing-table. From the larger of these he took out a diamond necklet of exquisitely delicate design with bracelets of the same sort. These latter he clasped about her wrists then, motioning her to be seated, he placed the necklet around her throat while she watched him in the mirror, as if unable to believe what she saw. The second case contained a ring with a single diamond of a brilliance to make her blink as he slid it on to her finger. Then, cupping her chin in his hand, he raised it so that she was forced to meet his gaze.

'What a lovely wife have I won for myself,' he mused, nor was there trace of that sardonic inflection in his words that she so disliked. 'I have bespoken a table for us in the dining-room,' he went on, smiling at her in the most friendly way imaginable, 'but, should you wish for it, we can be private here.'

Julienne-Eve was very sure she did not wish for it. There was going to be a deal of privacy to be contended with before the night was spent and the longer it could be postponed the better pleased she would be. His smile became a shade more pronounced at her vehemently expressed preference to eat belowstairs, but he offered her his arm without further comment and they descended to the dining-room.

Having surveyed the company through his quizzing-glass and bowed slightly to one or two persons of his acquaintance, Rotherham seated himself opposite his wife and consulted the menu while she envied him his unruffled composure. Did she but know, his mind was in hardly less of a turmoil than was her own.

A certain natural fastidiousness, coupled with a not over-plump purse, had hitherto restricted his connections with the muslin company though, on occasion, he had been encouraged to exploit the deplorable fact that many ladies of the beaumonde, who scorned to be called Cyprians, yet displayed all the dubious attributes of their less exalted sisters, were happy to receive his advances. But that was a game played by those who knew the rules and the only sin was to be found out. Marriage was a very different kettle of fish and one that he had been prepared to leave in abeyance until that happy—and hopefully, far-off—day when some eligible female should present herself to his notice. One moment of impulse had shattered this comfortable complacency. He still did not know just why he had acted as he did, yet he could not bring himself to regret it. Seeing Julienne-Eve's anxious gaze bent upon him, he applied himself to setting her at her ease.

'You being in such beauty, my lady, causes me to regret my choice of a table in so discreet a corner,' he teased her.

'You wish to flaunt me, my lord?' she responded gallantly. 'I—I feared that when you discovered persons of your acquaintance to be present that—that you would have preferred to be private.'

'They don't signify,' he assured her, keeping to himself the knowledge that those gentlemen had, undoubtedly, taken her to be a high-flying *chère-amie*, and were even now avidly discussing with their companions her possible identity.

Despite the ample meal she had consumed earlier in the day, Julienne-Eve found her appetite to be unaffected, and endorsed his choice of *truites au bleu à la Provençale*, preceded by caviar from Russia, a delicacy quite unknown to her, and followed by a sauté of pheasant with truffles.

'I have not called for vodka,' he said, sampling the wine that stood cooling by the table. 'I understand it is the accepted drink to take with caviar, but it is an excessively powerful spirit and I have no wish to see either or both of us carried from the room in a drunken stupor!'

Privately, Julienne-Eve considered it might not be at all a bad notion, but she obediently sipped the excellent hock he had provided and found it much more to her liking than champagne.

'You have but lately come back from the Peninsula, my lord?' she ventured, feeling that some conversational effort was required of her.

'Yes, but before returning to England I spent some months in Brussels until summoned home by our good Ainsley. An uneasy, fraught city, full of people trying to remember other days, and an equal number trying to forget.'

She did not like to press for an explanation of what he meant by that, so said: 'Shall you remain in England?'

His dark eyes rested on her reflectively. 'That would depend upon circumstances,' he said, and she was thankful that the waiter chose that moment to place the first course of their choice in front of her. 'Your father was a naval officer, so Ainsley tells me,' he resumed when the man had left them, 'but you could scarce have known him. What was his ship?'

His manner was so unforced and amiable that, unbelievably as it seemed to her, they talked together as naturally as if they had known each other for years and were merely seeking to establish every possible facet of mutual interest that existed between them. For his part, he saw with no small pleasure, the anxiety on her face give way to animation and even to laughter. Towards the end of the meal he said: 'I have engaged a box for the theatre tonight. The play is an old thing—*Wild Oats* by Mr O'Keeffe, an Irishman thought well of by Hazlitt, who has described him—rather erroneously, I would have thought—as our *English* Molière. Would it please you to put his theory to the test?'

Needless to say, it pleased her well and she sat, ent-ranced, throughout the entertainment, occasionally turning to him to express her delight or to ask his opinion of a passage or character in the play.

Her absorption in this make-believe world sustained her until they returned to the Pulteney. There her maid was waiting to take off the beautiful gown and hang it reverently away, talking brightly the while and asking how her ladyship had enjoyed the play. Julienne-Eve wished the kindly woman to the devil while, at the same time, dreading the moment of her departure.

That moment inevitably came and she was left alone, sitting in the middle of the vast bed, clad in a nightgown consisting of layers of sheerest tiffany, the very sight of which had put her to the blush.

'The perfect get-out for the bridal bed!' she taunted herself, burying her face in her hands. 'Dear God, what have I done?'

'Poor frightened child!' He was beside her, magnificent in a scarlet and gold dressing robe and, drawing her hands from her cheeks, kissed each before clasping them in his. 'I promise you to do nothing you don't wish for.'

'But—but, my lord—'

'Nathan,' he suggested whimsically.

'Nathan?' she repeated, momentarily diverted.

'If you had been paying strict attention in church,' said he with mock severity, 'you would have learned that my given names are Jonathan Edward Alexander. My mama dubbed me Nathan when I was in shortcoats.'

She tried again. 'My—Nathan, we made an agreement!' she asserted firmly.

'Why, so we did,' he allowed, gentling her as he would any timid young creature.

'I must honour my—my part of it.' Her chin went up proudly at his sudden laugh. 'Yes, my lord, females, too, can honour their word!'

Impulsively he clasped her to him. 'Word of a lady, you absurd infant?'

'I am *not* an infant!' she protested indignantly.

'By God, you're not!' His eyes dropped to her too

revealing nightrobe. Then, roughly, he kissed her and rose. 'That's enough of husbandly attention for tonight. Sleep well, my lady.'

Her cry, hardly above a whisper, checked him. 'Don't go! Don't leave me!'

Slowly he came back to the bedside. 'Oh, you foolish little wife!' he mocked her, but very kindly.

'Foolish I may be,' she flashed at him spiritedly. 'But if that Lucy is to get her just deserts, my lord, you have your part to play!'

Being thus strongly reminded of his duties, his lordship was obliged to concede that her ladyship was in the right of it and time was not on their side so, with a shrug of half-amused resignation, he applied himself to assuaging her very natural anxieties.

CHAPTER
EIGHT

SIGHTSEEING excursions on the following day were largely
abandoned in favour of visits to milliners and mantua-
makers. Mr Ainsley had insisted on advancing an allo-
wance to his newest client and she, possessed of wealth
hitherto unknown to her, seemed bent on spending it in the
shortest possible time.

'Depend upon it, I shall have pockets to let before my
next quarter is due,' said she ruefully, surveying the mound
of parcels heaped about her feet.

Rotherham, edging his phaeton with inches to spare
between a sporting curricle whose owner gave the appearance of being bent on self-destruction, and a slow-moving
town chariot whose elderly occupants, together with their
coachman, seemed to be asleep and oblivious to all danger,
chuckled sympathetically.

'If you have quite finished sporting your blunt, ma'am,
we can take a turn in the park before dusk.'

'Oh, how delightful that would be! I do believe—the
Park is in that direction, is it not? Why, then, do we not
drive along that street?'

'That,' said Rotherham with lofty scorn for her ignorance, 'is St James's Street, the hub of London's clubland,
and no lady of quality may be seen there.'

'Well, I think it looks excessively genteel, with so many
gentlemen of fashion strolling up and down,' said she,
deliberately provocative.

'Bucks on the strut, more like!' he growled, his attention
momentarily distracted from his pair who instantly took
exception to a fountain of water issuing from a broken pipe
at the side of the street and broke into a canter. Her
ladyship advised her husband to pay heed to his horses and
when Rotherham, who was thought to be a very fair whip,
bit his lip in supposed chagrin, she added graciously that

she considered in general he handled the ribbons very well.

The day had passed with the utmost amiability, once only was there a hint of discord and that scarce worthy of the name, when her fancy had lit upon an Angoulême bonnet that accorded perfectly with her pelisse. He contended that to complete the ensemble was his concern and, seeing he was resolved to do it, she yielded gracefully.

'Though where I am to wear it,' she lamented as they left the shop, 'Heaven alone knows.'

'You will wear it here in London when we come to visit at our town house.'

'H-have we a town house?' she asked doubtfully.

'Yes, in St James's Square. It is let now, but the lease falls due at the end of the year. Ainsley thinks I may just be able to stand the nonsense if I take it up for the season.'

'You mean—a season in London?'

'You'd like that, wouldn't you?'

'You are very kind, my lord, but—' She lowered her voice so that his groom, a taciturn retainer from Peninsular days, should not hear. 'I thought our marriage was to be kept private.'

'Oh, by March or April I doubt it will be a secret for I must tell my mother and she'll not be able to keep a guard on her tongue. There could be other ways of its being known also,' he added, glancing slyly at her.

Julienne-Eve decided that the moment was not opportune for going into detail about those other ways, and began to talk away like a very jaw-me-dead until he stretched out a hand and placed it over hers, pressing it briefly and reducing her to silence.

Back once more at the Pulteney, he tossed the reins to his groom and came to hand her down. A hotel servant hurried to gather up the parcels and, laughing, her hand on Rotherham's arm, she walked through the foyer of the hotel and was about to ascend the stairs when his name was called out in a clear female voice.

She heard his sharp intake of breath, then he said calmly: 'Go on up to our rooms, ma'am, I shall join you presently.'

Accepting the command as being a perfectly reasonable one, since to be made known to any of his friends would defeat their wish for secrecy, she continued upstairs, but could not resist glancing back when she reached the half-landing. What she saw quite arrested her attention, for Rotherham was talking to the most ravishingly lovely creature imaginable. Curls as bright as new-minted gold peeped out from under a bonnet that seemed to be composed solely of ostrich feathers and ribbons in every shade of blue, all framing an enchanting face of which no feature was less perfect than another. Her complexion was beyond compare, her eyes a deep sparkling violet, and her lips, just then parted to reveal pearl-like teeth as she smiled up at Rotherham, were as exquisitely curved as could be hoped for. Her voice, silvery as a bell, carried clearly to Julienne-Eve's ears.

'Nathan! Where have you been hiding? I have been back from Brussels a full se'ennight and becoming bored already, I declare, for lack of your company!' He said something indistinguishable and she swept on. 'Oh, I have heard all about it—your matrimonial race! Poor Nathan! How unfortunate that I cannot enter the contest on your behalf! But I fear that even my dear Henry's complacency would not survive such a shock!'

As she spoke, the lady looked up at Julienne-Eve, and her cloak swung open to reveal the fact that she was in expectation of a happy event and that at no very distant future date.

For a long moment they stared at each other, then Julienne-Eve, her cheeks aflame, went on her way followed by a tinkling laugh and the silvery voice remarking: 'Shame on you, Nathan! But she's a pretty little pigeon, I'll allow, and they do say the smaller the pony, the harder the gallop!' The voice hardened perceptibly. 'Unless—can it be that you have entered the race and wed the chit?'

Julienne-Eve, hastening to her room, gestured to the servant to lay her parcels on a table and stood, pulling off her gloves, her eyes snapping dangerously. After a few minutes of pacing to and fro, all heaving bosom and tight-clenched hands, she took herself to task. Gentlemen, as her mother had often warned her, were unpredictable, and kindly Mrs Crawford had also endeavoured to prepare her for future matrimonial disillusionment by explaining that husbands, even the best of them, were apt to maintain their irregular connections after the knot had been tied. If she pleased her husband well, perhaps she would be fortunate in that respect, but with the Royal brothers, from the Regent down, setting an example of dedicated promiscuity, who could wonder if lesser gentlemen regarded such behaviour as being nothing out of the way?

Putting off her bonnet, her ladyship sat before her mirror and shook out her flattened curls while she endeavoured to regain her composure. If this brazen creature was his fancy-piece—well, in a marriage such as theirs she had no right to expect more than token fidelity, but when she allowed her mind to dwell upon his tender love-making, his care for her innocence, she had to struggle very hard to hold back the tears and inform herself sternly that no doubt he had had ample opportunity for practising the art of seduction, and the pleasing of a wife would be the most trivial matter to one so versed in the skills of Venus.

On descending to dinner a little later, they discovered the foyer and public rooms of the hotel to be as full as they could hold with ladies and gentlemen all speaking French. An enquiry elicited the information that there had been a gathering of French royalists, given in part to compensate for the fact that not all of them could be included in the Ambassador's reception being held that evening. Rotherham went at once to enquire for his table and Julienne-Eve looked about her with lively interest, listening appreciatively to the conversations being conducted in her vicinity.

One gentleman in particular caught her attention, a tall silver-haired exquisite, with eyes as cold and black as agates, who spoke for the most part in lightly-accented English. He and his lady, whose back was turned to Julienne-Eve, were taking their leave of another couple and deploring the fact that they were obliged to return to the Continent almost immediately.

'We leave for Dover about noon tomorrow and will rest there for a night.' The lady spoke in French and Julienne-

Eve started in recognition of a half-forgotten memory. 'If you have any messages you would wish us to deliver to your family, we are lodged at Grillon's.'

The other couple expressed their thanks, farewells were exchanged and the tall gentleman, who was addressed as M. le Marquis, took his lady on his arm and prepared to leave the hotel. She, in turning, gave the astounded Julienne-Eve a clear view of her profile.

'Maman!' The word burst from her lips, but so great was the clamour around her that it passed quite unnoticed. Then Rotherham came to claim her and, as one in a trance, she allowed him lead her into the dining-room.

Dinner was a markedly silent meal in strong contrast to the hub-bub going on all around them. Rotherham seemed immersed in thoughts that, to judge from his rather set expression, were not wholly felicitous, while his lady was so taken aback by this unexpected comeabout that it drove every other notion from her mind. Towards the end of the meal the waiter, murmuring something in his ear, handed his lordship a letter.

He glanced at it, frowning, and thrust it into his pocket unopened, but not before she had caught a waft of perfume from the pink scented writing paper, and again her hands clenched under cover of the tablecloth.

'If you don't mind, my lord, I think I would like to rest in my room. I—I have the headache.' At least, she felt, the lack of colour in her cheeks would bear out her statement.

'My dear, why did you not say so? We need not have entered this parrot-cage. A little too much shopping to-day, perhaps?'

How dared he sound so fondly solicitous with that note burning a hole in his pocket! Languidly, she permitted him to lead her upstairs and make her comfortable upon a chaise-longue with pillows behind her head.

'Is there anything you wish for?' He was looking as concerned as if he really cared for the welfare of his tiresome but necessary wife.

'A glass of water only, if you would.'

He was gone rather longer than seemed needful to perform so simple a service and when he returned she sensed a tenseness about him, as if he was hard put to it to keep his temper in check.

'I regret, ma'am, I shall have to leave you for a few hours. A private matter that I must attend to.'

A private matter, indeed, thought she, one with yellow curls and violet-blue eyes! Aloud, she said in the coolest manner imaginable: 'How fortunate then that I have no wish to move from here this evening.'

'Shall I send your maid to you? I do not care to leave you alone like this.'

Really, he was playing his hand very well! Difficult for him to have his mistress—and she *enceinte* at that!—and his wife demanding his attention at the same time!

'No, no.' She smiled sweetly at him. 'I assure you a few hours' quiet and I shall be perfectly recovered. Oh—if you could place my Imperial Water by my hand. Thank you.'

Swiftly he bent to kiss her forehead, then, on receiving her repeated assurances that she would do very well without him, he left her.

For a time she lay unmoving, trying to comprehend the full significance of all that was happening. Of one thing she was very certain, she was not going to be waiting meekly for her husband when he returned, hot from the embraces of his lightskirt! Suddenly she sat up and put her feet to the ground. It was all very well saying she was not going to be here, but where was she to go? To ask for another apartment at the Pulteney would be too humiliating and should she lock her door he had but to call on whoever had a master-key and explain that my lady had mislaid hers. But, of course! She clapped her hands together in silent triumph. No doubt Grillon's could house her for the night! And with her mother and stepfather lodging there everything would be eminently respectable. To be sure, certain difficulties had to be overcome. She could hardly walk out of the Pulteney carrying her baggage, and she had no notion of what her mother's married name might be. The name she had given when she had left England had been a false one, this she had explained, was necessary to preserve her husband's anonymity. Julienne-Eve paused in the act of changing into the trim olive-green princetta walking-dress she had worn throughout the day to wonder how it came about that her stepfather, at that time a Bonapartist, was now, to judge from the scraps of conversation she had overheard, being received by His Majesty of France's Ambassador to England.

Pulling on her bonnet and pelisse, she went into the saloon and, seating herself at the handsome Carlton House desk, she drew out a sheet of writing-paper.

'My lord,' she began, then chewed the end of her quill doubtfully. How did one tell one's husband of little more than a day that one was leaving him? And she had to return on the morrow to change into her own clothes before journeying back to Tunbridge Wells. There was no question of wearing them to-night when she went to Grillon's—that, added to the fact that she had no baggage, would present a very off appearance. Drawing a deep breath, her lower lip protruding in a most determined way, she settled down to write. When she had finished she read it over, nodded as if satisfied, and dusted it off with sand. Then, sealing it with a wafer, she went on tiptoe into his lordship's bedchamber and set it in a prominent place on the chimneypiece.

He had obviously changed his dress in a great hurry before going out, and the sight of his long-tailed coat, satin inexpressibles, and silk stockings thrown carelessly upon the bed, brought a lump to her throat. He had not, he had explained, brought his valet with him because that worthy was a loquacious individual who could not be relied upon to hold his tongue, but she, if she had thought about it at all, had supposed that some member of the hotel staff was attending to his needs. Carefully she picked up the coat and tidied everything away, then, returning to her own room, she put what money she had into her reticule and, with a last unhappy glance about her, she went down to the foyer.

This she found to be still full of voluble French royalists, most of whom were emerging from the dining-room, among them the couple to whom her mother and the Marquis had been speaking.

Summoning up her courage, she stepped forward and addressed them in French. 'Pardon me, if you please, m'sieu, madame, but I observed you bidding adieu to a lady and gentleman before dinner, and I am very sure I made her acquaintance some years ago in this country. Could I be right?'

'Yes, you very well could, madame,' returned the lady pleasantly enough. 'Madame la Marquise Colomb d'Hauteville lived in this country for many years during the time of her first marriage, I understand.'

'Oh, then, perhaps she is indeed the Mrs Lawrence I once knew!' exclaimed Julienne-Eve, marvelling at her own duplicity.

'Law-rence? Yes, that was her name, I believe, the same as your famous painter of portraits.'

'I heard her say they were lodging at Grillon's. I am on my way there now and shall hope to see her.'

'Yes, well, it is possible.' The lady looked doubtful. 'They are engaged to attend at the Embassy tonight, but not, I imagine, before ten o'clock, and they leave England tomorrow. So you have not much time, madame.'

As the long-case clock standing near to her showed the time to be already past nine o'clock, Julienne-Eve could not but agree and, with suitable expressions of appreciation, she bowed herself out of the hotel. She was fortunate enough to discover a hack-carriage disgorging its load at the door so that it was a matter of a few minutes only before she was stepping out at Grillon's Hotel in Albemarle Street and requiring the porter to send up her name to Madame la Marquise Colomb d'Hauteville.

'Lady Rotherham—but she'll not know that, of course. I was Miss Lawrence when last I met Madame la Marquise,' said Julienne-Eve, carrying things off with a high hand. The porter, suitably impressed, begged her ladyship to be seated and sent a waiter with her message. After rather a long time, during which the fear that her parent might not wish to receive her took possession of Julienne-Eve's agitated imagination, he came back to escort her upstairs to a set of apartments which, though less spacious, in all other respects was quite the equal of that at the Pulteney, and she was ushered into her mother's bedchamber.

Madame la Marquise, seated at her dressing-table amid a

profusion of silks, laces, ribbons and jewels, met her daughter's eye for a significant moment in the mirror before waving away her hovering dresser.

'Thank you, Françoise. I will ring when I need you again. Come here, my child.' Obediently Julienne-Eve advanced and submitted to being saluted on both cheeks. Then her mother held her at arm's length and looked her up and down in the dispassionately appraising manner that the girl remembered so well. 'So you are married now? Tell me about it, and how you found me to be in London.'

Without any great shock of surprise, Julienne-Eve understood that, had she not sought her out, her mother would not have raised a finger to discover her. When she had made her new life she had buried the old one nor, was it plain, was she overjoyed at its resurrection in the shape of her discarded daughter. For the first time Julienne-Eve began to doubt the wisdom of her precipitate departure from the Pulteney and to wonder if it would not have been wiser, after all, to have stayed under Rotherham's protection, even if forced to share it with untold numbers of Cyprians, demi-reps, and their like. Compelling herself to be calm, she sat down and explained her situation with admirable lucidity.

'I thought to ask you, maman, to give me shelter for tonight. Then, tomorrow, I can return and inform his lordship of my intention.'

'My good child, have you taken leave of your senses?' The Marquise rose and began to pace the room impatiently. 'You have made a *mariage de convenance*—what do you expect? A husband prepared to give up all his old convenients—pouff! Just like that?' She snapped her fingers. 'I find you altogether absurd! Is he young—personable, your husband?'

'Yes,' admitted Julienne-Eve miserably.

'So that is it!' The Marquise came to stand in front of her. 'Because he pleasured you well on your wedding night you fancy yourself to be in love with him! Don't be a fool, girl! Think yourself fortunate if you bear him an heir and secure him a fortune. That way you may gain his approval, his affections do not concern you. My advice to you is to go back before he discovers your absence and play the complaisant wife.'

This callous indifference to her plight touched off a spark of rebellion in Julienne-Eve and roused her to retort: 'A rôle you, no doubt, play to perfection, madame!'

'Don't be impertinent!' The Marquise, all pretence at amiability cast aside, spat catlike at her. 'My husband is the head of my mother's family—the sole survivor, in fact, apart from myself. It was logical that he should marry me.'

Very French, thought her daughter sarcastically, undeterred by the rebuke. 'But he is not the man you ran away with, is he?'

'Of course not!' The Marquise's voice held a contemptuous note. 'The man I *escaped* with unhappily perished of injuries sustained during the flight. That is an episode in my life to which I never refer—do you understand me?'

'Yes,' said Julienne-Eve slowly. 'You mean the Marquis knows nothing about it. Did you also keep from him the fact of my existence?'

Her mother sat down again at her dressing-table and began to select the jewels she wished to wear with her elegant gown of sheerest gauze over a pearl-embroidered petticoat, cut daringly low at the neck to display her fine bosom and throat.

'No,' she said curtly. 'I told him that you were left provided for and in good hands.' She raised her head as a light tap sounded on the door. 'Here he is—not a word of that other, if you please. *Entrez*!' She was all smiles as the Marquis came into the room. 'Is not this a delightful surprise, *mon cher* Antoine? Here she is—our daughter, Julienne-Eve!'

'What joy to discover I possess so lovely a child!' Dropping his quizzing-glass through which he had been inspecting her minutely, he took both her hands in his and kissed each in turn. He was a great deal older than Julienne-Eve had first supposed, and of a dignity and presence that she could only describe as daunting. When the circumstances of her being there had been told him, he at once demanded to know where her husband was. 'Business affairs? On his honeymoon?' he exclaimed in utter disbelief when she had stumbled through some sort of explanation. '*Mon Dieu!* These English are too much the—how d'you say?—the cold fish for me! How can you forgive him such inattention?'

'She cannot, that is the whole point,' interposed her mother sweetly. 'She wishes to teach him a lesson for his lack of gallantry and stay here with us tonight.'

His curiously opaque black eyes studied his new-found daughter's troubled face for a moment. 'I think it an excellent idea,' he declared gravely. 'This young man must assuredly be brought to understand the enormity of his crime and what better way than to deny him the privileges he enjoyed last night? But, *ma vie*, why should not our daughter accompany us to the reception?'

'I cannot believe that, with so many more worthy of the honour being denied entry, any such notion would be acceptable,' returned his wife with a touch of asperity. 'And unless she has a suitable gown with her—for I fear nothing of mine would answer the purpose, such a shrimp as she is—we shall be obliged to leave her here alone for the evening.'

Julienne-Eve hastily declared that nothing would suit her better. The day had been full of incident and she wished only for an early bed.

'A pity.' The Marquis shook his head regretfully. 'It would give me much pleasure to escort two such beautiful ladies.' He shot a glance, vibrant with malice, towards his spouse. 'I will instruct my man to arrange for a room for you, my dear child. Doubtless your maman can provide you with the necessary night attire and whatever else you ladies consider indispensable to your comfort.'

'But, Antoine,' protested the Marquise. 'It is not at all the thing that we should connive at this—this deception. Lord Rotherham is a person of some consequence. Depend upon it, he will consider our readiness to assist his errant wife to be far beyond the line of what is pleasing.'

The Marquis's eyes gleamed ominously. 'So am I a person of some consequence, *ma chére*,' he murmured, deceptively gentle. 'The child shall stay here tonight if she so pleases.'

Then, with a bow, he withdrew, leaving the mother and

daughter to stare at each other, the one balefully, and the other with a sort of hopeful defiance.

'So your *beau-pére* admires your pretty face! Well for you he is as old as he is!'

The venom in her mother's voice startled Julienne-Eve into exclaiming: 'You make him sound the veriest rake, maman!'

'He was,' said the Marquise grimly. 'And, suddenly at the end, like all such men, he wished to secure an heir before his powers were quite spent. Why else do you think he married me—a penniless nobody? At least I was of a breeding to match his own, and no other of like birth would have him, so ill was his reputation. Since the birth of our son, of course, his conduct has been irreproachable.'

'You have a son?' gasped Julienne-Eve, and then wondered why she should be so astonished. Her mother had been very young when first married, she could be scarce past forty now and could be taken for ten years younger. 'How old is he?'

'Close on three years. The Marquis quite dotes on him.'

Which is a deal more than his mother does, ruminated Julienne-Eve grimly. She had always imagined that her mother's lack of affection for her stemmed from the fact of her being a girl but, apparently, this was not so. The Marquise was one of those women who possessed no maternal instincts whatsoever, and Julienne-Eve could not help but pity the little boy who must, in the course of Nature, soon be deprived of his adoring father and left in his mother's care.

At this point the Marquise, plainly deeming the audience to be at an end, summoned her dresser and the conversation turned to less personal topics. Wayward daughters notwithstanding, it was clear the Ambassador's reception was of prime importance and Julienne-Eve was obliged to discourse upon unexceptionable subjects while her mother was perfumed and hung about with so many diamonds that she glittered like a Christmas tree. Watching her progress through the hotel and out to her waiting carriage, with the Marquis resplendent in black and silver at her side, her daughter was profoundly thankful that it had not been possible for her to accompany them. To be shone down by her own mama was something not even the most sweet-natured of young ladies could endure.

Nonetheless, it was very mortifying to be in London, at the hub of the fashionable world, and be sitting in one's bedchamber with nothing other than a rather dubious French novel, unearthed for her by her mother's dresser, for company. When she allowed her mind to dwell upon the delights of the previous evening she found the printed words to blur and merge into each other in a most disconcerting manner. Finally, abandoning all hope of reading, she endeavoured to compose herself for sleep. But the noise and movement of the hotel had died away and the first faint glimmerings of dawn were paling the shadows before she fell into a fitful slumber, only to be awakened very soon after by the strident voices of the street-traders and the bustle of carriages as the Metropolis resumed its busy life.

Marvelling at how anyone could sleep in London, she gave up the effort and, having consumed a cup of chocolate brought her by a sleepy chambermaid, she presented herself belowstairs at the unheard-of hour of half-past eight. Her farewells to her mother and stepfather had been made on the previous night, and it was with a wildly beating heart that she called for a hack-carriage and presently stepped out in front of the now familiar portals of the Pulteney.

Ignoring the astonished stares of the staff, she swept up to her room to find her portmanteau ready packed and was about to summon a porter to carry it down when her hope of escaping undetected was dashed by the opening of the door into the saloon.

'So, my lady wife, you have returned?'

'And you also, I perceive, my lord.'

He advanced into the room, dressed for the road in riding-coat and buckskins. She dared to look at him and was appalled at what she saw. His eyes were slits of shadowed menace, deep-sunk in a colourless face; his mouth was a thin, relentless line, and his whole attitude as he strolled towards her, his hands thrust deep into his pockets, was one of calculated contempt.

'Where, am I permitted to ask, did you spend last night?'

'At Grillon's, in the care of my mama and stepfather,' she flung at him defiantly.

'Since when have you acquired these convenient relatives? You made no mention of them in your—ah, farewell message.'

It was plain that he did not believe a word of what she said, but she persevered bravely. 'No, because I could not be certain whether or not I should find them.' She was about to add, 'and whether or not my mother would receive me,' but decided against it and instead told him of how she had heard of the d'Hautevilles, presence in London. He heard her out, still with that air of scornful disbelief.

'How very fluently you lie, my dear,' he said admiringly when she had finished. 'Almost do you convince me. Now tell me why you decided to leave me in the first place.'

'Because, my lord, it seemed to me that you could do very well without me! The lady in whose company you spent last night is, it would seem, an old friend who, to judge by her—her generous form has granted you her favours long since!'

'I spent last night here alone,' he rapped out harshly. 'That lady is certainly one I have known for some time. The child she bears could have been fathered by any of a dozen gentlemen I could name—or even by her husband.'

'I don't believe you!' she said flatly, having made up her mind not to do so. 'I heard her as near as makes no matter admit it was yours.'

He laughed shortly. 'She'd have a piece of work to prove it.'

'Then why did you go to see her?'

'You are mighty persistent, ma'am,' he drawled. 'Downright touching, this wifely display of jealousy, damn me if it ain't! If you will have it, she guessed at our marriage and threatened to make it known. I had to turn her up sweet to still her tongue.'

'I have no doubt of that!' she retorted hotly and, for a moment, thought he was going to strike her. Controlling himself with an effort, he went on speaking in a perfectly level tone.

'May I be informed of your plans, ma'am?'

'To return to Tunbridge Wells and later to visit my mother and stepfather in France.'

'So our married life is at an end?'

'Yes, my lord.'

'You cheating little vixen!' he ground out. 'How much are you being paid for this by my dear aunt?'

'Wh-what can you mean?' she stammered, quite taken aback.

'If you will not play the wife to me then I cannot get an heir in any other way, so Trevor's path is clear. Very clever, 'pon my word!' Taking his hands out of his pockets, he strode towards her. 'But there's an answer to that, my lady!'

'D-don't touch me!' She retreated until her back was against the end of the fourposter. Very deliberately he took off his coat and flung it on a chair.

'Sweet innocence won't serve you now, ma'am!'

His strength was immeasurably greater than hers and she made no move to oppose him, submitting to his savage embrace until his fury abated and he almost flung her from him.

'Devil take it! Not even to such a shameless jade as you can I—why had you to be such a one?'

Desperately she wanted to cry out: 'I'm not! I'm not!' but, snatching up his coat, he was gone. With shaking hands, she smoothed her attire and, picking up her portmanteau, crept from the room.

CHAPTER
NINE

'I AM sure I do not know what has come over Nathan.' Mrs Saville tossed the letter she had been reading on to the table beside her and resumed her needlework. 'I tell him of our impending nuptials and he scarce even makes comment upon the matter.'

Sir Peregrine, emerging with manifest reluctance from a post-prandial nap, opened one wary eye. 'All to the good, ain't it?' he hazarded.

'Not at all!' Mrs Saville was very emphatic. 'Depend upon it, he'll come round to it in time but, at the moment, his mind is quite taken up by something other. What can it be, I wonder?'

Both of Sir Peregrine's eyes opened wide. 'A female?' he suggested hopefully.

His bride-to-be made a face of disgust. 'Then he's far behind the fair!' she declared tartly. 'With February all but spent and my sister-in-law announcing that they are in expectation of a happy event at Hever Court around mid-summer, there's no need for him to put himself out in such a way.'

'It could well be a girl,' he was moved to remind her.

She stared at him, needle poised in mid-air, absorbed in her thoughts. 'What should have happened to her, d'you suppose, Miss Julienne-Eve Lawrence? She disappeared so very completely.'

'No, no.' Sir Peregrine endeavoured to explain himself. 'I meant the Heathcott brat could well be a girl.'

'Oh, as to that, it would not be beyond Elspeth's powers to smuggle in a child of the mist in a warming pan, so be it was a boy.' She set down her tambour with a snap. 'Perry, we must go at once to Leyswood Towers. I conceive it to be my duty to call upon my sister-in-law and congratulate her upon the prospect of a grandchild.'

'Assure yourself there really is one on the way, d'you mean?' He chuckled. 'Awake upon every suit, ain't you, m'love?'

His love nodded complacently. 'I would be perfectly bird-witted did I not take simple precautions.' she agreed.

'Yes—hmmm! Perhaps it would be best if we visited Leyswood Towers,' allowed Sir Peregrine grudgingly. 'And, at least, discover what mischief that young rakehell of yours is brewing.'

She dimpled at him. 'Bless you, Perry dear, I must kiss you for that!'

'No—I beg of you—my neckcloth! Have a care, my dear!' moaned the unhappy gentleman, but to no avail, his lady continuing to express her gratification in what seemed to her to be a fitting manner.

Once having formed a decision, Mrs Saville allowed nothing to stand in the way of her arrangements. She did, however, take the precaution of sending a message to Rotherham warning him of their imminent arrival so that his lordship was on hand to greet them; a tight-lipped Rotherham who offered his congratulations to his prospective stepfather with punctilious courtesy. Sir Peregrine, who had been prepared for a less cordial reception, was touched by this unexpected civility and was pleased to accept a glass of steaming 'bishop' to counteract the rigors of the journey. His lady, more accustomed than he to her son's starts, took note of his shadowed eyes and brittle manner and resolved to have the truth from him before the day was out.

The small miracle of the book-room fire burning clear and strong with no evidence of smoke, and the general air of comfort that prevailed throughout the house caused her to raise her eyebrows in speculation, while the dinner set before them was of an excellence further to excite her curiosity.

'I cannot believe, Nathan, that Mrs Challis has had the dressing of so many dishes,' she remarked, as the first course of barrelled oysters and veal olives gave place to jugged hare and a turkey poult, flanked by a ragout of potato balls, with sprouts and creamed spinach, and for those who still had the appetite for them, a lemon soufflé and a Welsh rarebit.

'An acquaintance of mine had occasion to turn off his chef by reason of his advancing years. As I have neither the appetite of a cormorant nor the digestion of an ostrich, the old man pleases me well, nor can it be said that his strength is taxed beyond endurance in this household. You will join us in a glass of port, mama? We three would rattle like peas together in the saloon. You'll be more snug here.'

'Indeed, it is a deal more cosy than ever I remember it.' She looked about her. 'New drapes, I see, and heavy ones, good fires, good food, and plenty of the best wax candles. You like your comfort, my son.'

'I haven't enjoyed a surfeit of it these last years in the Peninsula,' he reminded her dryly.

'True,' she granted, and waited until the butler had set the decanters on the table and withdrawn. 'But how do you propose to support it?'

'Doubtless the Lord will provide,' said he in what she considered to be a very whimsical manner.

'Forgive me if I appear sceptical of Almighty intervention on your behalf,' she returned with cool sarcasm, 'but would not a wife have been a more certain insurance?'

'As it turned out, no.'

His words fell into a silence that was broken only by the soft swirl of the port as it filled the glasses and the gentle hissing of a damp log upon the fire. Mrs Saville, realising that an ill-judged show of concern might prohibit any further confidences, phrased her next question with care.

'Do I understand that you have entered into the married state and found it to be less than satisfactory?'

All trace of amusement had vanished from his face and when he replied it was with a touch of constriction.

'A salutary experience, I assure you, ma'am, and an excessively mortifying one.'

'May I know—who is the lady?'

'Your entry for the Nursery Stakes, dear mama. Miss Julienne-Eve Lawrence.'

Mrs Saville directed a warning glare at the dumbfounded

Sir Peregrine. 'Indeed?' she said politely. 'And when did the marriage take place?'

'Oh, some four months ago,' he replied, a shade impatiently, as if the matter was of small account. 'And we have been parted for all but two days of that time.'

'But why, Nathan, in Heaven's name?' his mother so far forgot herself as to exclaim. 'She's no vapourish female, I dare swear, and you're no greenhead! What threw things out of joint?'

Sir Peregrine, eyeing his scarce-tasted glass of port with regret, cleared his throat and suggested he withdrew to the book-room while this delicate question was being resolved, but Rotherham motioned him to remain seated.

'You're of the family now, sir, it's best you know the whole of it.'

In a few short sentences he gave them the story of his brief essay into matrimony. Mrs Saville did not take her eyes from his face during the telling, seeing in its taut lines the wounded pride and beneath, the deeper hurt. At the end, Sir Peregrine was first to break the hush.

'Confounded bad luck, that woman showing up just then,' he growled. 'Who was it? Not little Harriet or one of her girls?'

'God, no! Chastity Fanshawe.'

'Chastity indeed!' exploded Mrs Saville. 'When all the world knows her nursery is as varied as the Harleian Miscellany!'

'Not my wife! She is a simple innocent, I'd have you know—or would have me believe she is.' Something in the way he spoke caused his mother to rise and go to stand behind his chair, her hands resting lightly on his shoulders. He turned his head to look up at her. 'Have I misjudged her, d'you suppose, mama?'

Much though she longed to offer him consolation, she knew her son too well for that, and wrinkled her brow as if giving the question much thought.

'To such a girl London, an inheritance, marriage to you, all must have come as something of a shock. Then, to cap it, the lovely Lady Fanshawe in a state of expectancy, claiming you for her own—yes, enough to disenchant any young wife, I do declare.' She patted his cheek reprovingly and returned to her chair. 'But I think that you, too, my son, were not fully awake upon that suit. Indifference makes no display of emotion; jealousy stems from a stronger source.'

'I did think of that later,' he admitted, drawing a hand tiredly over his brow. 'Just before Christmas I called at Culver Lodge to—to give my wife greeting. I was received civilly enough by Miss Beresford, the lady of the house, who infomed me that Jul—my lady had taken boat for France two days previously to join her parents. But other than that they resided in Paris, she could tell me no more.'

'So that part of her story was true?'

'Yes.' He hesitated. 'Although I wonder if Miss Beresford was being quite open with me. Perhaps she had been asked to keep a guard on her tongue.'

'Did she know who you were?'

'I believe my name occasioned some surprise, but no more than that. And she spoke always of Miss Lawrence, never of Lady Rotherham.'

'Who are your wife's parents?'

'That I do not know either. They were lodged at Grillon's on the night of her—her flight, but half of London was speaking French that night.'

'If she stayed there she would have been registered as Lady Rotherham, stands to reason,' put in Sir Peregrine. 'Perhaps someone at the hotel would remember.'

Rotherham shrugged with a fatalistic acceptance quite foreign to his nature. 'Small chance after so long a time.'

'Nonetheless you will go to London tomorrow, Nathan, and enquire at Grillon's.' Mrs Saville emphasised her point with an imperatively tapping forefinger upon the table. 'For my part, I will call upon this Miss Beresford. A female asking questions need not occasion alarm as might a gentleman, and it is possible that, by now, she has had a message from your wife.' She paused, then steeled herself to continue. 'It was on the second night of your marriage that she left you, was it not?'

He laughed shortly. 'Your sensitivity does you credit, mama! The answer to your unspoken question is—yes!'

'Nathan!' His mother sat bolt upright, gripping the arms

of her chair. 'She may now be carrying your child!'

'Maybe—how should I know?'

For an instant his face showed wistfully tender, then he seized the decanter and splashed port into his glass with an unsteady hand. Sir Peregrine and Mrs Saville exchanged glances.

'I will go to London tomorrow,' announced the stout baronet with rare decision. 'If you start making enquiries about your wife's whereabouts at Grillon's they'll guess there's a screw loose somewhere. Better that I should do it—aged uncle, not seen the girl in years, thought maybe she'd tripped off to France with her parents—something of that sort.' He waved away Rotherham's thanks. 'Glad to be of service, m'boy. Devilish awkward, mislaying a wife.'

'Indeed, Nathan,' said Mrs Saville with the suspicion of a twinkle in her eye. 'I am persuaded you have made a perfect mull of the whole business!'

'Yes, mama,' confessed his lorship humbly. 'I suspect I have.'

The Marquis Colomb d'Hauteville, among others of his privileged class, had his hôtel in the Faubourg St Germain. Julienne-Eve found herself to be admitted to this exalted society solely by reason of being the Marquis's stepdaughter, for her English title counted for less than nothing, and beauty had quite gone out of fashion since the great ladies of the *ancien régime* could not measure up in face or form to the galaxy of lovely creatures that had thronged the Emperor's court. But she was soon to discover that, however autocratic and disapproving their ladies, the gentlemen of the 'noble faubourg' were not unappreciative of a pretty face and, in addition, many distinguished Englishmen were to be found mingling with the élite of Parisien society.

The Marquise viewed her daughter's social triumphs with a calculating eye. Julienne-Eve had been more than doubtful about accepting her stepfather's invitation to visit them in Paris, sensing that it lacked her mother's approval, but her period of usefulness to Miss Beresford was at an end and she had to admit to a certain curiosity about the Colomb d'Hauteville ménage. Also, she needed a little

time to make her dispositions for the future. To discreet
queries about her husband, she allowed it to be understood
that his affairs detained him in England and, heartsore and
lonely though she might be, she would have been less than
human did she not enjoy her conquests among the many
gentlemen who came to call at the Hôtel d'Hauteville.

Among her more constant admirers was an elegant
exquisite, the Vicomte de Beaumanoir. This nobleman
claimed old acquaintance with her mother and the Marquis, though she suspected the latter cared little for the
connection. The Vicomte's conduct towards her was at all
times irreproachable, and if she sometimes experienced a
qualm of doubt about the occasional predatory glint in his
alert grey eyes or the petulant pout of his full lower lip when
she lightly turned aside some extravagantly-phrased com-
pliment, her experience of such fashionable beaux was too
slight to warn her of danger. There were those who might
well have done had they not been lost in speculation as to
why the Marquise should relinquish her cicisbeo in favour
of her daughter with every appearance of complaisance,
while the Marquis, whose years prohibited him from regular attendance at the innumerable social events to which
they were bidden, seemed well content that so acceptable
an escort should offer in his stead.

On one such occasion the ladies had attended the theatre
in the Vicomte's company and after had gone to sup at the
Beauvilliers Restaurant in the Rue de Richelieu, when a
party of English ladies and gentlemen entered and seated
themselves at an adjacent table. The sound of the familiar
tongue so worked upon Julienne-Eve's imagination that
she had to turn away in order to conceal the onrush of
home-sickness that swept over her. Then a chance remark
caught her attention and, looking up, she discovered that
one of the ladies in the party was regarding her with more
than ordinary interest. Her confusion was intensified when
this person smiled and raised a hand in greeting. Though
she had seen her but once, and then only for a few minutes,
she was in no doubt that she was looking at her husband's
mother.

Stumbling to her feet, she made hurried excuse. 'Forgive

me, maman, M. le Vicomte, but there is a lady to whom I must pay my respects.'

Mrs Saville at once rose to greet her. 'My dear child, the very one I wish to see!'

'You—you know, ma'am?'

'Nathan told me the whole.' Mrs Saville's voice was vibrant with understanding while her keen glance missed no detail of her daughter-in-law's appearance. 'Is it possible for us to speak privately together? I am lodged with Lady Oxford in the Rue de Clichy.'

Julienne-Eve gulped slightly. 'I am with my mother and—and a friend. If you would care to—'

'I should be enchanted to make your mother's acquaintance.'

The introductions were effected, neither the Vicomte nor the Marquise expressing other than well-bred gratification at the unexpected encounter. It was arranged that Mrs Saville should call at the Hôtel d'Hauteville on the following day and, having seen her rejoin her party, Julienne-Eye was congratulating herself that things had passed off very smoothly when the Marquise suddenly declared she felt uncommonly tired.

'Do not let me mar the enjoyment of your evening, my dear Vicomte. I see the Gontauts are about to leave and will, I am sure, take me up in their carriage. I trust you to return me my daughter safely before too long.'

Giving Julienne-Eve no chance of protest, she then left the table to join her neighbours who at once signified their willingness to escort her home. The Vicomte laughed, a soft chilling sound that set all Julienne-Eve's nerves jangling.

'I grieve for Madame la Marquise's distress, but allow it to be a most happy circumstance for me. If you are concerned, my lady, as to the propriety of my driving you home unescorted in my carriage, then I have but to call a chair and walk by your side.'

Her ladyship could only blush and disclaim that any such ridiculous notion had entered her head. The Vicomte sat back, well-satisfied. He had made the offer and she had declined it, now she must be held as much to blame as he should anything irregular occur. Julienne-Eve, for her part, knew not what to make of her mother's behaviour and sought to reassure herself by assuming a lightly flirtatious manner.

'Indeed, with both maman and mama-in-law here tonight, poor Madame Propriety must be quite shone down,' she quipped.

'Madame Propriety,' he mused, 'how great an influence does she have over all our actions.'

Again, Julienne-Eve felt a tremor of warning. 'And rightly so, M. le Vicomte, do you not agree?'

'Ah, there speaks the virtuous wife!' he quizzed her, taking her fan from her hand and gently waving it by her flushed cheeks. 'I think I could find it in my heart to pink your English husband just a little with my sword for his neglect of you.' His tone changed subtly as their waiter came at that moment with their *cotelettes à la Soubise*. 'It is to be hoped that the excellence of the dish will excuse the time endured in waiting for it.'

Softly though the words were spoken the reproof was very clear and the waiter bent almost double in his anxiety to placate his client.

'Je m'excuse, M. le Vicomte, mais il y a trop de monde ce soir.'

'So?' The Vicomte closed the fan with a snap and Julienne-Eve had the foolish fancy that, had it been the unfortunate waiter's neck in his fingers, he would have thought no more of it. Restraining an impulse to throw herself upon Mrs Saville's kindness and beg her company, she contrived to maintain an air of composure, though she scarce tasted a mouthful of the delicious food placed before her. The Vicomte kept up a flow of easy conversation throughout the meal so that when they rose to leave the restaurant she was almost persuaded that her doubts of his behaviour existed only in her imagination.

'My lady is as sweet and fresh as an English rose,' he whispered in that language as he took his seat beside her in the carriage, having privily instructed his driver to take the longest route imaginable to the Faubourg St Germain.

'But roses do have thorns!' said Julienne-Eve firmly,

determined to stamp out any amorous pretensions. 'I cannot but feel concern for poor maman. She has ever been subject to the headache and has, I fear, exerted herself overmuch on my behalf.'

The Vicomte, who very well knew that the Marquise's malaise stemmed from an excess of temper, brought about by his whispered command to leave him alone with her daughter, smiled complacently. The handling of such ageing and capricious beauties was simplicity itself for a man of his resource. One hint that unwillingness to oblige him would result in the loss of his attentions and the thing was done. He wondered if the daughter would prove as complaisant as the mother and slid a caressing hand up her arm.

'M. le Vicomte! I beg of you—' Julienne-Eve shrank back into her corner against the squabs.

'How lovely you are when your eyes flash fire!' he murmured, pressing closer to her.

The strong perfume with which his clothes were drenched almost suffocated her as he clasped her to him, while her struggles only further excited his passions. Then, when she felt herself to be nearing exhaustion, a sound from outside wiped the anticipatory smile from his lips and, releasing her, he lowered the window to listen attentively. It came again, loud and clear, repeated by several voices.

'*Vive l'Empereur! Vive Napoléon!*'

With a half-uttered curse, Beaumanoir ordered the horses to a halt and slipped out of the carriage to mingle with the jostling crowd. Julienne-Eve, grateful for her deliverance though, as yet, unaware of the reason for it, peered out into the dark busy street, and debated the advisability of making a dash for freedom. But the fact of her being in an entirely strange quarter of Paris and that, by the sounds of it, a disturbed one, gave her pause and, in a moment, he was with her again.

'To the Faubourg St Germain with all speed,' he snapped, slamming the door to behind him.

'What is it, M. le Vicomte?' she asked, bewildered at his changed demeanour. 'Is something amiss?'

'Yes, my lady, something is very far amiss,' he replied

furiously. 'The Corsican has escaped from Elba and all his *vieux moustaches* are rallying to his banner! France is at war within herself again, and you had best play least in sight for the name of Colomb d'Hauteville is no prime favourite with Bonaparte!'

This alarming disclosure produced no more than a deep feeling of relief in its recipient, and she silently blessed the Emperor who, on this momentous night, would never know how he had foiled an attempt at seduction and earned an English lady's heartfelt gratitude.

CHAPTER
TEN

'TAKE the child—I beg this of you, madame. If the Emperor wishes to wreak his spite upon me, so be it, but my son—' The Marquis who, like most of his household, had been about since dawn, flung his arms wide in a gesture of total despair.

'Surely he would not harm a little boy?' expostulated Julienne-Eve, unable to drag her gaze away from her step-father's ravaged countenance.

'Not physically, perhaps, but he would have him reared in his beliefs, his disloyalties. A Colomb d'Hauteville to be other than the servant of the Kings of France is inconceivable!'

'The addition of one small child to our party is no great matter, after all,' pronounced Mrs Saville. 'He can be passed off as your son, my dear.' She smiled reassuringly at Julienne-Eve before addressing the Marquise. 'And you, madame, is it your wish to accompany us also?'

'My place is at my husband's side.' The Marquise's eyes were fixed upon her daughter. 'If aught should happen to us, I rely upon you to care for the boy.'

Privately wondering how she was to provide for her half-brother when her own future was so uncertain, Julienne-Eve nevertheless realised that this was no time to be finical about details and readily assented. The Marquise permitted herself a thin smile.

'It will be good experience for you when setting up your own nursery. Oh, no point in dissembling further, very soon the whole world must know that you are enlarging.'

Julienne-Eve attempted to assume an air of unconcern, while wishing that she might be absorbed into the close pattern of the needlework carpet beneath her feet. As nothing so obliging could be hoped for she forced herself to face the company to discover the Marquis and Mrs Saville regarding her with tolerant understanding and no hint of surprise.

'My felicitations, my dear child.' The Marquis patted her shoulder. 'When my wife told me of her suspicions, I was overjoyed. It is all the more fitting that you should now return to your husband's side.'

'Then that is agreed.' Mrs Saville rose briskly to her feet. 'I will return within the hour and must beg that you are ready with as few encumbrances as possible.'

'I will have my travelling chaise prepared,' said the Marquise at once. 'With a team of six horses you should make good time to the coast.'

'With your crest emblazoned on the panels, no doubt, and liveried postilions and outriders to support us?' she asked caustically. He was obliged to agree.

'You are in the right of it, madame. But how do you propose to travel?'

'By diligence, of course. A party of three women and a child are far less likely to attract attention in that way than travelling post.'

'My son travelling by the common diligence?' The Marquis's horror was almost ludicrous. 'And what of his nurse—his tutor?'

'My daughter-in-law and I shall be nurse and tutor until he is safe in England.' Mrs Saville held her irritation on a tight rein. 'My maid, Parsons, must come with us, since she accompanied me to France, and her presence will add an air of verisimilitude to the picture of two English ladies hastening home, away from possible danger.'

'Very true, madame,' he acknowledged ruefully. 'I will see that the child is awaiting your return.'

The parting between the Marquis and his son was one of the utmost poignancy. Julienne-Eve had seen little of the small Philippe during her stay in Paris, for he had his own suite of rooms and his own servants. This inevitably resulted in a strangely adult infant, whose bewilderment at the sudden change in his circumstances nonetheless broke through his carefully schooled composure.

'You will be in the charge of my lady Rotherham,' his father instructed him, 'and you must regard yourself as her son throughout the journey and not fail to address her as *maman*.'

'Mama would be better if he is to pass off as an English boy,' volunteered Julienne-Eve. 'How good is your English, Philippe?'

The child turned wondering eyes upon her. 'How do you do? Is it not a beautiful day?' he lisped with so pronounced a French accent that even the Marquis had to smile.

'I think, my son, you had better have a sore throat and not be able to speak at all,' he decreed. 'Come, a little scarf about your neck and—no, no, Philippe, no tears.'

'Papa, papa, why must I go? Cannot I stay with you?'

'I have told you, it is best that you go. We will be re-united when I consider it advisable. You need to know no more.'

The calm authority in his father's voice steadied the boy at once and, bidding his parents a formal farewell, he put his hand into Julienne-Eve's and walked with her from the room. Much though she longed to snatch him up and comfort him, she knew she dared not lest the fragile balance of control be overset. The only one of the four to be in perfect command of herself was the Marquise, who had said goodbye to her son as coolly as if he was going out for his daily promenade, and to her daughter with a finality that seemed to postulate that she had no expectation of their ever meeting again. This, too, Julienne-Eve had sensed in the Marquis's leavetaking of her and, while allowing it to be reasonable that, at his age, he well might not see either her or the boy again, her mother was a relatively young woman nor, outside of the bedroom, was the Emperor reputed to make war upon females.

Mrs Saville and her maid drove up prompt to the minute in a decrepit fiacre of such unsavoury appearance as to cause the fastidious Philippe to wrinkle his aristocratic small nose in disgust.

'We have seats bespoken on the Dunkerque diligence, no others were to be had. It is no great distance to Calais from there,' Mrs Saville added, forestalling the objection forming on Julienne-Eve's lips, 'so that if we find ourselves unable to get away from the one port, then we must attempt the other. Is this the boy? Does he have a fever?' Julienne-Eve quickly explained the reason for Philippe's invalidish appearance and her mother-in-law agreed that some such subterfuge was advisable. 'It is the best thing we can hit on, I suppose, but to restrain so young a child from speaking his own tongue for all of three days will be difficult.'

'Three days?' exclaimed Julienne-Eve in dismay.

'Yes, we do not arrive at Dunkerque until the evening of the third day from now and then there is the question of obtaining a passage to England. We will not be the only ones in a hurry to leave France.'

The truth of this remark was amply borne out by the number of persons thronging the Place des Victoires in the hope of securing a place on any coach leaving Paris. Indeed, the guard of the diligence was obliged to descend from his perch and brandish his whip in the most threatening manner to discourage unlawful attempts at entering or climbing upon his vehicle. Parsons, in order to make room for one distraught lady, handsomely offered to take Philippe upon her knee which attention, it was clear, did not meet with her charge's approval. Fortunately, his rebellious mutterings passed unnoticed in the general confusion.

At Lille, they discovered they had to change vehicles, and the town was in such a turmoil of excitement from conflicting rumours and fears that they quite expected their journey to be brought to a premature conclusion. Then it was that Parsons' goodheartedness was amply repaid, for the lady to whom she had rendered assistance was a resident of the town. She took them in charge, guiding them to an unpretentious inn, where she was received with great respect by the landlord who informed them that a second diligence would set out for Dunkerque from that very place in an hour's time.

It was almost dark when they at last arrived at their destination and Julienne-Eve's heart sank when she perceived the number of persons abroad in the streets and the general air of alarm that prevailed. They speedily ascertained that there was not a bed to be had in the place nor, because of a strong contrary wind, any possibility of a vessel being able to leave the harbour. Even Mrs Saville's buoyant spirits suffered a reverse at this unwelcome news, but she soon enlisted the sympathy of a respectable-looking towns-

woman to whom, despite the difficulties of communica-
tion—since a form of low Dutch appeared to be the language generally spoken in the town—she managed to
convey their need of somewhere to rest, the little boy's
indifferent health, and Julienne-Eve's interesting condition. The good woman's pocket being then amply lined, she
led them at once to her home, a simple enough place, but
clean and warm, where several sleepy children were turned
out of an upstairs chamber and fresh linen put upon the
beds.

As it was plain that food was not to be included in this
arrangement, once having assured herself that Julienne-
Eve and Philippe were comfortably disposed, Mrs Saville
with Parsons and their hostess in attendance, went in search
of something to eat. The little boy was so exhausted that he
slept almost before his head had settled into the pillow, but
Julienne-Eve, despite her weariness, lay wakeful, listening
to the unaccustomed sounds from the street outside and
wondering if it was hunger that was causing such odd
flutters beneath her heart. She smiled to herself in the
darkness. Even if too late to secure him his fortune, surely a
son would soften his animosity towards her? His mother,
though she rarely referred to the curious situation obtaining between her son and his wife, gave the impression that
she considered them to be behaving like a pair of irres-
ponsible children who needed taking in hand. Dear Mrs
Saville! Were it not for the natural anxiety attendant upon
such a journey, she would be enjoying herself hugely,
mused her daughter-in-law, and straightaway fell asleep.

She was roused some time later by the murmur of voices,
and opened her eyes to find the room bathed in candlelight.

'A little wine, my dear.' Mrs Saville looked to be as
collected as if dispensing refreshment in her own home.
'The food, I fear, is less than appetising, scarce a thing to be
bought in the town. We were fortunate to get milk for
Philippe and half a cold chicken.'

She was at pains to conceal her concern as she watched
the wan little face on the pillow. Cheerful and uncomplain-
ing though the girl had been, the jolting of the diligence, the
strain and the makeshift arrangements had taken their toll.

Where, in heaven's name, was Rotherham? It had been agreed that he should remain at Calais until he received word from her. That the message she had sent from Paris on the day of their departure had not reached him now seemed alarmingly probable, in which case there was nothing for it but to get herself to Calais on the morrow, on horseback if necessary. She had lodged word of their whereabouts in every possible place in Dunkerque that a traveller might enquire at, and could only hope that nothing disastrous had occurred to prevent his joining them.

Julienne-Eve was the first to awake on the following morning and, tempted by the faint gleam of sunlight showing from under the flimsy drapes and the mounting sound of the town bestirring itself to cope with another day, she stole from her bed to draw aside a curtain and peep down at the scene beneath the window. There were one or two hawkers beginning to call their wares in their strange, guttural tongue, and several housewives had already appeared at their doorways, on the look for food. The neighbourhood was clearly one occupied by the respectable poor so that it was almost with a feeling of outrage that she perceived the tall, lithe figure striding down the street, drab driving-coat swinging free, beaver tilted at a jaunty angle on his dark head. He was looking from side to side as if checking the houses, and as he approached that in which they were lodged, he consulted a piece of paper held in his hand.

With a smothered gasp, Julienne-Eve dropped the curtain back into place and returned to her bed where she lay with wildly beating heart, telling herself not to be so missish. It was inevitable that Rotherham should come in search of them, his mother must be acting with his knowledge, and she could well be grateful for it. Then the sound of his knock upon the street-door sent her under the bedcovers with tight-shut eyes, desperately feigning sleep throughout the following sequence of murmured question and answer below. Their landlady's call brought a ready response from Mrs Saville. Julienne-Eve lifted a chink of eyelid to observe her mother-in-law, still wearing her night-cap and enveloped in her voluminous travelling cloak, hasten from the room. Then Parsons was moving about, calming the little boy who had been awakened by the disturbance, so she deemed it prudent to sit up, yawning widely.

'I thought I heard something—where is Mrs Saville?' she exclaimed with a nice assumption of surprise.

'A gentleman has called to see her, she is speaking with him now,' said the maid repressively, endeavouring to animate the sulky ashes in the small grate with a broken-winded bellows. 'Drat this fire! I'll never get Master Philippe's milk warmed, and it's not likely we'll get more before we leave.'

'Are we leaving?' asked Julienne-Eve brightly.

'No doubt of it, m'lady. His—madam's friend will take us in hand now.'

So the identity of 'madam's friend' was to be withheld from her! Julienne-Eve mentally shrugged and began to assume her crumpled and far from fresh garments.

'Oh, what would I not give for a bath!' she sighed, surveying herself in the one fly-spotted mirror that was all the room could provide.

'Yes, well, it may be some time yet before you can enjoy that, m'lady.' Parsons gave up the losing battle with the ashes and directed her attention to coaxing the reluctant Philippe to partake of cold milk. 'But I'll give your hair a good brushing-out, and with a fresh tucker and a dash of honey-water, you'll feel more the thing.'

At that point Mrs Saville returned to the room, emanating enough energy to bestir the whole party. 'The gentleman declares that we are all about in our heads to attempt the seacrossing at this time, with so many resolved on it. Brussels should be our objective and, since I have many friends in that city, I am persuaded that it is the most sensible course. He is holding a carriage for us but begs we waste no time in taking it up since such vehicles are beyond price. He counts himself most fortunate to have obtained one at all. Can you be ready in fifteen minutes?'

They could, even to the point of standing waiting by the street-door when the commodious travelling chaise, drawn by a team of four strengthy bays, drew up before them. A young gentleman who, by his military bearing, looked likely to be more at home on a cavalry charger than on the box-seat of a carriage, sprang down to assist them with their possessions. The coachman, his broad-brimmed hat drawn well down over his face, merely touched the brim in acknowledgment of their presence and sat hunched over the reins but, from her previous meeting with him, Julienne-Eve was reasonably convinced that he was none other than her husband's groom.

Then, with a handsome douceur to their landlady who was understandably distressed by the sudden departure of such affluent guests, they were away at a brisk pace. Presently the noise of the *pavé* ceased and, to Julienne-Eve's amazement, they proceeded for miles over firm sand, with the sea almost touching the flying hoofs of the horses. Leaning a little out of the window to breathe in the fresh, clean air, she observed a horseman following them at no great distance. Assuming that he would shortly forge ahead, she set back in her seat to await his passing but when, after some time had elapsed, he had not appeared, she looked back again to see him still following them and was conscious of a warm glow of gratitude towards him for not intruding upon her while satisfying himself as to the safety of the party.

At Bruges, where they rested for a night, they parted from their comfortable carriage and, to Julienne-Eve's secret dismay, their discreet escort. They then proceeded by canal to Ghent, accompanied only by Mr Jones, the young cornet, who had, after the fashion of impressionable young gentlemen, quite lost his heart to her ladyship.

This delightfully leisurely method of progression was in such contrast to anything they had previously experienced that Julienne-Eve, watching the gentle landscape slide by, longed for the peaceful day to go on for ever, but she was recalled to the difficulties of the present when Mrs Saville, leaving Philippe in grave discourse with Mr Jones, came to sit beside her.

'He is so fascinated by all that is new about him that I truly believe he has forgotten his poor father already,' she sighed. Julienne-Eve made some suitable response and they sat in companionable silence for a time before Mrs

Saville resumed the conversation. 'Forgive me, my dear, if I touch upon a subject that may be displeasing to you, but tomorrow evening should see us in Brussels and time for discussion will be past.'

'You wish to speak of—of Rotherham, do you not, ma'am?'

'Yes. He has every expectation of being appointed to Lord Wellington's staff when—I beg his pardon!—the Duke comes to Brussels. In the meantime, he is under the command of Lord Hill who is there, as far as I can ascertain, for the sole purpose of restraining the young Prince of Orange's martial enthusiasm. A delightful boy and wholly devoted to the English interest, but a shade over-impulsive. Just consider what might have resulted had he married the Princess Charlotte!' She paused to reflect on that unlikely outcome and Julienne-Eve waited, suspecting what was to follow. 'As you may imagine, with all the military pouring into Brussels, to say nothing of persons like ourselves, the town is excessively overcrowded. Through the good offices of Lord Fitzroy Somerset, Rotherham has secured us a house which I understand to be set a little way out in the country.' She hesitated again, as if uncertain of how to express herself. 'I am sure I do not have to explain to you, my dear, that in so close a community as Brussels, where speculation and gossip are rife, the nicety of one's conduct is of prime importance. It would give a very off appearance indeed if Rotherham did not join our household.'

'I understand perfectly, ma'am.' Julienne-Eve's calm acceptance of the situation surprised even herself. 'I am content to be guided by you in whatever outward semblance of domestic harmony you think proper to assume. For my part, I shall be happy to live retired and, to be sure, my condition should provide sufficient excuse for such a course.'

In this comfortable assumption she soon found herself to be at fault. They sped through Brussels without pause, exclaiming in delight at the handsome buildings and unfamiliar costumes worn by the ladies, before entering the grounds of a considerable mansion, set amid trees upon an eminence over-looking a stretch of water. Here they were received by a most respectable English couple, acting as butler and housekeeper, and were enchanted to find the house to be as elegantly furnished and spacious as could be wished for.

As she reclined upon the couch-bed in her large and airy bedchamber, while a bright-eyed Belgian maid bore off her clothes with horrified exclamations at their bedraggled appearance, she could only feel relief at their safe arrival and thankfulness that Rotherham had been on hand to ease their journey. In this beautiful quiet place she could exist in a sort of limbo of inaction until they could continue on their way to England.

The following morning quite cut up these illusions when a perfect host of callers descended upon them. Lady Fitzroy Somerset, herself expecting a child in May, was the first to arrive, and in no time at all Julienne-Eve and this amiable niece of the Duke of Wellington were calling each other by their given names. Mrs Saville was well pleased to renew her acquaintance with Lady Caroline Capel who, with her numerous and lively progeny, lived at no very great distance from them, and who was attended by her second daughter, Georgiana. This young lady seized with delight upon Julienne-Eve who eventually had to cry out in protest that her poor brain could not take in any more names or details of the diverse society into which she had been dropped like ripe fruit from off a tree.

'Oh, but how fortunate you are to have such an interesting husband! We are all quite in love with him!' declared the mischievous Georgiana, her head on one side to judge how this sally would be taken. Julienne-Eve, who had been in some dread of first setting eyes on this so-interesting husband, reminded herself that he had spent some months in Brussels the previous year and must be well-known to its English circle. 'Our little Prince, you know, thinks the world of him,' went on her cheerful informant, 'so that we will be losing him to you, I don't doubt! Why—speak of the devil!'

Julienne-Eve had been about to protest that His Highness was more likely to attend upon a household of lively young ladies rather than that of a mother-to-be, when the door to the saloon opened to admit the Prince of Orange, with Rotherham and another gentleman in attendance.

The Prince, a slender eager young man, at once claimed her interest, announcing his intention of giving a ball for her as soon as she felt sufficiently rested to undertake such frivolity. Rotherham, his eyes steady upon her, kissed her hand as if they had but parted a few hours before, and presented Lord Hill, to whom she took an instant liking. Then they were honoured by the arrival of the Duchess of Richmond who looked her up and down and asked, with the bland rudeness peculiar to the highly-born, why Rotherham had kept his wife a secret for so long. To her relief, he turned off Her Grace's question with some jesting remark, but it was plain her curiosity was not appeased.

'Oh, to be sure, there was that dreadful will of your grandfather's—enough to send any young wife into hiding, I do declare! I hear from a friend in England that Lady Heathcott is expecting to be confined at the end of June. Your wife is to be in July? How very interesting!'

'She is a perfect cat and a dreadful mischief-maker into the bargain!' hissed the irrepressible Georgiana into Julienne-Eve's ear.

That young woman, who had never before spoken to a Duchess and who was a trifle overpowered by meeting all these important personages, felt the hot colour burning her cheeks. Catching Rotherham's eye, she found him watching her with a sort of pity in his regard, and understood at once that he had had this sort of situation in mind when he had wished to keep their marriage a secret.

Then Emily Fitzroy Somerset was taking her leave and inviting them to sup on the following evening. 'You will find the hours of eating here most strange,' she informed Mrs Saville. 'Dinner at three o'clock and all other meals accordingly—hence these late and lengthy morning calls.'

It was close upon that hour before the last of their visitors departed and Julienne-Eve sighed for a chair and the opportunity to put up her feet, but Mrs Saville was asking her son if he would not stay and dine with them.

'Thank you, mama, I should be glad to, but after I must wait upon Lord Hill who tells me he has received a despatch from the Duke in confidence for our eyes alone. And, no doubt, the Prince will wish me to assist him in making out his list of guests for his ball in your honour.' He inclined his head slightly towards his wife.

'He—he is a most engaging young man, is he not?' she ventured.

'Yes,' he responded rather drily. 'Now that we have persuaded him to conceal some of his British fervour and show more marked attention to the Belgians. But I would value your opinion of this house. Do you think it will serve for a time until the opportunity presents itself for your return to England?'

To her surprise she realised that he was asking for her approval, not that of his mother, and she hastened to assure him that she found their situation to be admirable in every way. 'Save only that I had not expected to find so much entertainment being engaged upon at such a time.'

He laughed shortly. 'The Prince would dance on his head sooner than not at all. Nor, when the Duke arrives, can we expect any diminution in our amusement, for he is a great dancing man also.'

Dinner passed pleasantly enough, with Mrs Saville eagerly plying her son with questions about the prices and customs that obtained in Brussels.

'Think of it, lace at only three and sixpence the yard—we must visit the lace manufactory, my dear—and Lady Caroline tells me that food stuffs are absurdly cheap,' she enthused.

'Prices may be low, but politics run very high,' Rotherham warned her. 'I would like you to steer a middle course, if you please, mama.'

She promised to be everything that was tactful and, having finished their meal, they withdrew to the saloon for coffee. Here, to Julienne-Eve's alarm, Mrs Saville presently excused herself on the grounds of seeing that all was well with Philippe and she found herself alone with her husband.

He rose to take her empty cup and place it on a table. 'I believe I owe you another apology, ma'am,' he said stiffly.

'Indeed, my lord, whatever for?' she asked, as if it was the least thing in the world.

'For my disbelief of—of your story. But you must allow that the sudden appearance of a set of parents when you were supposed to be alone in the world took a little swallowing!'

That was not why he had been so furious, but she let it pass. This attempt at reconciliation, she knew, was on account of the child, and as such she would accept it.

'The discovery that my mother was in London came as a shock to me too, for I did not entertain any hope of her still being alive, let alone wed to so distinguished a nobleman as M. le Marquis.'

'Did the Marquis approve your choice of escort on the evening you met my mother in Paris?'

She felt the telltale colour rising again and turned her head to look out of the window at the sunlit vista of woods and water. So he had been discussing her with his mother yet had not thought to call upon his wife!

'You mean the Vicomte de Beaumanoir? My mother holds him in high esteem.'

'There are others who do not,' he said, his voice harsh with disapproval. 'For all his noble quarterings, the man is no better than a libertine and adventurer. I myself was close to crossing swords with him when last I was in Brussels. There are many of his sort in this troubled town.'

She rounded on him, prepared to do battle. 'Let us be clear upon this, my lord! While I am in Brussels do I have to submit to you a list of any possible cicisbeos for your approval?'

'You will have no cicisbeos here,' he said shortly. 'If not I, then my mother will attend you.'

'A gentleman is a useful accessory at a ball,' she pointed out.

'Surely, ma'am, your dancing days are numbered?' It was the first time he had alluded to their child, either directly or indirectly.

'Oh, I don't know that,' she retorted. 'Lady Emily is still dancing and her time is closer than mine by two months.'

'I wish you to have the child in England, at Leyswood

Towers,' he said with an arrogant finality that made her long to rake him down. 'I shall arrange for you to get away as soon as I think it safe.'

'Thank you, my lord,' she said meekly enough then, spurred on by some demon of mischief, she added, 'but with such a despicable character as myself, how can you be sure that it is your child?'

Dear God, what had she said? Now, surely, he would turn from her in disgust! To her surprise, he did nothing of the sort, there was even the hint of a laugh in his voice when he replied.

'I never entertained any doubts on that head, ma'am. Unless, of course, Miss Beresford conducts a very different sort of establishment than I would have expected of her!'

She stared at him, open-mouthed. 'You—you met her?'

'Indeed, yes. A most respectable lady.' Involuntarily, she began to smile as he went on in a mock-ferocious manner. 'But should the babe make its appearance indiscreetly late, then I promise you I shall seek out its progenitor and call him to account.'

'Would that not be an extravagant gesture, my lord, if it should be a boy and Lady Lucy's a girl?'

'Fiend take Lady Lucy—and fiend take the time, for I must be gone!' Sketching a brief bow, he left her.

She stood there for a time, still half-smiling at the exchange. So he was confident that she had not played him false, that was something at least. It also accounted for his attempting to overcome his aversion towards her.

'Only,' whispered a tiresome little voice inside her head, 'until the child is born. After that, he is free to do as he pleases.'

With a smothered sigh she glanced at the mantel-clock and, reminding herself that it was time for Philippe's English lesson, she hurried away in search of her small stepbrother.

CHAPTER
ELEVEN

DESPITE the gathering clouds of war the long-awaited arrival of the Duke of Wellington did much to calm the
apprehensions of the inhabitants of Brussels, and the city
resumed its old gaiety with reviews, receptions, picnics,
fêtes champêtres, and always dancing, dancing into the
dawn of the glorious early summer days. As Rotherham
had predicted, the tempo of life increased, although it was
remarked that His Grace had not improved the morality of
Brussels society by inviting some ladies of dubious reputation to his entertainments.

'I am given to understand,' Mrs Saville informed her
daughter-in-law, 'that, it having been represented to the
Duke that a certain lady was not generally received, her
character being a trifle shady, he promptly put on his hat
and said: "Is it, by God? Then I will go and ask her myself!"
which he went out and did.'

Julienne-Eve was inclined to dismiss this and other such
tales as being mere 'Bruxelles stories', and was greatly
taken aback when she found herself to be in a fair way to
becoming the object of the Duke's gallantries. Even
Rotherham quizzed her on being one of His Grace's flirts,
and complimented her on her conquest.

'I cannot but be astonished that so great a man should
interest himself in such a way,' she objected.

'You rate yourself too low, my lady,' he told her solemn-
ly. 'And there are more facets to the Duke's character than
that of bluff soldier.'

They were sitting upon the terrace outside the saloon,
enjoying the late afternoon sunshine and watching Philippe
playing with a puppy of nondescript origin which had
mysteriously insinuated itself into the household. Though
there always must be constraint between them, Julienne-
Eve felt more at her ease with Rotherham than ever she had
since their coming to Brussels. His duties took him away for
the greater part of each day, yet he held himself ready to

attend upon her in whatever time he had available, nor did he enter her apartments except in the company of his mother or some other lady.

So tranquil had the situation become that it was with a distinct sense of shock she heard him say: 'I have made arrangements for you to resume your journey to England this week.'

'But—but—' she stammered, 'do you not believe that the Duke can bring us handsomely off against Bonaparte?'

'I have every faith in the Duke's military competence,' he said deliberately. 'But, whatever the outcome, it is bound to be a close-run thing. I would prefer my family to be safe away.'

'Yes, of course,' she agreed, believing him to be concerned solely for the welfare of his hoped-for son and his mother, then added saucily, 'but with Sir Peregrine threatening to join us, who could doubt the issue?'

At that, he had to laugh for it had taken weeks of entreaty on Mrs Saville's part to induce her timorous suitor even to consider leaving the safety of his native shores.

'And now I have written him to say he had best stay in England to receive you. The Duke has granted me permission to escort you to Ostend, and the captain of the packet I have engaged is well-known to me, a good Kentish man, who will take every care of you.'

'When do we go?' she asked, trying to emulate his casual manner.

'We leave here on Wednesday next.'

Julienne-Eve felt a wave of despair flood over her and pressed her hands tightly together to conceal their trembling. Wednesday—and today was already Monday! The truth was that the prospect of being separated from him was having a most adverse effect upon her spirits. To be sure he was autocratic and utterly provoking at times, but his mere presence gave her a feeling of security of which she had but vaguely been aware until this moment when that protection was about to be taken from her. There had been times, too, when he had even given the appearance of being resigned to his unsatisfactory marriage.

'Cannot you come with us?' she besought him, very low.

He looked at her in surprise. 'Do you fear for the child? You need not, I think, with mama and Parsons to watch over you.'

'I—I fear for you,' she whispered.

'I am obliged to you, ma'am, but I am a soldier. My place is here with my commander.' There was a note of surprise in his voice, as if her concern for him had taken him unawares. 'In any case,' he added on a lighter note, 'mama is resolved to be home for Lady Lucy's lying-in. I'll wager she'll disguise herself as the accoucheur's assistant if needs be in order to be in at the birth!' She said nothing and he leaned over to lay a hand on her clenched ones where they rested on her lap. 'Above anything I would wish to be with you when your time comes, but it cannot be.' He raised a finger to brush the swelling curve of her robe. 'I'll be thinking of you both, be assured of that.' The intimate gesture, the caress implicit in his manner, were too much for her resolution. Suppose she were to lose him now, just when she felt herself to be on the point of winning him? She raised tear-wet eyes to his, meeting the same question in their depths as must surely be in her own. 'You'll stay with mama, will you not? She has formed a very great affection for you. Should anything happen to me—'

'Of course, I'll stay with her, I love her dearly,' Her hands clasped convulsively over his. 'And even if we do not defeat Lady Lucy, I promise you your son will be the most cossetted infant in all England!'

He wore an expression on his face that she had not glimpsed since the first day of their marriage. 'I could almost wish for a daughter, were she the speaking likeness of her mother!'

The idyllic moment was rudely interrupted by a loud scream and a splash.

'Philippe!' cried Julienne-Eve, springing to her feet.

'God! The brat's fallen into the lake!'

In a flash, Rotherham had plunged into the water, seized the small boy in one hand and the wriggling puppy which had been the cause of the disaster in the other, and had hauled them both, dripping, on to the grass. The uproar had brought Mrs Saville and half the household running to the scene.

'Dear goodness, I had supposed you two to be in charge of them!' she complained, stripping off the sobbing little boy's shirt and trousers and wrapping his shivering pinkness up in a towel, but not before rendering the appropriate portion of his anatomy a shade pinker by the administration of a couple of smart slaps, which attention redoubled the young gentleman's vociferous complaints. 'You know you have been told not to play near the lake, Philippe!'

'It is quite our fault, mama Saville, please don't give him too great a scold,' pleaded Julienne-Eve. 'We—we were talking and forgot about him.'

Mrs Saville glanced from her son's intent face to her daughter-in-law's flushed one and drew her own conclusions, but all she said was: 'You'd best change your dress, Nathan. I can scarce do that for *you*!'

'No, nor give me a teasing, either!' he said, with a sympathetic grin for the unhappy Philippe, who was being borne off in the arms of his nursemaid.

'And don't forget we are bidden to sup at the de Beauforts' in an hour's time!' his mother fired off as a parting shot, which had the effect of sending Julienne-Eve hurrying to her bedchamber, calling out for Parsons to assist her.

Two days later they stood on the windswept quay at Ostend in readiness to board the sturdy little packet straining at her moorings beside them.

'The wind is in your favour, you should have a fast passage.' Rotherham was frowning as he looked across the white-capped waves. 'Adieu, mama. My thanks, and look to yourself.'

'And you, my son.' She embraced him briefly. 'Let us have news as often as you may.'

'That might not be very often,' he warned her and turned to his wife. 'I may come no further with you, but my thoughts are ever your servants.'

'And our prayers are with you.' She stepped forward and raised her face to his in a shy, half-inviting gesture. He hesitated, then quickly kissed her on the corner of the mouth, as awkwardly as any schoolboy.

'God bless you—both.'

Then he was gone and she stood, the wind lashing her cloak about her, her eyes following his tall figure until he was lost to her sight. Mrs Saville touched her arm.

'We had best be getting aboard,' she counselled. 'The tide is on the turn and the captain is anxious to lose no moment of it.'

The sea crossing was a mercifully brief one, none of the party suffering any indisposition from the brisk motion of the waves, and at Dover they found a beaming Sir Peregrine awaiting them who had secured lodgings for all the party at the Ship Inn.

'Been waiting here close on a se'ennight,' he informed them cheerfully. 'Ever since Rotherham warned me he was going to pack you off. Had a mind to come over and fetch you myself only—' He looked shamefacedly at Mrs Saville. 'Got a touch of the old trouble—gout, y'know,' he added confidentially to Julienne-Eve.

'Port!' His lady waved a reprimanding finger at him. 'How many bottles a day, Perry?'

'No more than two, I give you my word! And I have had the greatest good fortune,' he hurried on, ignoring her upflung hands. 'When visiting m'nephew at Bristol t'other week, came across a little tavern with as well-stocked a cellar as could be wished for, including several dozen of the smoothest port that ever I tasted.'

'All of which you bought!' Mrs Saville sighed in half-humorous despair.

'Had it sent to Leyswood Towers, thought it would be a good thing for—er, wetting the baby's head!' said he, twinkling at Julienne-Eve, who was hard put to it to keep a straight face in view of Mrs Saville's disapprobation.

The sight of Leyswood Towers on the following day imbued my lady Rotherham with a comfortable sense of homecoming. The massive solidity of the great house seemed to enfold her as if welcoming its new mistress and the child she carried. Adam, too, though looking a deal older than she remembered him, left her in no doubt as to his sentiments towards Lucy's offspring.

'My own great-grandchild or no, be it a boy, I'd drown it

in a bucket as easy as I'd do a kitten!' he avowed.

'We hope it won't come to that!' said Mrs Saville in the tone of one who thought it might not be such a bad notion after all. 'When is it due?'

'At the month's end, 'tis said, but it'd not surprise me if 'twas before. You'll be wanting your carriage tomorrow, ma'am, I don't doubt.'

'I must assure myself of your dear granddaughter's good health,' said Mrs Saville reprovingly, and had to smile at his indignant back as he stalked away. 'Poor Adam!' she murmured to Julienne-Eve, 'I cannot blame him for riding rusty. The possibility of his great-grandson stepping into Nathan's shoes here goes against the pluck. Now, there is another thing I must attend to—my own long-postponed nuptials. I am going to suggest to Perry that, as he is here and there is no likelihood of Nathan coming home until the Corsican is overcome, we dispense with ceremony and wed without delay. I shall, of course, send an invitation to my dear sister-in-law, though I doubt the younger Lady Heath-cott will be feeling sufficiently the thing to accompany her.'

She returned from her call at Hever Court the following day with her colour high and eyes snapping dangerously.

'Smug as a cat that's had the cream, is dear Elspeth! The only glimpse I had of Madam Lucy was when I was leaving and she strutted across the drive into the gardens without so much as a glance at us. I can tell you I had much ado to restrain Adam from dropping his hands and driving over her!'

The succeeding June days were fully occupied by the two ladies in engaging the services of a doctor and a midwife, in refurbishing the old nurseries, and in making arrangements for Mrs Saville and Sir Peregrine to be wed in some style, if very quietly. This ceremony was to take place in the private chapel at Leyswood Towers, with only the immediate household and one or two old friends to attend them.

'Not so grand an affair as it would have been in Brussels, when the dear Duke offered me his own chaplain, and we should have had Rotherham and all our acquaintance to stand up with us,' lamented Mrs Saville. At mention of Rotherham Julienne-Eve's face clouded over for there had been no word from him since their return. Deep in her heart, she had a premonition that all was not well, but kept reminding herself severely that such fancies were peculiar to her condition and had nothing to say to anything. Her mother-in-law was quick to comfort her. 'Depend upon it, the Duke has him running thither and yon, he'll have no time to set pen to paper. No news, one is always assured, is good news, so let us turn our attention to our own small affairs and leave the greater ones to resolve themselves.'

The wedding-day dawned bright and clear and, by mid-day, the sun was blazing down from as cloudless a sky as anyone in England had a right to expect. Julienne-Eve, assisting Parsons to put the final touches to Mrs Saville's ensemble of a hyacinth blue satin robe, worn open in front to reveal a petticoat of toning blue lace, with a perfectly ravishing French bonnet and pale lemon-coloured kid shoes and gloves, felt a lump come into her throat and could not resist hugging her mother-in-law warmly to the extreme danger of her elaborate coiffure.

Sir Peregrine, his corpulence tightly corsetted, cut a splendid figure in white pantaloons and blue coat, with a waistcoat intricately embroidered in gold and silver thread, while Berlin gloves and a tall, amber-topped cane completed a picture of elegance impossible to fault.

Julienne-Eve was delighted to greet her old friend, Mr Ainsley, who had made the journey from London that morning, and whose cheerful commonsense did much to dispel her fears.

'Put your faith in the Duke,' he advised her, 'I would be prepared to wager any amount that there will be no great confrontation after all. When it comes to it, Napoleon will find that his countrymen have had their fill of war.' Though he might say this to reassure the ladies, privately to Sir Peregrine he voiced a very different opinion. 'From what I hear, it is all building up and must presently explode like some great firecracker. London is alive with rumours, the most prevalent being that Bonaparte has caught Wellington napping and has won a famous victory. Pray Heaven his lordship has come off safe.'

It was not until they were seated in the chapel that

Julienne-Eve realised that no one from Hever Court was present, although a card had been duly despatched there. The brief ceremony over, Sir Peregrine with his lady on his arm, walked out into the sunshine and they were smilingly receiving the good wishes of the estate workers gathered outside when a carriage came hurtling up the drive and stopped amid a flurry of gravel. From this stepped Lady Heathcott, her apparel complete to a shade, who came hastening to offer apologies for her tardy arrival.

'My excuse must be that my lawyer has just come from London with most disturbing news. There has been a prodigious battle, it would appear, but nothing is very clear nor even who has been victorious, though 'tis thought Bonaparte has prevailed.' Her cold eyes darted to Julienne-Eve's anguished countenance. 'Many lives have been lost, particularly among the Duke's own staff and senior officers.'

The whole strangely unreal scene of bride and bridegroom in all their finery, belated wedding guest relating such unacceptable tidings, and background of gaping rustics and servants, swam before Julienne-Eve's eyes and, with a low moan, she sank to the ground, saved only from a heavier fall by Mr Ainsley's arm.

'Devil take it, Elspeth, you could have broken that more gently!' The new Lady Whittinghame was beside her daughter-in-law in a moment. ''T would serve you well if this undid you!'

Lady Heathcott smiled triumphantly. 'Lucy is already in labour,' she said sweetly, 'and so I must return at once. My felicitations, dear Sybilla, and to you, sir.' Her glance flickered over Sir Peregrine's impressive bulk. 'The companionship of so amiable a spouse throughout your declining years will, no doubt, compensate for the lack of—ah, the more youthful pleasures of the marriage-bed.'

With which parting shot, she ascended into her carriage, leaving Sir Peregrine gobbling like a turkey-cock in his fury.

'Devil take the woman! Does she think me beat to a standstill!' he spluttered.

'Never mind that now!' His bride, regardless of her

gown, was on her knees beside Julienne-Eve. 'Someone get something upon which to carry her ladyship into the house—make haste, if you please!'

Later that day, a tired but vastly relieved Lady Whitting-hame bore her grandson in her arms to the book-room to display him to her husband. Sir Peregrine, a trifle muddled from the amount of port he had consumed in order to console himself for so unsatisfactory a wedding-day, prodded the small bundle with a cautious forefinger.

'Boy, is it? Got the exact time of birth, I daresay? Need to, with that woman!'

'I have—and three independent witnesses!' said his lady grimly. 'And I have despatched Ainsley over to Hever Court to discover what Madame Lucy has produced. There, my little love,' she cooed, 'quite perfect despite your sudden appearance! Even to having the third finger of your left hand of a length to match the second! Nathan's is just the same, and his father's and grandfather's before him.'

Mr Ainsley, on his return from Hever Court, looked more despondent than she had ever before seen him.

'It's a boy. We've lost by a short head, I'd say. Didn't tell anyone over there that, of course, pretended I didn't know our exact time.'

'Did you see the child?' demanded Lady Whittinghame fiercely.

'No. Baynton is there, all smiles and legal quibbles. Some bad news, ma'am.'

'What can be worse than that?' she snapped.

Mr Ainsley drew a deep breath and plunged resolutely on. 'Baynton's had further word of this battle. It seems to have taken place near Brussels, by a small town or hamlet called Waterloo. We won, but at a terrible price. The names of the dead and missing are beginning to come through.'

'Yes?' She stood, rock-still, eyes fixed on his troubled countenance.

'Picton, Maitland, and young Lord Hay are dead; Uxbridge gravely wounded. Rotherham is set down as missing.'

'Missing? Well, that's not the end of the world, after all.' She squared her shoulders and drained at one gulp the glass of wine Sir Peregrine thrust at her. 'But do not be troubling Julienne-Eve with any of this. Yes, what is it, Challis?'

The old butler looked as if he could not find words to express his sense of outrage at being asked to announce so lowly a person as a groom, but Adam solved his problem by thrusting him aside and walking into the saloon.

'Forgive me, m'lady, but there is something you should know, and at once.'

'You bring the odour of the stables with you, Adam!' she reproved him frostily. 'Thank you, Challis.' The moment the door had closed behind the butler's rigidly disapproving back her tone changed. 'What is it? What have you found out?'

'I went to Hever Court, as you instructed me, m'lady. 'Tis all in a bit o' confusion but I was fortunate to see Sir Trevor a-walkin' alone in his privy garden. He greeted me as if it had been but yestereve since last we met. I doubt he even knows I've left his service or, if he does, today's doings have put it clean out o' his mind. He's as bobbish as you like over the birth o' his daughter.' Exhausted by so much rhetoric, he stood silent while his audience digested his words.

'Nothing to signify,' declared her ladyship, but without any great conviction. 'He's such a hubble-bubble fellow— they would never tell him the truth.'

'Someone might have let it slip in his hearing,' said Mr Ainsley thoughtfully. 'His is a tenacious mind, once plant a seed of information there and it is the devil to uproot it.'

'Plenty of virgin soil for it to flourish in!' she snorted. 'But what to do? We can hardly expect him to stand witness to his own misfortune—indeed, if it came to a court of law, I doubt not his mother would have him clapped into a madhouse rather than have him testify,' She rounded on Mr Ainsley. 'Who was present at the birth?'

'Baynton, a local doctor—Hogben, I think the name is—Lady Heathcott's chaplain and a midwife.'

'Hogben? He's a drunken sot and could be bought with a cask of brandy. Baynton, we know—but the chaplain?'

'Is very stricken in years and almost totally blind.'

'Which leaves the midwife,' she mused. Adam spoke up.

'Your pardon, m'lady, but I had a word with young Jem. He'd just got back from leavin' the midwife to the London coach.'

'Not a local woman then.' Lady Whittinghame consulted her watch. 'The coach will be on its way by now. Take the chaise, Adam, and—yes, take Parsons with you. I'll prime her with a story. The woman might not care to entrust herself to you alone.'

'You cannot wrest her from off the stage!' protested Mr Ainsley, his legal hackles rising at so improper a notion.

'Not forcibly, but if Adam gets to the posting-house while the horses are being changed, Parsons can go to the coach, wringing her hands and asking if, by chance, anyone skilled in midwifery is travelling. Upon the woman declaring herself, she will then spin a tale of how her young mistress has been brought to bed prematurely and could the midwife render what aid she can.'

'Suppose she won't?' objected Mr Ainsley.

'Then the rustle of a roll of soft should stir her conscience!' said her ladyship as she left the room, closely followed by her groom. A few minutes later saw her giving him final instructions as he brought the chaise to the door to collect Parsons. 'Spring 'em, Adam. Lathered cattle will give a greater appearance of urgency. Now, Parsons, you have your story ready to your tongue?'

'I have that, m'lady.' Parsons, tying her bonnet strings somewhat askew, was as sternly composed as ever and her mistress eyed her doubtfully.

'No, don't straighten it! Look as distraught as you may. Here is some money.'

'Great Heavens, m'lady, you're never going to give her all that?' gasped the scandalised maid.

'I'd give her a deal more if she'd stand witness for us! But, for the moment, ten pounds should suffice to entice her. Keep up the pretence until you get here, use my name— Lady Whittinghame—if you must, not Lady Rotherham's, she may have heard it spoken at Hever Court. Now away with you.'

Parsons nodded and, stuffing the notes into her reticule, stepped up into the chaise. The vehicle sped away while Lady Whittinghame returned to the saloon to be confronted by a very dubious Mr Ainsley.

'If they do succeed and return with the woman, what do you propose to do?' he asked.

'Inform Lady Heathcott that we understand her daughter-in-law was delivered of a girl. Convince her that we have two witnesses, the midwife who we will keep safe here, and another. Best not to mention Sir Trevor by name, he is too uncertain and I'd not wish ill to come to him.'

'It could be said that you bribed the midwife.'

'It *will* be said that I bribed the midwife,' corrected her ladyship, 'but once we have the facts we can lay them before a magistrate in Tunbridge Wells. Now, I suggest we dine since we cannot expect Adam and Parsons back for several hours.'

In this assumption she was shown to be correct for dusk was falling before the rattle of wheels came to the ears of the anxious party in the saloon. The midwife, who gave every appearance of being a sensible body, seemed remarkably unconcerned when she discovered the purpose of her removal from the stage-coach was other than had first been told her.

'Thought as 'ow there was sommat out o' kelter over there,' said she, with a jerk of the head presumably in the direction of Hever Court. 'The 'usband dancin' about like a caper merchant an' the law gemelman makin' me sign a paper sayin' as 'ow I'd attended the birth.'

'The birth of what—a boy or a girl?' rapped out Mr Ainsley.

'Can't say what was written, sir, I ain't got no learnin',' said the woman simply. 'Set down m'name, I can, that's all. But he pushed more blunt into m'fist than ever I'd seen afore—and for why? 'Twas an easy birth enough, a nice little girl, though she didn't seem to give no pleasure to her grandmama. But 'tis often like that with the gentry,' she added philosophically, 'a boy is all they care for.'

'I would like you to see my grandson who was also born to-day.' Lady Whittinghame took the woman by the arm in the most friendly way. 'And I'm afraid I must detain you here for a time until this thing is resolved, but rest assured you will be well recompensed for your trouble.'

'Well, I 'adn't expected to be turned off so sudden, and none of my other ladies is comin' due yet.' The midwife, allowing herself to be led from the room, seemed resigned to her fate. 'But what's to do 'ere, m'lady? I ain't ever been mixed up in any sharp business, y'know.'

The door closed on Lady Whittinghame's voice, soothing down this predictably tender conscience. Sir Peregrine, who had retreated into a corner during the preceding discussion, then stepped forward and produced a newspaper from behind his back.

'Adam got this in Tunbridge Wells—the full despatch from Waterloo.'

He spread *The Times* open on the table and together the two gentlemen studied it in silence. At length Mr Ainsley raised his head to stare at the darkening scene outside the undraped windows.

'It would appear to have been a most bloody encounter,' he said.

'And the victors as cut about as the vanquished, like as not.' Sir Peregrine folded up the paper and tucked it under his coat. 'I'll not show this to Sybilla to-night.'

'No, do not,' agreed Mr Ainsley absently, then, 'I doubt we'll get news of Rotherham for some days.'

'Know a fellow in London who might help,' volunteered Sir Peregrine. 'Could go up to-morrow and see what's what. Feel infernally in the way down here.'

'Confoundedly wretched wedding-day you are having, sir,' deplored Mr Ainsley. 'May I pour you a glass of your superb port?'

'Thank 'e.' Sir Peregrine managed a nonchalant shrug. 'Well, that's how it goes, y'know, but I shall come about, never fear. It's Rotherham, if anything's happened to him, we're in the suds.'

'We have his son's inheritance to fight for,' said Mr Ainsley, a rarely stern expression on his cherubic countenance. 'And, come what may, I'll not be had on that suit!'

CHAPTER
TWELVE

'WHILE I am willing to allow you every degree of consideration because of your great affliction, dear Sybilla, such an
accusation is the outside of enough. I have a grandson, a
perfectly normal little boy, as you are very welcome to
come and see for yourself.'

'Yes, you have had time to substitute some peasant's
by-blow for your granddaughter, I don't doubt!' Lady
Whittinghame, looking tired and drawn as well she might
with the Duke's letter, written in his own hand, expressing
his deep regret at the loss of her son fresh in her mind, still
retained enough spirit to outface her sister-in-law. 'The
midwife's testimony—'

'The midwife!' Lady Heathcott's laugh tinkled incon-
gruously through the silent house. 'A stupid, ignorant
woman! How much did you pay her?'

'More, it would seem, than you.'

'Come, Sybilla!' Lady Heathcott assumed a briskly
businesslike manner. 'Our affairs cannot be at a stand
forever, and for all the world to see us pulling caps like a
couple of fishwives is no very dignified spectacle. If money
is the problem I have no doubt I can persuade Trevor to
make over sufficient to your daughter-in-law to grant her an
easy independence for the rest of her life.'

Lady Whittinghame, exercising unbelievable self-
restraint, drew in a deep shuddering breath. 'Trevor,' she
said with dangerous calm. 'You, of course, can make him
do and say what you please?'

'Within reason, I can, yes.'

'Even to affirming that the daughter born to him was a
son?' The moment the words were spoken she knew from
the quick flicker of alarm in the colourless eyes regarding
her, that they should not have been.

'Trevor is in no doubt that he has a son,' said his mother
smoothly. 'Now, do we settle this affair amicably, Sybilla,

or do we have to go through the misery of dragging it through the courts? Depend upon it, no one will profit from that save the lawyers, and we shall be held up to ridicule by the *beau monde.*'

'There is much in what you say, Elspeth.' Lady Whittinghame looked to be giving this viewpoint serious consideration. 'But the decision is not mine to make. My grandson's mother must be consulted and she, as may be imagined, is not in prime twig at the moment.'

'Indeed no, how should she be, poor young woman!' Lady Heathcott was all compassionate understanding. 'To suffer such a cruel blow and not a year married! I'll not press now for an agreement—how should a week or more signify?—and so to use a stricken household would be an unkindness not in my nature.'

Her sister-in-law seemed as if about to dispute that last statement but held herself well in control until her visitor had left her, then, instructing Challis that she was receiving no one else that day, she dragged herself wearily upstairs.

When the news of Rotherham had been broken to Julienne-Eve she had received it with a sort of passive acceptance, as if expecting no less, that was more painful to observe than any violent outburst of grief could have been. Repulsing all attempts at consolation, she withdrew into herself, existing only it would seem, for her child. Happily, the little boy thrived, apparently not a whit put out by his precipitate entry into the world. She was resting in her bedchamber on a chaise-longue by the open windows and made to rise as Lady Whittinghame entered.

'No, please do not move, my dear. Are you quite alone? Where is Jonathan?'

'I permitted the nursemaid to take him for a little airing. She is so devoted to his interest and it is such a beautiful day.'

'But a premature baby, scarce a month old!' remonstrated her horrified mother-in-law.

'Come, mama!' Julienne-Eve essayed a playful wag of the finger. 'We vowed we'd not smother him with too much care! Besides, they have been in my sight for most of the time until they went into the rose-garden—here they come again, she is bringing him back. Who was your visitor?'

'Dear Elspeth, wishing all to be forgiven and forgotten, just so long as she has her way. Yet she is not comfortable in her mind, else she would not have offered money—oh, yes!' She nodded in response to Julienne-Eve's surprised exclamation. 'An "easy independence" for you was proposed, if you please! What an odious creature she is! I think I will accept her invitation to go over and see this brat for myself.'

'Was Lady Heathcott alone?' Julienne-Eve asked idly.

Lady Whittinghame looked at her sharply. 'As far as I am aware, she was.'

'Oh, I expect it was of no consequence. I saw a second carriage in the driveway, but it moved away before she left. Are not these roses exquisite? Parsons picked them at first light this morning.'

They discussed domestic affairs for a few minutes until they were joined by the nursemaid, carrying the baby.

'Good as gold he was, m'lady,' she crowed, laying her charge back in the cot, who promptly gave vent to a loud wail of protest. Julienne-Eve started, then got to her feet and walked slowly across the room. Something in the set intensity of her face drew Lady Whittinghame's attention.

'What is it, my dear? What troubles you?'

Julienne-Eve, bending over the cot, picked up the child and bore it to the window. There, swiftly unloosing the many shawls in which the infant was swaddled, she cried out in an anguished voice: 'This is not Jonathan! This is a baby girl!'

'What?' For a moment Lady Whittinghame was persuaded that an excess of grief had affected the young woman's reason, but one searching glance at the child assured her of the truth of the statement. 'Then who—what have you done?' she demanded of the open-mouthed nursemaid.

'N—nothing, I promise you, m'lady! I—I but set him down on a bench in the rose-garden while I—while I—'

'While you what? Speak up, you wretched ninnyhammer!' Her ladyship had seized the unfortunate girl by the shoulders and was shaking her so violently as almost to render her speechless. Julienne-Eve mercifully intervened.

'No, no, let her be, mama. Now, Mary, tell us what happened—quickly, if you please.'

'Th-the lady said she'd have an eye to the baby,' quavered the terrified Mary, 'while I p-pointed out the way to her groom. They had mistook this house for another and were lost, she said.'

Julienne-Eve and her mother-in-law exchanged grief-stricken glances. 'And she substituted this child for Jonathan while you were doing so. Can it be—it must be Lucy's daughter!'

Lady Whittinghame scrutinised the baby closely. 'Yes, there's no doubt of it. See—she has the Saville defect! The third finger of her left hand is, like Jonathan's, of a length with the second.' She turned to the nursemaid. 'Would you recognise this woman again?'

'Oh, yes, m'lady. Thin and dark she was, and ever so quiet-spoken.'

'Of course!' Julienne-Eve struck her hands together in despair. 'That other carriage I saw in the driveway while Lady Heathcott was with you!'

'Oh, to be sure, 'tis all now perfectly plain!' Lady Whittinghame held her spinning head. 'While Elspeth was holding my attention, the children were changed over. And now Jonathan's very life may depend upon our submission to her demands!'

'No, it will be to her advantage to care for him and to pass him off as her own grandson. Nonetheless, I am going to Hever Court to fetch back my child.' Julienne-Eve was as cold as ice and so ashen-faced that her mother-in-law took alarm.

'It isn't going to help our cause, my dear, if you fall ill—and what good do you think such a request would do? Let me have the handling of this and Mary will come with me and keep her eyes open for a sight of the woman who took Jonathan. What misfortune that Perry should have chosen this morning to go into Tunbridge Wells! His presence would give so much more weight to my accusations!'

Julienne-Eve thought it likely would, if not precisely in the way her mother-in-law had in mind. Left to herself, she

paced the room, a prey to every possible sort of
apprehension. All that she had left of Nathan, his son, to be
snatched from her in so heartless a fashion might reasonably have been supposed to have thrown her into utter
despair but, strangely, it had had quite the opposite effect.
Gone was her numbed submission to her misfortune; in its
place burned a fierce resolve to win back her child and
avenge herself on those who had taken him from her.

The sound of the chaise setting out for Hever Court
brought her to the window and, once it was out of her sight,
she selected from her armoire a hooded cloak of indeter-
minate colour. Then, with a last look around the room, as if
reminding herself of every detail of it, she went out, closing
the door softly behind her. Outside her mother-in-law's
bedchamber she met Parsons.

'You're going out, m'lady?'

'Just for a turn about the garden, I cannot sit idle. It is so
warm, perhaps I might read—oh, my book! Could you
fetch it for me, Parsons, if you please? It is Lady Morgan's
latest novel. I must have left it by the window when—' Her
voice broke and Parsons was quick to offer comfort.

'There, m'lady! Sit you here while I go seek it. Never
fear, m'lady, the mistress will know what to do. We'll have
our little lamb back safe before ever he knows he's gone.'

The moment the good woman had left her, Julienne-Eve
was on her feet and had darted to the swivel-topped
rosewood Davenport in the corner of the room. Here a
swift search brought to light a small, silver-mounted pistol
which she knew her mother-in-law had had by her during
the days of their flight from France. Knowing well that it
was never loaded, being retained merely for appearances'
sake, she slid it into the inner pocket of her cloak and was
sitting with demurely folded hands when Parsons returned
with her book.

It took a deal of persuasion to induce the maid to allow
her go out unattended, but at last she was free and in the
open air. Suspecting that Parsons would be watching her
progress from a window, she walked slowly to the rose-
garden, most of which she knew to be shielded from
observation by the immense yew hedge that bounded it on

all sides. Once confident that she was out of sight of the house, she slipped through an archway cut deep in the hedge, along a shady walk at the back of an orchard, and from thence into the stableyard.

Her appearance there and request for the whisky to be made ready for her occasioned no surprise, for she had been taking a drive in the little vehicle for the past few days. The stableboy's only concern was that Adam was not on hand to accompany her as he had gone to Hever Court in attendance upon Lady Whittinghame.

'I believe I am perfectly capable of handling Sorrel,' Julienne-Eve assured him. 'She is not likely to run away with me and I expect to meet up with her ladyship on her return.'

He watched her doubtfully as she took up the reins and the docile Sorrel trotted meekly enough out of the yard and down the drive. Pulling her hood over her head, she prayed that Parsons had given up her vigil at the window and gone about her duties. However, no warning cry assailed her ears and when she reached her next obstacle, the entrance gates, she discovered, as she had hoped, that they had been left standing wide for the chaise's return. She was through them without pause and away down the road before the aged gatekeeper could bestir his rheumatic limbs to challenge her passing.

It was yet another glorious day, the hedgerows rich with flowers and tall, waving grasses; the birds already muting their songs and seeking the shade of the trees as the sun climbed to its noonday heat, but there was little joy in the beauty of her surroundings in Julienne-Eve's heart as she urged Sorrel to give of her best. When nearing Hever Court, she judged it prudent to turn off the main road and approach the house by a little-used track, for the last thing she wished for was to encounter Lady Whittinghame on her way back, a likely occurrence since she could not visualise the interview with Lady Heathcott being of long duration.

Quite what she had in mind to do she had no very clear idea, but when she came to the outbuildings that lay to the east of Hever Court and discovered the first barn she approached to be standing open and deserted, she led the mare inside and made her secure before setting out on foot towards the house. On her way she encountered only one under-gardener, busily snipping away at a hedge, who gave her an incurious 'Goodmorning' and went on with his work. Then she heard the sound of voices. One she instantly identified as that of Lady Heathcott and concluded that Lady Whittinghame had had her say and departed. The other was a man's voice, low and grumbling. Concealing herself behind a clump of thick-growing rhododendrons, she strained to hear what was being said.

The two were perambulating about the sunken garden beneath her and, as they turned, they came within her line of vision. Although she had seen him but rarely during her sojourn at Hever Court, she at once recognised the man to be Stapleton, Sir Trevor's valet.

'But who could have told him? I made sure he was informed that it was a male infant.' Never had Julienne-Eve known Lady Heathcott to be so agitated.

'Heard someone talking, I don't doubt. He can be sharp enough when it don't suit.' Stapleton was a low-browed, powerfully built man, with more of the air of a pugilist than a valet.

'And to boast of his daughter to Adam! Who knows who else he may have spoken to? He must be silenced.'

They then turned away from Julienne-Eve and she could hear nothing of what was said until they came near to her again.

'And what's in it for me, m'lady?' The man sounded reluctant, as if being urged to something against his will.

'A generous reward if you bring it off safe. But it must give all the appearance of an accident.'

'It's not to my liking, I tell you straight, m'lady,' he growled. 'Too many questions can be asked with all that money at stake.' She could be heard soothing him down as they left the garden and went out of Julienne-Eve's sight.

Feeling that her knees might not continue to support her, Julienne-Eve tottered to a nearby stone bench which commanded a view of the park and gardens, all looking as if freshly swept, the lawns combed, the flower-beds bright with blossom; the whole scene as perfect as if it had been painted by the hand of a master, with no hint of the evil that lay at the heart of this perfection. It was several moments before she had regained control of her emotions and, reminding herself that this was no place to be sitting where anyone might discover her, she continued on her way towards the house. It did occur to her that her most sensible course would be to return to Leyswood Towers and tell what she had overheard, but she was urged on by an irresistible impulse that could not be denied.

Taking advantage of the ample coverage provided by the verdant midsummer foliage, she stole nearer to the East wing of the house and there was arrested in her progress by the sight of a man's figure climbing out of a second-floor window and descending to the ground by the aid of an old and immensely strong ivy that covered most of the wall.

He scrambled down quickly, dropping the last few feet to the ground. As he stood, brushing pieces of ivy and lichen from his person, he looked about him as if to assure himself that no one had observed his irregular mode of egress, and she almost cried out in astonishment as she recognised Sir Trevor.

After a few moments he moved away from the house and began to make his way through the gardens in as cautious a manner as her own. Julienne-Eve found herself at Point Non-Plus. What this development might mean, she could not be perfectly sure, but it was evident from Sir Trevor's confident descent that it was not the first time he had employed that method of eluding Stapleton's vigilance. It was also obvious that, as he was proceeding in her direction, she would be obliged either to conceal herself and observe his movements, or to meet him face to face.

The whimsical notion of kidnapping him and holding him in exchange for little Jonathan brought a fleeting smile to her taut mouth, and she toyed with the fancy of marching him off at the point of her unloaded pistol. 'And why not?' she ruminated, half-aloud. ''Twould keep the poor young man safe from his mother's villainy at least. If I could but persuade him of his danger.'

Throwing back the hood of her cloak, she stepped forward into his path. At first she feared she had been too hasty, so violent was his reaction to her appearance, and she at once discarded the idea of threatening so timid a creature with a weapon. He had turned and was poised for flight when she held out a hand, saying in the most cordial way: 'Good-day to you, Sir Trevor. Do you remember me, I wonder? I was engaged as your mother's companion for a short time last year, but it did not answer.'

At that he checked and looked over his shoulder at her. Then a sly expression stole across his vacuous countenance and he laid a knowing finger to his nose.

'Miss Lawrence, is it not? But you ran away, as I remember. Mama was very put out. She wished me to marry you.'

'But you married Lucy instead, didn't you?'

'Yes, Lucy.' Mention of his wife seemed to disconcert him. 'She is not as pretty as you are.'

He took a step in her direction and she caught that predatory gleam in his eye that she had witnessed once before. Hastily she said: 'I am married now also. To your cousin, Rotherham.'

He became suddenly agitated. 'Rotherham! Got to see Rotherham! Must tell him something!'

'Well, I can take you to him,' declared Julienne-Eve, hoping she would be forgiven the deception. He hesitated, plainly unsure of her. Steeling herself to take his arm, she went on talking brightly. 'You have got a little daughter now, have you not?'

At that a look of pained bewilderment came over his face. 'Yes, but I am not to speak of her. I told Adam, d'you see, and mama heard about it and went up in the boughs. She said she'd have Stapleton flog me if I did it again.'

Julienne-Eve, thinking of Stapleton's powerful frame, gulped back her indignation and refrained from making further comment. This poor creature was no better than an overgrown child and used to being treated as such. 'If you'll come with me I'll keep you safe from him,' she entreated.

'I'll come with you, Miss Lawrence,' he agreed happily.

'Lady Rotherham,' she corrected him.

'Rotherham! Yes, I must see Rotherham!' Again he became distressed and began to wring his hands. 'I asked to see my little girl but mama said it was a boy and showed me a boy-baby. But it wasn't mine, you know, it was the finished likeness of Rotherham.' He giggled nervously. 'Should make a match of it, my girl and his boy. Then the money would be all one anyway.'

In Julienne-Eve's opinion, for a gazetted addle-pate, Sir Trevor was displaying a deal of common sense. 'What a good idea,' she said, drawing him out through the gardens in the direction of the barn where she had left Sorrel. 'But your mama might not approve. She has the intention of passing off Rotherham's son as yours.'

'But what of my little girl?' he asked querulously, as she pulled him down a side alley to avoid observation by the gardener, still intent upon his topiary.

'She is quite safe,' Julienne-Eve promised him. 'You can see her for yourself, she is at Leyswood Towers.'

His face brightened at once and he trotted along obediently by her side until they were back at the barn. To her relief, he then mounted without protest into the whisky and they set off along the lane. Arrived without mishap at the main road, she was about to turn Sorrel's head towards Leyswood Towers when they almost collided with another vehicle proceeding from that direction at great speed.

'Why—m'lady! Sir Trevor!'

'Adam! Adam!' Julienne-Eve choked with emotion at sight of his homely face. 'Quickly, there is no time to lose! Take Sir Trevor to Leyswood Towers and conceal him. He may be in danger of his life.'

'Yes, m'lady. But what of you?'

'I am going back to Hever Court. I—I forgot something,' said she glibly, assisting Sir Trevor to alight and seat himself in the other vehicle. 'Tell Lady Whittinghame to take great care of him, Adam, and bid her not to worry about me.'

'When I've done that, m'lady, I'll come back to you.'

'Give me two hours at the least,' she adjured him. 'If I do not return here after that time, then you may come in search of me. But come alone and keep hid.'

With that, she turned the whisky adroitly and, urging the reluctant Sorrel back the way she had come, left Adam with no choice but to carry out her instructions and convey Sir Trevor safe to Leyswood Towers.

CHAPTER
THIRTEEN

THE room in which he lay was a small low-ceilinged apartment, scantily furnished, with white-washed stone walls. Over his head light filtered through an iron grill that guarded the long narrow window. Rotherham had no means of judging how long he had been there for, at first, his moments of awareness had been too fleeting to allow of coherent thought, but after a time he came to recognise voices and dimly to comprehend that he was gravely ill.

There had been a battle, that he knew, for short vivid episodes flashed across his visual memory like pictures in a kaleidoscope, but to weld them together was a task beyond his powers. Putting out a hand, he touched a stone pitcher standing, icy-cold, beside the bed. As the room was oppressively warm this seemed to postulate that whoever had him in their charge had recently come and gone so that he might expect to be left alone for a time. Slowly, fearful of putting any strain upon his injuries, he drew himself up in the bed and, stretching up his right arm, secured a hold on the grill above his head. Then, by pressing hard against the wall to give himself support, he contrived to stand upright.

He at once found his strength to be unequal to such exertion and had time only to perceive that outside the window lay woods as thick as a primeval forest, through the foliage of which the sun's rays penetrated hazily, when his senses began to leave him again, and he sank back upon the bed.

So intent was he in endeavouring to direct his fall so as to cause the least hurt to himself, that he did not hear the door opening and quick footsteps crossing the flagged floor. The next thing he knew his head was being supported while a mug of water was held to his lips. The drink cleared his whirling senses and he opened his eyes to look up at a countenance almost entirely concealed by a mask.

'I had not thought to find you so eager to leave me, my lord.'

The English was impeccable though the accent was undeniably French, with a clipped resonance to it that was vaguely familiar to his ear.

'Hardly that, sir.' Rotherham scarce recognised the slow, stumbling tones for his own. 'While the spirit may be willing, the flesh lags far behind.' His words faded away and his head dropped back as if the holding of it upright was too great an effort.

'Try this, it will give you strength.'

This time he smelled the sharp odour of brandy and gratefully gulped down the fiery liquid before speaking with something of his normal clarity.

'How came I here? Who are you?'

The other put up a hand and removed his mask. 'Forgive this charade, my lord, but I have my reasons for not wishing to be recognised in these parts.'

Rotherham rubbed his aching brow as if to stave off the memories crowding closely upon him. 'You are surely— Beaumanoir, is it not?'

'I am honoured that your lordship should recall our meeting.' Seating himself on a stool by the bed, the Vicomte went on in the most amicable way. 'To answer the first of your questions, I found you after the battle lying atop a pile of dead Frenchmen, and carried you here. Only I and a doctor who, apart from his own barbarous tongue, speaks but a smattering of French, know of your where-abouts. Good fortune, was it not, that I chanced upon you?'

Painfully recalling the circumstances in which they had last met, when he had been within ames ace of calling the fellow out for some slighting reference to the Duke, Rotherham reserved judgment on that remark, saying merely: 'What are my injuries?'

'A shrewd sabre cut to the side of your head and neck which should, in all fairness, have put a period to your existence. It left you all about in your head and has cost you half an ear, but I fancy if you wear your hair a shade longer 'twill mask the defect so that it need not cause heartrend-ings amongst the ladies. Your adversary with the sabre, or some other, also struck you below the left shoulder and we feared for your arm but I understand it to be mending well.

As to the outcome of the battle, about which you are no doubt concerned, your Duke was victorious, but at some cost.'

The faint sneer implicit in the indolent voice caused Rotherham to wonder, not for the first time, how much reliance could be placed on the loyalty of these Royalist Frenchmen. When all was said, it must go against the pluck to see a foreign army defeat a French one whether led by a Corsican upstart or the generals of the Most Christian King. Aloud he said:

'Where is this place, if you please?'

'Within a short march of the French border. But you'll not be in sufficient health to attempt the journey yet, my lord. The country is overrun with lawless bands of soldiers, deserters from both armies. I have in mind that we might pass ourselves off as such, in the hope that dog will not prey upon dog.'

'And our destination?'

'Why, Paris, to be sure, and—but I have intelligence of another sort which I hope will not distress you.'

Rotherham felt a tightening of the muscles in the back of his neck as if they would warn him of danger. 'And that is, monsieur?'

'M. le Marquis Colomb d'Hauteville has—joined his forefathers. I think you never knew him so that cannot cause you more than passing regret. Madame la Marquise, your wife's mother, is now Madame la Vicomtesse de Beaumanoir.'

His words hung expectantly on the air and Rotherham, on whom the dual effort of recollection and concentration was having a predictable effect, forced himself to make suitable reply.

'My felicitations, monsieur. So we are, in some sort, related?'

The Vicomte's teeth flashed whitely. 'I suppose I have as much right to call myself Lady Rotherham's stepfather as had the Marquis. Now, my lord, I will leave you to rest. That, I am assured, is what you are most in need of.'

'One thing more.' Rotherham detained him with up-raised hand. 'Have you any news of my wife?'

'As yet, none of the sort you are hoping for—oh, yes, her mother has told me the whole. But Lady Rotherham is at Leyswood Towers, a letter was received from her assuring us of her safety and also of that of the small Philippe and of your lady mother. The moment it is possible I will send her news of you, but that must wait awhile, I fear. First, you must be got to Paris and into my wife's care. Sleep now, my lord, I will be bringing the doctor to see you later.'

After he had gone Rotherham lay, cursing his bodily weakness and tortured with conjecture at what might have happened at home. Had Julienne-Eve given him up for lost and, if so, how would she receive the news of his continued existence? And what of her own well-being and that of the child she carried?

Some hours later—just how long or whether it was even the same day he hardly knew, so little notion had he of the passage of time—he became aware of a discordant conversation going on by his bedside. At first he thought his brain had become perfectly addled for nothing of what was said made sense to him, then a few words of French were uttered and he opened his eyes to find himself the object of contention between the Vicomte and an individual of full habit and slovenly dress. At once this personage addressed him in a flood of execrable French, of which he could not understand more than one word in ten.

'This, my lord, in spite of his unprepossessing appearance, is your doctor, and he is informing you that you are remarkably fortunate to be breathing and you have him to thank for it. He also begs that you will refrain from undoing all his handiwork by listening to my urgings and putting too premature a strain on either your mind or your body.'

His lordship, looking at the doctor's coarse, powerful hands with their filthy fingernails, suppressed a shudder at thought of being touched by them.

'I am vastly obliged to him,' he managed to say.

'Despite your understandable revulsion,' murmured the Vicomte, 'he is a good doctor and most likely did save your life.'

'Who does he think I am?'

'I've told him you are a Brandenburger and that English

is our sole common tongue. That satisfies him well enough for these people are concerned only with their own survival, the greater issues pass them by. He is, however, tolerably well pleased with your progress, and hopes to see you out of your bed within the week.'

'Please convey to him my thanks.' Rotherham's mouth twisted wryly. 'That is all I can offer him for his services.'

'No need to concern yourself on that head, my lord. I have attended to it.' He laughed at Rotherham's protest. 'It will all go down to your account, never fear!'

The room fell silent after the two men had left their patient, and their voices faded away outside while Rotherham pondered over Beaumanoir's last words. So an account was to be rendered, was it, despite the newly-forged family connection? And, no doubt, the price of gratitude would be governed by the amount of money available. Did Julienne-Eve win what Sir Peregrine was pleased to call the Nursery Stakes, then that price could well be high. A libertine and an adventurer he had named Beaumanoir when speaking of him to her, and he saw no reason to believe that marriage to her mother might have improved his character. What sort of woman was her mother, he wondered, who had borne one of the most honoured names in France but, close upon the Marquis's death, had taken this well-bred scoundrel for husband?

He was soon to have the answer to this question for, in less than the prescribed week, he was on his feet and walking about, albeit uncertainly. The Vicomte was plainly much relieved to see him so improved but Rotherham, greatly though he longed to be on his way, warned himself not to appear to be making too rapid a recovery. That way Beaumanoir, believing his prisoner to be more helpless than was the case, might drop his guard and a chance for escape might present itself. For prisoner he was, of that Rotherham became increasingly more convinced, though quite what ploy his captor had in mind had yet to be ascertained. His present course must be to await the Vicomte's pleasure and try to show weakly willing. As another precaution he spoke to Beaumanoir only in English and to the doctor not at all, giving all the appearance of one who is unwilling to put himself to the trouble of struggling with an unfamiliar tongue.

'Well, my lord, we'll make a start tomorrow!' The Vicomte was almost voluble in his enthusiasm. 'You're not fit for any great exertion yet, so we must travel by slow stages. A sturdy cob and a small cart will serve the purpose of such vagrant fellows as we shall appear to be. I'd liefer have gone on horseback, but that could invite unwelcome attention, and you are in no case to go on foot.'

With this last Rotherham was in full agreement. 'You believe there is danger, then, of our being accosted?'

'If this should happen, my lord—and I confess I think it very likely—you are a wounded soldier of whichever army is appropriate, and too addled in the head to answer questions.' He tossed a pair of homespun breeches and a coarse shirt on to the bed. 'I regret the necessity for these unspeakable garments, but your own clothes must be destroyed. And—oh, your signet ring, if you please. The sight of that could cost you your life. I'll keep it hid for you.'

The memory of that journey stayed forever with Rotherham as one of infinite frustration and unbearable slowness. On several occasions their progress was halted by villainous-looking groups of miscreants, but each time the Vicomte talked his way out of the impasse. Clad in a ragged frieze coat, a shapeless hat pulled down over his face, tattered woollen mittens covering his hands, and a short clay pipe clamped between blackened teeth, he presented so sinister an appearance as to discourage all but the most intrepid, while Rotherham's groans and generally befuddled aspect supplied a further touch of authenticity to their story.

They lay concealed for most of a day on the outskirts of Paris so as to approach the Faubourg St Germain under cover of darkness. 'For,' as the Vicomte declared, 'even my wife might not readily recognise me in this guise and, as for you, my lord, daylight does you no good service at all!' Rotherham grunted drowsily and Beaumanoir glanced at him over his shoulder. 'A good meal and a good bed are what you need, this journey has been overlong. Ah, here we are. Now let us see if I can carry it off or if Madame's footmen will have me thrown down the steps!'

At first, to Rotherham's ears, it seemed as if the latter would be the Vicomte's fate, then a cool female voice sounded over the clamour, the cover of the cart was drawn back and he was assisted to alight. He stood swaying in the light of the flambeaux, tired in all truth but feigning a greater lassitude, until assisted into the house by a scandalised footman. Then the same voice addressed him in English, calling him by his name and making him welcome. He raised his head to look at her, Julienne-Eve's mother, a veritable *grande dame*, dressed in the first stare of elegance, who surveyed his bedraggled person with something like contempt in her regard.

'Your pardon, madame,' he muttered, 'but I—I cannot-'

'The devil!' The Vicomte caught him as he staggered. 'You—fellow! Take his legs! Where shall we lay him, Heloise?'

Madame gave clear instructions and, before many minutes had passed, Rotherham was stripped of his rough garments, bathed and laid between silken sheets in a bed of unbelievable softness. Food was brought him by a manservant who stayed to see him eat it, which he did with a careful show of disinterest despite his hunger. When the man had left him, he slid out of bed to inspect his surroundings.

It was a markedly feminine room, all glimmering silks and dainty furnishings, and he was tempted to wonder if it had been Julienne-Eve's bedchamber when she had resided in the house. He found the notion an uncommonly comforting one and, smiling a little at himself, he went to one of the tall windows but could make out little more than trees whipping in the wind against a cloud-tossed sky. He then tried the door of his room which gave on to a wide landing, and was about to investigate further when the sound of voices from the hall below sent him back in haste to his bed.

Presently soft footsteps announced the approach of the Vicomte and his lady to the bedside. Rotherham, deep beneath the covers, decided to feign sleep and even produced the semblance of a snore.

'It would seem that the God of Dreams has claimed our

guest.' His mother-in-law sounded amused, but the Vicomte leaned over him in some concern. He straightened up with a satisfied nod as Rotherham permitted himself to sigh and turn a little as if disturbed in his slumber. 'Yes, but he is worn to the bone and, though his wounds are healing well, he is uncommonly low in spirits. He will need constant attention.'

'Your care for my daughter's husband does you credit, Thierry.' She laughed softly and touched her husband's cheek with a fondness that told its own story. 'Come, let him have his rest. You have been away from our nuptial couch for too long, my love.'

The Vicomte treated this advance with marked lack of gallantry. 'If you would trouble to apply your undoubted good sense to the matter, madame,' he rapped out, 'you would realise that his health is of prime importance to our plans.'

'Oh, so we have plans?' she murmured.

'But of course! Think of your daughter's gratitude when we restore to her her husband.'

'What of it? You are requiring us to stand with hands outstretched in expectation of a *pourboire* for the service?'

'The situation may be quite otherwise,' the Vicomte informed her. 'If she should produce a son in good time then the re-union between my lord and my lady may prove a costly one.'

'You mean you would hold him until—Thierry, are you mad? And to bring him here—to this house!' Rotherham felt her fingers on the coverlet, drawing it away from his face. 'Are you sure he is asleep?'

'I tell you he is at the point of collapse, I feared he would not survive the journey. In any case, his command of French is negligible, what little he knows he cannot remember so confused is his understanding. I shall leave for England tomorrow to carry the glad news of his survival to your dear daughter. Should she not prove sufficiently grateful—and you may trust me to spin a tale of heartrending distress brought about by your late husband's inconsiderate will—why then I must regretfully inform her that, if she wishes his lordship back at her side, she must pay for the privilege.'

'Suppose she cannot? What if this other woman, his cousin's wife, has been brought to bed of a son before her?'

'That, of course, would be unfortunate,' he agreed. 'But I cannot conceive of Rotherham being short of the needful. And there is always Philippe.'

'Oh, yes,' she said bitterly, 'and my nursemaid's pittance for taking him in charge!'

'Too bad, my dear,' he purred, drawing her arm through his and leading her from the room, 'that you did not play your cards with a little more finesse!'

The door closed on her decidedly astringent reply and, as Rotherham sat up in bed, his brain whirling with the intelligence it has received, he heard the key turn in the lock. So he was to be held prisoner until Julienne-Eve found the money for his release! But to think that her mother would lend herself to such a design was the outside of anything, however little she had benefitted from the Marquis's estate. Understandably, this was a sad set-back for the Vicomte, who had seized upon her evident affection for him to secure for himself what he had hoped would prove to be a wealthy wife. What would be her fate when he had no further use for her?

That, Rotherham decided, was no immediate concern of his, there were more urgent matters deserving of his attention, the first of which was his escape from the trap closing about him. His knowledge of Paris was not extensive but sufficient, he hoped, to allow him make his way to the Rue de Clichy, where resided his mother's friend, Lady Oxford. There, at least, he could be sure of shelter and money to help him on his way. He had no doubt that the Duke or the Allied commanders had set up a military headquarters in the city, but the business of establishing his identity in that way might take up more time than he could afford for, if he was to defeat Beaumanoir's purpose, then he must follow hard upon his heels. Nothing, however, could be attempted until the Vicomte had gone, when he must convince Madame la Vicomtesse of his inability to walk further than the street door.

This, he discovered, the next morning, was not as easy of attainment as he had hoped. Aided by the Vicomte's valet, he had risen late and dressed in clothes which, he gathered, had belonged to the late Marquis. By reason of the privations he had endured in the past weeks, they fitted him tolerably well and, thus attired, he made his unsteady way downstairs to a handsomely appointed saloon opening out upon a secluded garden. Here he was received with every consideration by his mother-in-law.

'I beg that you will be seated, my lord,' said she in her faultless English. 'My husband has told me of the grievous hurts you have sustained and by how slight a chance you come to be alive.'

'Indeed, madame, were it not for his timely rescue of me no doubt I should have suffered the fate of many others less fortunate.' Rotherham spoke slowly, as would a man who found it difficult to collect his thoughts.

'He was, as doubtless he has told you, seeking a fallen friend on the battlefield, and so discovered you.' More likely seeking what he could pick up from the bodies of the slain, thought the recipient of this confidence, compelling himself to listen with an air of gratitude to what she had to say. 'He has left for England—did you know? But, of course, you could not since he departed early this morning and did not wish to disturb your rest. He bade me tell you that he will spare no effort in hastening to relieve my poor daughter's agony of mind.'

From her gracious manner he concluded that the pretence of all being done in a perfectly amiable way was to be observed for the time at least. Encouraged by his hostess, he made a praiseworthy effort to enjoy the luncheon presently set before them, while she maintained a ready flow of conversation without saying anything of particular consequence. When the meal came at last to an end, she summoned the valet to assist him back to his room.

'Indeed I think that is enough effort for one day, my lord, but if you feel so disposed we will meet again at dinner.'

He thanked her with distant civility and allowed himself be led away. He was not so far gone in exhaustion, however, as not to observe a footman seated on a chair outside his door—for his convenience, the valet informed him, he had but to call out and the man would be with him in an instant. He could scarce suppress a smile. She could not keep him locked in his room without explanation and, doubtless, his physical fraility would serve as sufficient excuse for such surveillance.

The afternoon wore interminably on and, grateful though he was for the enforced rest, he came no nearer to a solution of his difficulties. The footman, a cheerfully garrulous young man, looked in from time to time to light his candles and enquire his pleasure. Feeling himself to be unequal to the strain of supporting another *tête-a-tête* with his mama-in-law, he elected to take his dinner in his room. This led unexpectedly to a swift resolving of his dilemma.

He had finished his meal and the valet was preparing him for bed when the footman came in once more, bearing a glass of fine brandy with his mistress's compliments and wishes for a sound night's sleep. One sip convinced Rotherham that there would be no doubt of his sleeping sound did he drink the whole, and he was about to pour it away when he thought of a better use for it.

Waiting until the house was quiet and its occupants hopefully abed, he called the footman to him and explained in halting French that, while not wishing to offend the Vicomtesse, brandy unhappily gave him a disorder of the stomach. Would the young man be so kind as to drink it on his behalf? It went without saying that his offer was readily accepted and, less than half-an-hour later, Rotherham stepped out of his room, walked past his unconscious guard, down the stairs and out into the rainswept darkness.

'The thing is, Sybilla, you cannot hold the fellow here against his will. 'Tain't legal!' Sir Peregrine looked as outraged as if his lady had offered him violence.

'But it is not against his will!' she assured him sweetly. 'He is perfectly content, cosing away with Adam—and who better to look after him than his grandfather-in-law?'

'That's all my eye and Dick's hatband!' Sir Peregrine spoke with unwonted asperity. 'What are you going to tell his mother?'

'Nothing as yet. It is plain she has no idea of his whereabouts since she has not arrived upon our doorstep, demanding his return. Besides,' she pointed out very reasonably, 'he is of age, he can come and go as he pleases. If she denies him such freedom of movement, then she must justify her actions.'

'Assign him to Bedlam, d'you mean? She could do that and leave you without a trick in your hand,' countered Sir Peregrine astutely.

'Ye-es.' For once Lady Whittinghame sounded less than confident. 'At least I am hopeful that little Jonathan is safe. He is too necessary to their schemes to be harmed.'

Sir Peregrine brushed some snuff off the front of his waistcoat. 'How did you fare this morning?' he asked.

'Nothing was admitted, she'll not be had on that suit, though everything was implied and all in the most complacent way. She's devilish sure of herself. One thing only, the nursemaid had a glimpse of that dresser of Elspeth's, Marchant her name is, and was satisfied that she was the woman who took Jonathan. But that is nothing to the point now—what can Julienne-Eve be about? Where is she?'

'Confined too, I shouldn't wonder! Of all the bird-brained notions to go back to Hever Court when a kindly Fate had dropped Trevor into her lap—' Sir Peregrine raised his eyes to Heaven as if imploring Divine guidance on such inexplicable conduct when the sound of carriage wheels approaching the house drew his attention to the window. 'Who the devil's calling at this hour? Can it be—no, by Jupiter, it is a perfect stranger! Never saw the fellow before. Hoped it might be Ainsley,' he elaborated, 'but there's small chance of seeing him before morning.'

'You've sent for him?'

'Only thing to do, m'dear. He's the man to unravel all the legalities and decide who gets the money.'

'Yes, I had forgotten that,' she said in a subdued way. 'I look upon him as being one of us but he is in duty bound to show no preference.'

'Oh, I'll wager he'll do that if he can. But can he? And if Julienne-Eve has fallen into that woman's hands, there'll be no bearing it. Two hostages against one, and that one dicked in the nob! It won't answer, Sybilla, I tell you it won't answer!'

Her ladyship, though greatly perturbed in spirit, was about to demonstrate that she, at least, could answer, when Challis came to announce their visitor.

'A French gentleman, m'lady, wishful of seeing Lady Rotherham. I told him as how she wasn't receiving so he asked to see you. His card, m'lady.'

Lady Whittinghame picked up the small piece of pasteboard proffered her upon a silver salver with reluctant fingertips, as if fearing it might snap at her.

'The Vicomte de Beaumanoir,' she read aloud. 'I don't know him—oh, yes, I do!' She turned to her frowning spouse. 'I think, Perry, we must see this gentleman. He may have news of Julienne-Eve's parents.'

'Let us hope it is cheerful news then,' said he with resignation. 'We have had a deal too much of t'other sort around here of late.'

The Vicomte had taken care with his appearance, preferring to assume a sober elegance in dress that could be made to suit whatever rôle circumstances forced upon him. Pale pantaloons clung smoothly to his well-rounded limbs, a mulberry-hued coat fitted his shoulders to perfection, and only the smallest of diamonds were permitted to glitter discreetly in the folds of his neckcloth. He saw, from the guarded approval in Sir Peregrine's eye as he inspected the visitor through his quizzing-glass, that he had not been at fault in his judgment.

When preliminary courtesies had been exchanged and the gentlemen made known to each other, Lady Whittinghame explained that her daughter-in-law had been delivered of a premature child not long since and was not yet quite up to snuff. The Vicomte's lively countenance assumed a grave expression. 'A son, I trust? And in good time?' At her look of surprise he added quickly, 'Madame—Lady Rotherham's mother—told me it all.'

'A son, yes, but whether in time has yet to be resolved.' Lady Whittinghame did not feel obliged to disclose any further details on so private a matter. 'But what tidings do you bring of the Colomb d'Hautevilles? Philippe, I must tell you, is very well and has become amazingly fluent in English, though perhaps not quite the English his parents would have chosen for him.'

'Argot of the stables, more like,' confirmed Sir Peregrine, busying himself at the wine table. 'Can't keep the lad away from them.'

'How happy his father would have been to know that,' said the Vicomte with an air of profound melancholy.

'Would have been? Then—the Marquis—'

'Alas, madame, his heart and his years did not prove equal to the strain imposed upon them.'

Lady Whittinghame murmured her regrets. 'And the Marquise?'

'Is no longer the Marquise, I am happy to inform you, but has done me the incomparable honour of becoming my wife.'

Her ladyship got the impression that events were moving more quickly than she quite liked, but she suppressed her astonishment and wished the Vicomte every joy in his marriage with well-simulated enthusiasm.

'A droll situation, is it not?' he twinkled but, despite his affability, she formed the opinion that Julienne-Eve had in no way benefitted from the change of stepfather. Further conjecture was swept from her mind by his next words. 'That, of course, is in part my reason for wishing to see Lady Rotherham. My other message for her is of an even more joyous nature, and for you, too, madame.' As he spoke he held out his hand and she cried aloud at sight of the ring resting upon his open palm.

'Nathan! He lives!'

He nodded. 'Sadly wounded, but he will survive.'

Lady Whittinghame, her limbs trembling as with ague, sank into the nearest chair and sat there, speechless, while the Vicomte, with all the hesitancy of one who deplores being the extoller of his own virtues, told them of his rescue of her son. When he had finished his recital and had received their thanks with becoming modesty, he looked keenly from one to the other.

'This matter of the child—may I be informed of how things stand in that respect?' Seeing her indecision, he earnestly emphasised his point. 'I may well be of service to you in this also. If so, I am yours to command.'

'Can't see why not.' Sir Peregrine filled their guest's glass and his own with a fine disregard for Rotherham's best Madeira. 'The way things are shaping, m'dear, we'll need all the new recruits we can muster.'

She had to allow that he had a point there, and told the Vicomte the full story with commendable brevity. He sat for a time, rolling the wine-glass between his fingers, before giving her the benefit of his opinion.

'The child must be got back, that is the first essential.' The crisp decision in his voice was in strong contrast to his former diffidence. 'And where, do you suppose, is Lady Rotherham?'

'I greatly fear she has thought fit to attempt the rescue herself,' admitted Lady Whittinghame worriedly.

'It should not have been permitted, madame. Should she have been taken, then it complicates our task unduly.'

She bit her lip, resenting his high-handed manner, but unable to dispute the truth of his reasoning. 'Adam, my groom, has gone to seek her,' she began then, once again, the sound of carriage wheels drew Sir Peregrine to the window. 'Perhaps that is their return now?'

'No, by God, it's Ainsley! How in thunder could he—I'll go fetch him.' Sir Peregrine hurried from the room while she explained to the Vicomte who Mr Ainsley was and his importance in the matter of the inheritance. Clearly the latter was also being brought up to date with the latest developments for it was some minutes before the little man came in hard upon Sir Peregrine's heels. 'Here's a piece of luck! Ainsley was on his way here when he encountered my messenger in mid-stream, as it were.'

'I am more happy than I can say, my lady, to learn of his lordship's survival.' Mr Ainsley made his bow to her ladyship while his sharp eyes assessed the visitor. 'This morning I received a letter from Lady Heathcott requiring me to fulfil the conditions of the late Lord Rotherham's will. I thought it best to consult you before proceeding to Hever Court.'

'Where you will be shown my grandson as proof of—oh,

Nathan, Nathan, how we have failed you!'

Seeing her dissolve into most uncharacteristic tears, Sir Peregrine rallied to her comfort. 'At least, m'dear, we know the boy's alive, we have the Vicomte's word on that. As for the rest, we've got Trevor safe, and there's the midwife, too.'

'Ah, yes, the midwife.' Mr Ainsley set down a bulky leather portfolio upon a table and fiddled with the straps. 'I implored her, for her own safety, to ply her trade in some place other than that where she was known until all this had been resolved. Unhappily, she did not take my advice.'

'You mean—' Lady Whittinghame's eyes dilated in horror. 'Oh, no, not that poor woman!'

Mr Ainsley gave a slight affirmative nod. 'Yestere'en she was discovered, a short distance from my office, foully murdered. I had asked her to come to see me, both to assure myself of her well-being and to recompense her for any loss in income owing to have moved away from her regular haunts. By so doing, I played into the hands of those who must certainly be watching my every move.'

The Vicomte whistled softly between his teeth. 'It would seem that they mean business, these people.'

'Aye, and if Julienne-Eve is in their power, then the trap's down with a vengeance,' supplemented Sir Peregrine gloomily.

'We will best know the answer to that,' said Lady Whittinghame, whose keen ears had heard the sound of movement in the hall, 'if we hear it from the lady herself. And, unless I mistake the matter, here she is!'

CHAPTER
FOURTEEN

WHEN she had left Adam and Sir Trevor to return to Hever Court in search of her son, Julienne-Eve had no notion of how she might fulfill this task. Once more tying up the disapproving Sorrel in the barn, she secreted the pistol inside her bodice and stepped out of the cool gloom of the building into the noonday heat.

Everywhere seemed deserted under the scorching sun, but she was brought up with a jolt by a low laugh and a murmur of voices from almost under her feet to discover two of Lady Heathcott's staff disporting themselves in a manner that would have earned them their mistress's severe disapprobation had she been privileged to witness their activities. A footman's coat was hung upon a bush and a mob-cap and apron lay beneath it. As she debated what best to do other garments arrived to join these, and one of a pair of slippers struck her so that she was minded to request the owner to have a care for her person.

'That new wet-nurse, then—Sarah, her name is—I thought she'd be to your fancy.' It was the girl speaking. 'Pretty enough piece, ain't she?'

'I've no taste for the little 'uns. Sommat round and picksome's more to my liking!' The sound of a hearty slap produced a storm of giggles and protests. ''Sides, she's only come yestere'en, I scarce set eyes on her.'

'Time and enough for you, ain't it? Oh, Timothy!' The squeals increased in volume and Julienne-Eve, trusting that Timothy had all his attention directed upon what he was about, tiptoed around the bush and picked up the mob-cap and apron. The latter, being of generous size, covered her pink cambric gown, while every vestige of hair was tucked away under the cap. She had no means of knowing how long it would be before their loss was discovered, and could only wish Timothy every success in his improper advances so that his companion's interest might be wholly engaged for some time to come.

Then she stepped out confidently without any attempt at concealment. She was Sarah, the new wet-nurse, doubtless brought in for Jonathan's benefit, and probably not yet known to many more of the other servants. Hoping that ill fortune did not bring her face-to-face with the real Sarah, she entered the house by a side-door which gave on to the kitchen quarters. From thence she stole through the strangely silent house until she reached the entrance hall. Close to her a clock struck the hour and she started nervously. Then, catching sight of herself in a pier-glass, she had to smile. With the mob-cap pulled low over her forehead and her face pinched and wan beneath it, there seemed small likelihood of anyone recognising the radiant Miss Lawrence of the previous year in so undistinguished a figure.

The door to the dining-room stood ajar and she could see the table still littered with the remains of a cold repast. Wondering that her ladyship's servants should be so neglectful of their duties, she was about to go on when the sight of the food reminded her that she had not eaten that day and the unaccustomed exercise had stirred her appetite. Quickly she wrapped up a small parcel of cold meats and bread in a napkin for consumption at her leisure and put it in the pocket of her apron. Beneath it she laid the pistol, experiencing an odd sense of security from the very touch of it, and continued on her way upstairs.

Here, the tap of footsteps hastening in her direction sent her to cover behind the long window drapes. Then there came the sound of a stumble and the crash of falling china, followed by a stifled sob and the scuffling noises of the broken pieces being collected together.

'Sarah! What have you done now?' It was Marchant's voice, sharp with impatience. 'Oh, you clumsy wretch! Her ladyship'll be none too pleased at this!'

'I—I caught my foot on the rug, miss,' whimpered the unfortunate Sarah.

'That's plain to see for you've ripped it! You'll not be seeing much of your wages this month, my girl! Now be off with you and dispose of all this. You can replace the broken dish from the china store.'

'Please, miss, where is the china store?'

'Oh, fiddle! I'd best come with you I suppose. The child is safe enough for a few minutes.'

'In which assumption, my good woman, you are far and wide!' murmured Julienne-Eve as, the two having disappeared, Marchant still to be heard berating the wet-nurse, she stepped out from behind the protective curtain and almost ran in the direction from whence they had come. She had no difficulty in finding Jonathan for the door to his nursery stood wide and he lay there, crowing sleepily.

Snatching him up, she held him close while she considered what next to do. She was about to step out into the passage again when the sound of a door opening further down its length had her scanning the room in frantic search of a hiding-place. The only one that offered was a heavy mahogany tallboy, set across a corner so as to leave a small angle of space behind it. Edging herself around it, she stood clutching the mercifully somnolent Jonathan, the sound of her heartbeats so loud she was assured they must surely be heard throughout the room.

Someone was walking slowly down the passage. The footsteps came to the door of the room then hesitated and stopped. There was a faint sound as of surprise and Julienne-Eve held her breath, but nothing more was said and the footsteps moved away.

Slumping back against the wall in trembling relief she became aware of something pressing into the small of her back and released one hand from cradling Jonathan to feel about behind her. It was a small knob or handle and she realised that she must be leaning against a jib-door leading to a servants' stair, and plainly one that was never used. Frantically she tugged at it, but to no avail, and she was resigning herself to accepting that it had been papered over and quite closed up when it yielded with a suddenness that threw her back against the tallboy and caused Jonathan to make drowsy complaint as if requiring to be informed what his mama thought she was about. As she expected, a stairway led directly up and down from inside the opening and the only light was a faint glimmer coming from above. This, and the knowledge that she could not remain in her present hiding-place for very long without certain discovery, determined her to take the upward flight which, being both steep and narrow, she found to be no easy task, burdened as she was with the child. The light came from a slit window at the top where she was faced by a massive door.

Drawing back the protesting bolts that secured it, she found herself in a large attic room, empty save for a broken wickerwork chair. Setting Jonathan down in this, she advanced upon a door set in the farther wall of the room only to find, to her dismay, that it was secured on the other side. She then addressed herself to the small, dirt-encrusted windows and dimly perceived a low parapet, with a narrow walk lying between it and the wall of the room. The latches were solid with rust, but eventually one yielded to her efforts and a welcome waft of fresh air pervaded the attic. With a last look to assure herself that Jonathan was sleeping soundly, she emptied her pocket of food and pistol and climbed out of the window on to the walk to peer over the parapet.

This gave her a clear view of the stableyard and outbuildings and, even as she watched, the place burst into activity with figures running to and fro and shouted commands. Concluding that Jonathan's disappearance had been discovered, she dropped to her knees and crawled along the narrow walk to look in at the windows of the next room. This also was empty, and she was about to go back when she perceived that the windows of a further room were barred and a small vent was slightly open. Beyond this room the walk and parapet ended at an angle of the house and, hopeful of obtaining a better view of what was going on below, she continued to the corner.

This yielded a glimpse of the front of the house and her spirits suffered a sharp reverse when she saw Sorrel and the whisky being driven smartly into the forecourt. Slowly she began to wriggle backwards and, as she came level again with the partly-open window of the last room, she heard the rustle of movement within and a low groan. Then a woman's voice cried out from over her head.

'Who is that? Who are you?' Accepting that there was no

point in further concealment, Julienne-Eve sat back on her heels and looked in at the window to find herself staring into the wide terrified eyes of a white-faced Lucy. For a moment neither spoke, then it was Lucy who whispered: 'It is—it is Miss Lawrence, isn't it? Oh, miss, please help me!'

The young woman's whole demeanour was so alarming that Julienne-Eve could find no words to answer her. She was thin to the point of emaciation, her hair hung in snarled wisps about her bloodless cheeks, her dress was disordered and far from clean, while anyone observing the wildness of her expression might be forgiven for supposing her mind to be quite unhinged. Her next words supported this theory.

'Oh, miss, miss—your ladyship, I should say! Please get me away from here, I know she's going to kill me!'

While prepared to accept that Lady Heathcott's was not a conciliatory nature, Julienne-Eve felt that this accusation was pitching it a bit too strong. Then she remembered the threat against Sir Trevor and felt the spark of anger reviving within her. Forcing herself to speak in a calm, reasonable way, she said:

'But why should she wish to kill you, Lucy? Surely you are necessary to her?'

'Not any more, I'm not!' choked the girl. 'Her dear daughter-in-law I was, nothing too good for me—until I had my baby. Then she tried to make me swear it was a boy but I would not. Oh, I've done you much wrong, my lady, but I'd not do that! I thought that if Trevor and I both refused to play her game, 'twould send her to grass.'

'So it was you who told Trevor?'

'Yes. Oh, miss, where is he?'

'Safe in your grandfather's charge. Your little girl is safe also and I have Jonathan here. So all we have to do is release you and walk out of the house,' said Julienne-Eve, marvelling at her own inventiveness.

'The end bar there is loose, miss—but what's the use of that? The windows are locked and I cannot get out that small vent nor through a pane did we break one.'

'No, but—' Julienne-Eve shook the bar fiercely and was gratified to find it come away from its worn socket into her hands. 'Now, Lucy, stand away if you please. I am going to try to break the window hinges.' Thereupon, relying on the noise and confusion going on down below to cover any sounds issuing from above, she applied the iron bar to such good effect that presently the window sagged inwards, the weight of it breaking the lock as it fell down on to the bed beneath. 'There! Now all you have to do is to squeeze out through the gap left by the bar.' Her privations here stood Lucy in good stead and she inched her slender form through the small space to collapse in a sobbing heap at Julienne-Eve's feet. 'Quickly, we must not linger. Should anyone come up and find you gone, then it will be all holiday with us.'

The effort of climbing out had all but exhausted Lucy's frail store of strength, and Julienne-Eve was obliged to assist her along the walk and into the room where Jonathan lay sleeping. When she was sufficiently in command of herself to relate her somewhat incoherent story, it appeared that she had been confined to the attic for close on a month, with little more than gruel and water to sustain her.

'But did not someone remark upon your absence—the servants?'

'They'd not care if they did.' The girl's voice was bitter. 'They've no love for one of their own kind set over them. Anyway, there are few of the old staff left, her ladyship has seen to that.'

Julienne-Eve could well imagine Lucy being a tyrannical mistress but, despite that and her treacherous behaviour, she could not but feel pity for her one-time maid's unhappy plight.

'Food is what you need,' she declared, opening up the napkin and spreading it upon the floor. Lucy's eyes lit up at sight of its contents and Julienne-Eve had to turn her head away and pretend to occupy herself with the blissfully unconscious Jonathan so as not to witness the animal-like rapacity with which the food was despatched. When every last crumb had been devoured, Lucy continued her tale in a more composed manner.

'I wasn't up to snuff at first after my baby was born, I can't rightly remember for how long. I think her ladyship hoped I'd stick my spoon in the wall and save her the trouble. Then she tried to persuade me that I was all about in my head, and she showed me a baby boy, saying he was mine. But I knew he wasn't and I'd have none of him. So she locked me up here and told me I'd never see my baby again if I did not sing to her tune. 'Twas as well you came when you did, miss—m'lady. She came up here yesterday and told me I had 'til this evening to make up my mind. I—I don't know as how I could have held out against her any longer. I—I want my baby, y'see, I don't care if she is a girl.'

'You've been very brave, Lucy,' Julienne-Eve soothed her, marvelling at the power of mother-love in so unlikely a subject. 'Now, you remain here with Jonathan, I am going to steal down that stairway and listen for any sound from below.'

'Like as not they are all out, buzzing like bees about the place,' nodded Lucy with something of her old assurance. 'Take off your footgear and step close to the wall lest the stair should creak. Is that your pistol, m'lady?'

'Yes, but it is not loaded. I had thought to use it only to threaten should the need arise.'

Unlacing her shoes, Julienne-Eve crept in stockinged feet down the stair and stood, listening, before trying the jib-door. This gave way with a sufficient jerk to precipitate her into the narrow space behind the tallboy with rather more noise than was quite comfortable. No one, however, appeared to be at all interested in her movements and a glance into the room satisfied her that she was free of any company.

'My hope is that they will have searched all the upstairs rooms at the first,' she gasped when she rejoined Lucy.

'Maybe, but they'll know you cannot have gone far in the time.' However poor her physical condition, Lucy's mental processes were clearly not impaired. 'If you're not found outside by now then they'll know you're still in the house and, depend upon it, someone will remember that jib-door. Or, perhaps, call upon me and find me gone. And they know I'm in no state to get far on my own.'

Julienne-Eve straightened up from putting on her shoes. 'Lucy, we keep speaking of "they". Who, apart from her ladyship and Stapleton, is here?'

'That lawyer of hers, Mr Baynton, for one. Then there's Miss Marchant. She's the worst of the lot, I do believe. I swear she'd cut my throat if her ladyship gave the nod. There are very few servants. As I told you, she dismissed most of the old lot, not wishing to have witnesses to what she's doing, I'd say. But Stapleton is always with her like—like an evil shadow.'

Julienne-Eve repressed a strong desire to shudder and picked up the unprotesting Jonathan. 'You go down first and wait while I secure this door so that no one can come through from the attic in pursuit of us.'

This she did, but when she arrived at the foot of the stairs it was to find Lucy huddled on the lowest step.

'It's no good, m'lady,' she gulped. 'I'd only hold you back, I'm that feeble. Do you and the baby get away and when they find me I'll say I took him and hid him. But you'd best make haste for I doubt I'll hold out against her ladyship's persuasion for too long.'

For Jonathan's sake Julienne-Eve was sorely tempted, but the fact that the girl's testimony would clinch the case against her ladyship weighed the scales in favour of getting her out of the house at all costs. This, however, proved to be quite beyond her powers. She herself was near exhaustion and Lucy so desperately weak that they came to a stand by the door of Lady Heathcott's bedchamber.

'Here's one place they'd never think to look!' Lucy's eyes lit up with malicious delight. 'I'll hide behind the bed drapes until you can come back for me. Bring as many people with you as you can and demand to see me. When I hear your voice I'll come down. That's as good a plan as any.'

Privately Julienne-Eve considered it an excessively dubious plan, but Lucy plainly had reached the end of her rope. Also the two hours limit she had given Adam was almost spent and she had no wish for him to come in search of her before she was clear of the house. Reluctantly she deposited the girl behind Lady Heathcott's bed and let the heavy drapes fall over her before continuing on her way downstairs. A certain amount of disturbance coming from the direction of the kitchens decided her to leave boldly by the front door. The forecourt was deserted but she had scarce crossed it and moved into the cover of a shrubbery than Lady Heathcott's voice could be heard declaring that, as the child was not to be found in the grounds, then he must still be in the house.

Thanking Heaven for Lucy's quick wits and praying that she would be found to be equally fortunate in her choice of hiding-place, Julienne-Eve made what haste she could to the barn. It was then she discovered that the pistol was not in the pocket of her apron. This had her in a puzzle for, while she recalled laying it on the floor of the attic when she had climbed out of the window and seeing it on her return, she could not remember having picked it up. Yet it most certainly had not been there when she had left the room. Shaking her head perplexedly, she subsided on to a heap of straw and attempted to soothe Jonathan who, very properly, had begun to take exception to being hustled about in so unceremonious a fashion. His protests soon disturbed the still air and Julienne-Eve closed her eyes in despair. To have achieved so much and then to lose it all on the last throw was the outside of enough!

'Please, please, my darling, be patient a little longer!' she implored him and, tucking him under her arm, she left the shelter of the barn and started to trudge steadily towards the road. She had not gone a hundred yards when her foot caught in a tree-root and she stumbled to the ground, rolling over desperately in the effort to save her child from injury. For a moment she lay breathless, lacking the strength to pick herself up, and the mob-cap, being rather large, slipped down over her eyes. Impatiently she put up a hand to pull it off, releasing her hair about her shoulders.

'Thought it must be you, m'lady, but I couldn't be sure, not in that rig,' said Adam's voice at her elbow. 'I've got young Jem here with me, promised him he wouldn't be the loser if her ladyship turns him off for helping us. I hope I did right, m'lady.'

But Julienne-Eve was quite unable to give him any assurance on this point for the shock of seeing him and realising that she was safe had proved too much for her overstrained nerves and she had quietly fainted away.

CHAPTER
FIFTEEN

'So you see, the very first thing must be to rescue Lucy.' Julienne-Eve heard herself repeating this injunction in a parrot-like way several times over.

The events of the past hours had quite worn her down and, to cap it all, the unbelievable joy of knowing Rotherham to be alive had come as so great a shock that her tired brain could scarce accept the fact.

Seeing how it was with her, Lady Whittinghame called for wine to revive her; for Parsons to take charge of Jonathan; for Adam to tell his story; and all done in an inexorable bustle while Julienne-Eve sat, her eyes going from one to the other as if imploring to be assured that her ears had not deceived her.

'Never fear, m'dear, we'll winkle the girl out!' Sir Peregrine, sitting beside her on the sofa, held a glass to her lips. 'Come, try a sip of this, 'twill put heart into you.'

'No, no,' she protested feebly, pushing it away. 'I must go back to Lucy. I know where she is, you see, and she will be on the look for me.'

'You are not going anywhere, dear child,' said Lady Whittinghame fondly, putting an arm about her. 'Except to your bed. The gentlemen and I will see to all this. And when you are quite rested we will have a long cose about Nathan and how best to get him home.'

At that Julienne-Eve's composure, which had so nobly withstood all that had gone before, inexplicably deserted her. She burst into heartrending tears and allowed her mother-in-law to lead her, sobbing, from the room.

'Ah—hem!' Sir Peregrine tossed back the untasted glass of brandy with commendable regard for economy. 'What do we do now, Ainsley?'

'I suggest, sir, that you and I call upon Lady Heathcott at once, when I will inform her that I know her grandchild to be a girl and have the testimony of both the infant's parents to prove it.'

'Both?' echoed Sir Peregrine in some doubt.

'I will then stand at the foot of the stairway and call upon Lady Lucy to disclose herself,' declared Mr Ainsley in a very determined manner. 'But Lady Rotherham is in the right of it, we must waste no time lest Lady Heathcott should discover her.'

'I would remind you, gentlemen,' the Vicomte here intervened, 'that I stand *in loco parentis* to Lady Rotherham and another pair of hands may well be of assistance. Also, I have quite as strong an interest in the successful outcome of this affair as any.'

Mr Ainsley looked as if he would like to enquire further into the nature of that interest, but he was not a man to waste time in pointless argument; he also saw the force of the Vicomte's reasoning. 'True enough,' he acknowledged. 'Shall we go?'

'Er— just a moment, Ainsley.' Sir Peregrine looked a shade uncomfortable. 'Her ladyship—Sybilla—will be in a rare taking if we go without her.'

'Someone must stay here with Lady Rotherham,' insisted Mr Ainsley. 'Pretty fools we should look if the child was snatched away again in our absence!'

As they waited for the carriage to be brought to the door the Vicomte strolled out to the terrace to admire the handsomely landscaped gardens stretching down to a well-wooded park. Sir Peregrine pulled at the lawyer's sleeve.

'Tell me,' he hissed. 'why did the Marquise marry that fellow? Can't follow the reasoning there.'

'Nor I, to be plain with you, but I imagine her to be the sort of lady who must have a man to wait upon her and he is well-bred and personable enough. I'd say he surmised that Lady Rotherham would not see her mother without a feather to fly with if she succeeded in winning the Saville inheritance.'

'Rotherham might have something to say to that!' interjected Sir Peregrine. 'From all I hear, Julienne-Eve has no great cause to be grateful to her parent.'

'An understatement, sir, if I may be permitted to say so,' said Mr Ainsley primly.

Sir Peregrine seemed about to enlarge upon this theme,

but the Vicomte returned to the saloon at that moment and, with a shrug, his host led the way out to the waiting carriage.

Upstairs, Lady Whittinghame had persuaded Julienne-Eve to lie upon her bed and partake of some nourishment while they went over every small detail of what had passed between her and Lucy.

'And you are quite sure that her feelings towards us are benevolent?'

'Quite, quite sure. So you do see that I must go back. I doubt she would show herself did she not hear my voice. And I have to confess to you that I have lost your pistol.'

'You took my pistol?' Lady Whittinghame started as if stung by a nettle unwarily grasped.

'Yes, but only to use as an empty threat should I need to do so. Why, what troubles you?'

'It would not have been an empty threat, my dear. The first thing I did after Jonathan was taken was to prime it, but I decided against taking it to Hever Court this morning lest I should lose command of myself and shoot Elspeth down!'

'Dear God! You have never done so before—I never thought to check!'

'Why should you, indeed? And no harm's done, after all, though we had best find it. Yes, Parsons?'

'The gentlemen said to tell you they have left for Hever Court, m'lady.' The maid, entering at that moment, spoke in her usual unemotional way.

'They've gone without me? All three of them?'

'All three of them, m'lady,' corroborated Parsons but got no further because Julienne-Eve was off the bed and pushing away her half-tasted bowl of soup.

'We must follow them! Lucy does not know any one of them! And don't try to tell me that I cannot, because I can and I will!'

After that there seemed nothing more to be said and, since the gentlemen had not taken Adam with them, Sir Peregrine handling the ribbons himself, in no time the two ladies were bowling along in their wake, having left the most stringent instructions with Challis to admit no one and with Parsons to hide herself and Jonathan away.

It was plain from the moment they drew up before Hever Court that something was amiss. The doors stood wide and, apart from a scared-looking lad standing to the heads of Sir Peregrine's pair, no servants were to be seen.

'Great Heavens, what can have happened?' Lady Whittinghame scrambled from the carriage, followed closely by Julienne-Eve, and together they hurried up the steps to stop, transfixed, in the doorway.

The scene that greeted their gaze was, to say the least, unusual. Standing in the hall, their backs to the new arrivals, was a group of gentlemen comprised of the Vicomte, Mr Ainsley, Sir Peregrine, and two others whom Julienne-Eve recognised as Stapleton and Mr Baynton. They were all staring upwards to the head of the stairs where stood Lady Heathcott, motionless as a statue. A few steps away from her was Lucy, steadying herself with one hand resting upon the newel-post, while the other held a pistol trained upon her ladyship.

'Oh, no!' breathed Julienne-Eve in horror, 'I told her it wasn't loaded!' Then, stepping forward, she called out, 'I am here now, Lucy, it is quite safe to come down.'

The words stirred Lady Heathcott from her stupor and she swung round upon her daughter-in-law. 'So you have been in collusion with these others!' she accused her. 'You deceitful trollop!'

'Aye, I've had more kindness from them than ever from you!' sneered Lucy, the pistol waving dangerously in her weak clasp. 'Where is my baby?'

'She is safe at Leyswood Towers with her father,' Mr Ainsley intervened. 'And if you care to join them, ma'am, then the party will be complete.'

'Yes, dear lady, do put that pistol away,' begged Sir Peregrine. 'I declare it makes me quite nervous.'

'You needn't fear, 'tain't primed,' Lucy assured him and proceeded to demonstrate her belief by pulling the trigger. There came a flash and a report and the weapon fell from her hand as Lady Heathcott slowly sank to her knees and pitched headlong down the stairs to lie at the feet of the thunder-struck group below.

Mr Ainsley was the first to move and kneel beside her.

'You'd best send for a doctor,' he said after a brief inspection. 'The wound is slight but I think her arm is broken and, in falling, she has sustained a heavy blow to the head.'

With a little moan, Lucy subsided to the floor and Julienne-Eve, fearing she might meet a like fate, started forward up the stairs to comfort the distraught girl, while the others of the party busied themselves about Lady Heathcott's unconscious figure.

The doctor, who came within a very short time, confirmed what Mr Ainsley had told them. 'Of itself, the bullet would have done little harm. It is lodged here in the flesh of the shoulder. Her worst injuries were caused by the fall.'

'I still insist it was attempted murder!' Mr Baynton, looking thoroughly put out as well he might at the over-throwing of all his plans, was plainly determined to find a scapegoat on whom to vent his ill-temper.

'Fustian nonsense!' said Mr Ainsley, displaying not a vestige of sympathy. 'The whole affair was a deplorable accident, as well you know.'

'I know nothing of the sort! I intend to bring a charge of premeditated killing against this young woman!'

'Oh, cut line, Baynton!' snapped Mr Ainsley. He then leaned forward and said something very low into the other's ear, which caused Mr Baynton's pastily unhealthy countenance to assume an even more unhealthy hue and effectively stilled his tongue.

'I think there is no more for us to do here.' Lady Whittinghame rose and looked about her. 'You will acquaint me with whatever arrangements you find to be necessary, Mr Baynton. I would not wish to be behindhand in offering assistance during my sister-in-law's—er, enforced indisposition. Perry, your arm for Lady Heathcott.'

'What? Who? Oh, yes, to be sure!' Gallantly, Sir Peregrine supported the wilting Lucy to where her grandfather stood, grim-faced, by the chaise.

It was a very subdued party that gathered around the dining-table at Leyswood Towers that evening. The air was warm and still and the tall windows were opened wide to admit what breath of wind there was. Lucy, having first been reunited with husband and child, had been put to bed, but Julienne-Eve, eager to learn all she could of Nathan's condition, felt unable to take Lady Whittinghame's advice to do likewise.

It was not until the meal was over and the ladies about to withdraw that the Vicomte said pleasantly enough: 'If you will bear with me for a few moments, I wish to bring to your attention a matter of some delicacy.' Dismissing Challis with a nod, Lady Whittinghame re-seated herself and motioned to Julienne-Eve to do the same. All looked expectantly at the Vicomte, who smiled encouragingly upon them. 'The—ah, successful outcome of to-day's little engagement gives me to hope that what I have in mind may be amicably arranged.'

Mr Ainsley, who had taken the Vicomte in strong aversion for no reason other than a sharp nose for a rascal, slid the port along the table to Sir Peregrine and settled back in his chair.

'Would the delicate matter be in any way concerned with money?' he enquired tentatively.

'Well, there you have it, sir!' The Vicomte was all rueful candour. 'The Marquis saw fit to leave everything in trust for his son. My wife receives an income from the estate for just so long as she cares for the boy to the satisfaction of his trustees—not a very large income, I would add.' He sighed heavily, as if deploring such paternal foresight.

Lady Whittinghame thought the Marquis had shown great good sense in making this provision. 'Pockets to let, M. le Vicomte?' she enquired sweetly.

Beaumanoir spread his hands wide. 'One has to live, you understand. I am sure my new stepdaughter will be happy to have her husband restored to her at whatever price.'

Sir Peregrine gave vent to a snort of disgust. 'I knew it! There never was a Frenchie who didn't put his pocket before his honour!'

'I beg you, sir, do not be unduly severe upon my poor countrymen!' Beaumanoir mocked him. 'But, to quote your English saying, needs must when the devil drives!'

'How do we know you are telling us the truth?' demanded Lady Whittinghame. 'You may show us my son's ring but it could well have been picked up on the battlefield.'

'Or pulled off his finger while he lay—' began Sir Peregrine, but was silenced by a glare from his spouse.

'You have my word that Rotherham is in my wife's care and will be restored to you in as prime order as is possible.'

'Faugh!' exploded Sir Peregrine. 'And can we place any trust in that?'

'Not above half, I fear,' sighed Mr Ainsley. 'My dear Lady Rotherham, I am inclined to believe that your mother has much mistaken the matter if she thinks to mould this—ah, gentleman into a conformable husband.'

'My mother!' Julienne-Eve spoke for the first time in the discussion. 'Does she know of this demand of yours?'

Hardened sharp though he was, Beaumanoir found himself unable to meet her clear gaze. 'She is in hopes, of course, that you will of your own accord, offer to recompense us for our services.'

'And what would you consider a suitable recompense, monsieur?'

The Vicomte, one hand toying idly with a silver fruit-knife, appeared to be lost in thought while Julienne-Eve found her eyes following the movements of that white hand as if bewitched by it.

'Shall we say—fifty thousand pounds?'

There was a sharp intake of breath around the table, but nothing else broke the silence until a quiet voice spoke from outside the open French windows.

'I protest you do me too much honour, M. le Vicomte.' As he stepped inside, Rotherham's glance swept the room until it came to rest on the anguished face of his wife.

'Nathan!' burst out Lady Whittinghame, but he motioned her to silence, his attention centred upon Beaumanoir.

'You thought me done-up, did you not? As did your lady wife! I'll warrant she has her fellows still scouring the streets of Paris for me!'

'The stupid jade! She'll answer to me for this!' The Vicomte, his calm quite overset, was on his feet, glaring at the intruder.

'I have no doubt she will,' returned Rotherham drily, 'as you, sir, will answer to me.'

'No!' Sir Peregrine surprised them all by his authority. 'You'll not sully your sword by crossing it with that of a rogue! Bid him begone, Rotherham, and think himself lucky to get off so light!'

'There are more subtle means, of course, of terminating so hopeful a career.' Mr Ainsley, his head to one side, was considering the possibilities. 'Illegal detention could be proved no doubt, my lord? And as for this matter of demanding money by threat—well, we have witnesses a-plenty to set up a pretty case.'

The Vicomte, recovered from his initial shock, was once more in command of himself. 'Illegal detention, you say? And what of the small Philippe? Are you not holding him when he should be in his mother's care? With or without your permission, I will carry him back with me to Paris.'

A small cry of protest came from Julienne-Eve and Rotherham looked quickly at her. 'Not only will you not take Philippe,' he said levelly, 'but you will give me a written undertaking on behalf of you and your wife never to attempt to see either her son or her daughter again. Attend to that, if you please, Ainsley.'

'At once, my lord. If you will follow me, monsieur, we can deal with the matter now.' Seeing the Vicomte hesitate, plainly unwilling to accept defeat, Mr Ainsley added softly: 'Prisons can be uncommon uncomfortable places if you're short of the ready to smooth your way. I doubt you'd find the experience a pleasant one.'

Beaumanoir made a wry grimace. 'Very well,' he said at length. 'Lead on, little man, I'll sign your bit of paper for what it's worth. Your servant, ladies and gentlemen.'

Making the company an elegant leg, he followed Mr Ainsley out of the room, flirting his lace-edged handkerchief at a troublesome fly as if to stress his unconcern. With his departure, the others turned to Rotherham, his mother clasping him to her while Sir Peregrine urged him to sit down and thrust a glass of port into his hand.

'I'll vow the air feels cleaner for his going! Gad, you look hagged, my boy! How did you make your escape?'

Rotherham, his eyes never leaving Julienne-Eve's still white face, told them briefly.

'By great good luck, as I came to Lady Oxford's door, it opened to release two fellow officers, old friends of mine, who had come to take their congé of her before leaving for England that very night. Good fellows that they were, they accepted my need for haste and took me with them without question. I was fortunate again in that, thanks to a following wind, we made a speedy passage which had not been possible for several days, and so was no more than a few hours behind Beaumanoir when we landed at Dover. The rest you know, or can guess. Now for your news, if you please.'

'You are the father of a most beautiful little boy,' his mother told him proudly.

'And, by reason of that, more plump in the pocket than any man has a right to expect!' added Sir Peregrine. 'For all of which you have your lady wife to thank.'

'Yes.' Rotherham stepped towards her, his hands outstretched to take hers, but she faced him with such an air of defiant misery that Lady Whittinghame looked at her in alarm.

'My mother! She was part of his schemes but—but she *is* my mother!' The words burst out of her as if against her will.

'Your mother comes out of this better than she has a right to expect!' She flinched at his harsh tone and he went on more gently. 'Though I do believe she is so besotted with him, he can bend her to his will as he pleases.'

'Then will you not be lenient with her, my lord? It would seem that if Philippe is not restored to her, she has nothing.'

His expression hardened. 'Would you then pay her a handsome competence for her treachery? Perhaps you regret my untimely return and would have been happy for her to have fifty thousand pounds!'

She stared at him, bewildered by the accusation, not realising that it was his fatigue speaking. Then, stifling a sob, she ran from the room. Lady Whittinghame, with a reproachful look at her son, hurried after her.

Sir Peregrine cleared his throat tentatively. 'Best leave things until morning,' he counselled. 'It's all been a bit of a shock. She's a great gun, that girl of yours—but your mother'll want to tell you about it, I'll not spoil her story.'

For the rest of that evening Julienne-Eve was left undisturbed in her bedchamber, with Jonathan beside her in his crib for she would entrust him to no one else, while in the saloon below she could hear the rise and fall of voices far into the night. Much of this discussion, she was persuaded, was directed towards arranging her future. Well, the most she could hope for was to have her own apartments at Leyswood Towers and the chance of seeing her son each day, while his lordship, having achieved his aims, went his own way. To judge of his cool reception of her, he could well be thinking that she was in league with her mother and the Vicomte! At least, she was assured, she could rely upon Lady Whittinghame to put him right on that head and, in the midst of working out a powerful speech in her own defence which somehow became excessively involved, she fell asleep so did not hear the opening of the door, nor see her husband tip-toe across the room to look upon his son. Then, bending over his wife, he drew up the covers from where they had slipped from her shoulders and stood for a time, watching her, before leaving as silently as he had entered.

The only one to be in spirits on the following morning was Sir Peregrine, who took the party in hand and told them how they should go on.

'A picnic, that's the thing!' he declared. 'We'll never have a better day for it! You'll join us, Ainsley?'

'Nothing I'd like more,' said the little man wistfully, 'but—'

'No buts!' Sir Peregrine would not be denied. 'You have earned yourself a holiday! By the way, what did you say to that fellow Baynton yesterday to shut him up so sharp?'

'Oh, I just brought a certain legal irregularity to his notice which had quite slipped his memory,' murmured Mr Ainsley in the most innocent-seeming way.

Sir Peregrine chuckled. 'You lawyer fellows—always got a trick up your sleeves! But enough of all that, let us plan the day's expedition. Depend upon it, there's nothing like sunshine and fresh air for chasing away the blue devils!'

It said much for his resolution that the party was ready to set out before half the morning was spent, despite protestations from Lady Whittinghame that Julienne-Eve should keep to her bed, that Nathan was in no state to be indulging in such an excursion, and half-a-dozen other objections that sprang readily to her tongue. However, a few words in her ear from her sapient spouse sent her off, smiling, to see what the kitchens could produce at such short notice, and to persuade Julienne-Eve to bear her company for, of all things, she found picnics to be a tedious bore, but would not for the world disappoint dear Peregrine.

If her daughter-in-law doubted the veracity of this statement she was in no frame of mind to dispute it. The events of the previous day had left her as if suspended between a dream world and reality. She entertained no hope of a happy outcome and, with a sort of numb submissiveness, was merely existing until she should know what the future held for her.

'Do you and your lady lead the way in my curricle,' Sir Peregrine instructed Rotherham. 'Your shoulder will allow of handling it? Capital! Then away with you and we will follow at our leisure. We'll meet up at that folly not far from the Gallipot—you'll know the place.'

As Rotherham made no objection to this blatant attempt to segregate them from the others, Julienne-Eve allowed him to hand her up into the curricle and see to her comfort with every appearance of solicitude. At first, they kept reasonably ahead of the rest of the party but, very soon, the perfectly matched pair of chestnuts wearied of such slow progress and began to show their mettle. Julienne-Eve glanced doubtfully at his lordship to find him smiling at her in a very disarming way.

'Should we be drawing away so fast, my lord?' she enquired politely.

'If you wish for it we can pull off the road and allow them to catch us up,' he replied promptly. 'Ah, here is a turning of which we may avail ourselves.'

That was not precisely what she had in mind, but she accepted that, if her situation was to be made clear, the soonest done the better, and made no demur as they wheeled down a secluded lane.

Presently they came to a halt beside a delightful pool, deep in shadow from overhanging branches, its verges coloured with wild willow herb and meadowsweet. Here Rotherham spread a light rug over a fallen tree-trunk and, throwing off his coat, freed the horses from the pole and led them to the water.

Standing there in shirt and breeches, the dappled sunlight glinting off his dark locks, he looked strangely young and vulnerable and her heart ached at thought of what he was surely preparing to say to her. Unhurriedly, he tethered the chestnuts fetlock deep in thick grass to their great content, then came to cast himself down by her feet, his head resting on the tree-trunk so near to her hand that she had scarce to move it to touch his hair, springing afresh in crisp curls about his injured ear.

In the field beyond the trees a lark rose singing from the golden corn, and a hare stirred from its form to peer at them inquisitively. All the world seemed joyful and at peace save only she, who sat waiting to hear her fate. Then a horse snorted and the hare bounded away in sudden fright.

'Lucky fellow! Free, with never a care.' He turned on his side to look up at her. 'My mother has told me how much I am in your debt. It was not, as I remember, part of our bargain that you should hazard your person on my behalf or that of our son.'

She had a suspicion that he was quizzing her and answered him with formal courtesy. 'I did no more than would any mother for her child, my lord.'

'With the possible exception of my own mama, I can think of no other who would have displayed such courage and devotion,' he said quietly.

'You make too much of the matter, my lord, I—'

'Julienne-Eve,' he interruped her. 'Don't be forever arguing with me! It's an uncommon waste of time and there is so much we have to say to each other.'

Here it comes, she thought and, instinctively, her back stiffened and her chin came up in a characteristically defiant attitude. 'What is it you wish to say to me, my lord?'

He took her hands as they lay clasped in her lap and,

turning them over, pressed a kiss into each palm. 'Will you have me for husband, my darling? Can you forgive me for the way I have misused and misjudged you?'

The whole glowing summer scene swam before her eyes and she closed them to shut out the sight of his pleading face. He sounded as shy and uncertain as any stripling importuning his first love, but she knew him better than to believe that! He wished to make amends, to be sure, and to do it as graciously as circumstances would permit. She resolved to help him in this laudable aim.

'Our bargain, my lord, as I remember, did not extend beyond—beyond—' He took her up quickly.

'Beyond the birth of our child, you would say? Look at me, Julienne-Eve!' Kneeling beside her, with one swift movement he swept off her bonnet and tossed it aside, loosing her hair about her face. Startled, she put out her hands as if to ward him off and was caught up in an embrace so fierce as to crush the breath from her body. 'Oh, my foolish little love, don't you know that I adore you—have adored you from the very first! Nor,' he went on, leaving off kissing her for a moment, 'do I accept that you are entirely indifferent to me!'

'Wh-why should you think that?' she heard herself saying in a very small voice.

'Look at me!' he commanded again, yet in so entreating a tone that, shyly, she raised her eyes to his. What she saw there so confounded her that she was obliged to hide her face in his shoulder from whence emerged a muffled whisper.

'I—I never was indifferent to you! B-but I couldn't say so, could I?'

'No, sweetheart, of course you could not!' The laugh in his voice drew a responsive gurgle from her. 'But what a merry dance you've led me!'

'*I* have?' She drew away from him in assumed affront. 'And what of you, pray?'

He laid a finger to her lips. 'If I promise to be the most unexceptionable husband, to let you have your way in all things, to do nothing that you cannot approve—my lady, why are you laughing?'

'Because I know that the very first time our wills cross you will become imperious and arrogant and—oh, Nathan, Nathan!'

The inquisitive hare, returning to his form, supposed the two humans to be asleep, so quiet were they. Then he heard the deeper voice speak and stayed, listening, ears cocked.

'Philippe stays here with us, of course. I can arrange with his trustees for an agent to look after his estates until he is of an age to take them over himself.'

'And Lucy and Trevor?'

'They'd be best off away from Hever Court and my dear aunt, but that, I'd say, is for Lucy to decide.'

'Poor Lucy,' she murmured drowsily for the hot sun and his lordship's encroaching attentions were taking her mind from the matter in hand. 'She's not a bad girl, you know, only—only—'

'Over-susceptible to temptation, you would say?' he suggested mischievously then, seeing her eyelashes droop upon her cheeks, he kissed her long and tenderly. 'My poor tired little wife, tell me what I must do to make you happy?'

Julienne-Eve gave this proposal her full attention. 'I think, perhaps,' she began, then hesitated. 'No, if you would consider—' Another pause, while he studied her intent face, his eyes alight with amusement. 'I am of the opinion,' she said at last gravely, 'that if you would just *love* Jonathan and me, it would answer very well.'

Whereupon his lordship gave all his attention to proving to his lady how very conscientiously he proposed to fulfil her requirements so that she should have no possible cause for complaint.